# MY BEST FRIENDS' WIVES AND I

# MY BEST FRIENDS' WIVES AND I

Nicholas Vaughan

Order this book online at www.trafford.com
or email orders@trafford.com

Most Trafford titles are also available at major online book retailers.



Printed in the United States of America.

ISBN: 978-1-4251-0252-4 (sc)

Library of Congress Control Number: 2012901193

*Trafford rev. 03/02/2012*

**North America & international**
toll-free: 1 888 232 4444 (USA & Canada)
phone: 250 383 6864 • fax: 812 355 4082

This is a story about a bored married man, with his own business that is not doing too well.

For a 40th birthday present to himself, he wants a one-time affair with some of his best friends' wives. He commits a robbery, so he has enough money to give them the most romantic night out they have had for years.

Unfortunately, it starts to get complicated when some of the girls show feelings towards him; he harbours similar feelings for a couple of the girls. Then, to top it all, he decides to get rid of a drunken, abusive husband and friend.

www.tellastory1.co.uk

I was born into a to a hard working Birmingham family in the mid fifties. I have a mother and father who still love, respect and help each other, with two sisters one older and one younger.
We all grew up with a normal upbringing and when I left school at 15, I worked in a number of garages, striving and working hard to own one of my own.
I am now married with a wife and son who are my life.

It has always been my ambition to write a book, so over the years and with life being a large part of my education, I took my time and achieved it eventually.

# Chapter 1

It was 9.30, Saturday morning, the beginning of July, and it looked like it was going to be a blistering hot day again. There wasn't a cloud in the sky, just a long broken jet-stream trail.

I was on my way to work, travelling along the dual carriageway in my black Jaguar xj6. The air conditioning was on full and adjusted to blow straight in my face. I was destined for McDonalds; before I did anything else, I had to have something to eat.

My head was aching from the previous night: yes, I had a hangover, the mother of all hangovers. My mouth and throat were so sore from the amount of alcohol I'd drunk while playing a stupid game called Cardinal Puff-Puff.

After my failed first attempt, it was downhill all the way. Every time I didn't say, or do, the right thing in sequence, I had to drink a glass of red wine. In general I felt like a carrier bag full of shit and I didn't even become a Cardinal.

I drove around the red thin lane, clipping the kerb twice and stopped by the huge menu. I heard a faint Scottish voice say, "Welcome to McDonalds, can I take your order please?" It seemingly came from a small orange box on a pole.

Straining to see the board, I said, "Can I have a breakfast and a-"

I hadn't said orange juice, when the box said, "Welcome to McDonalds, can I take your order please?" in a more abrupt manner. It was then I realised I hadn't dropped the window and she hadn't heard me. Feeling a bit stupid, and looking around to see if anyone was watching me, I opened the window and started again.

After I ordered, I was told to go round to the next window to collect and pay for the food. Almost automatically as I pulled up, the little glass door opened and a head popped out. "It won't be ready for a couple of minutes. Can you drive over to the yellow boxes, park there and someone will bring your breakfast out to you," she said, without drawing a breath. I counted the money out into her little hand and collected my orange drink, thanking the girl.

I was beginning to lose interest by now and, as you can imagine, I was not feeling too good, but as instructed, I drove to the designated area. Then, with my engine still running, I sat with my head thrown back on the head rest and my eyes closed, saying those immortal words to myself: "Never, ever again."

I thought about the party. It was my 40th birthday and there were about eighty people enjoying themselves, drinking and dancing. It must have been a good night because the police came round twice. I vaguely recall someone in a uniform asking, "Can you turn the music down please? Next door are complaining about the noise." If I remember correctly, someone did turn it down and, when the police drove away, someone else turned it up again, even louder.

I sat quietly, reclined in my seat and almost falling asleep, when I heard the rustle of a carrier bag to my right. "At last, food," I thought. A different girl passed it through the window. "Sorry to keep you waiting, sir." She was long and thin, and had a complexion like a tomato pizza. I thanked her and drove off down the motorway towards work.

As I cruised along the inside lane carefully, I suddenly remembered my birthday present to myself. I had decided while I was sitting down to catch my breath after dancing with someone who I hadn't seen before at a party—let alone mine—that, as life begins at 40, or so they say, I was going to have a one-time affair with some of my best friends' wives—in secret of course—or at least try.

I am fortunate enough to have plenty of friends of all shapes and sizes. Some are rich, some are not so rich and some just get by. Most of them I've known for twenty years or more, some only about ten years. But I know them all very well . . . or so I thought.

The girls I had in mind had all been married for more than ten years, so it was a pretty safe bet that they hadn't got AIDS or anything like that.

Sometimes at parties, or when we went out somewhere and had all had vast amounts of alcohol, I'd kissed some of the girls and danced a bit closer than perhaps I should have. But no one slapped me that I can remember. In fact, I've said some things that I wished I hadn't the day after. Last night was no exception. So while I was sitting down and looking around the room, I began to wonder, if pushed, how many would say yes to a secret romantic, expensive night out?

Some people would probably say I had a death wish, me, I just crave excitement now and again. I am 40, as I said before. I have been married for fourteen years. I must have missed the first seven-year itch. My wife's name is Elizabeth. We have a son Michael, 7 years old, and I love them both dearly.

I'm six feet two, thick black hair, blue eyes, moustache, about thirteen stone, well built and hate shaving more than anything. I've got stubble for most of the week and only shave if I really have to, or if I'm going somewhere nice.

Like all other rampant red hot-blooded teenagers, I would always chat up an attractive girl in my younger years, perhaps in a bar or a club and ask them for a date. Sometimes they would turn me down, other times they would accept. I would arrange to meet one night for a drink or a meal, even a dance. As money was no object in those days, I didn't save any of my wages. I lived with my parents, so I would blow the lot almost straight away.

The night would arrive, eventually. I would be both nervous and very excited as I got myself ready. Throwing Brut aftershave on by the bottle, wondering what she was going to wear for our first night out, what she would be like, then driving off in my Ford Anglia that I had spent half the week washing, polishing and vacuuming. Making sure the passenger seat fully reclined easily, checking the radio worked and that the romantic cassette was loaded and ready to come on when the time was just right. Worrying whether the money I had would be enough. And then there was the butterfly feeling in my stomach: standing by the bar, alone, waiting, wondering if she had changed her mind; and then when she walked towards me smiling, and apologising for being late. Then the drinking, snogging, chatting about nothing, trying to work out whether or not I was going to get laid. That's what I missed; I wanted that excitement or buzz, whatever it was called. I loved to go to a dance, or a nightclub.

I met my wife Liz at a club called the Masons Bar. It was just outside the town where I lived, on a main street. It had a revolving circular dance floor that moved slowly in one direction and, as the night went on and everyone drank more and more, the disc jockey, as they were called in those days, would change the direction to see how many people would fall over. We've been going round and round together ever since.

Elizabeth is a very pretty woman, about five feet six, long black hair, big brown eyes and a will of her own. She has a good job, working long and hard hours, as a customs officer at the local airport.

We have a relationship where we hardly ever see each other. Liz gets up early while I'm asleep, and returns home in the afternoon, in time to collect Mick. I go to work after I have dropped Mick at school in the morning and when I get home late, Liz has gone to bed. We only speak to each other in the day on the phone, some weekends and when she is off. We are so busy trying to pay the bills and make a living; we seem to be drifting apart.

I have a country garage, not doing too well. I sell petrol, repair cars, offer a twenty-four hour rescue service, a body shop, and sometimes I sell the odd car from there. In total there are six employees and, as you can imagine, wages day is a bit expensive. We have been there for seven years. Sometimes things are good and other times things are not so good. But that's how it is in the car trade.

When I first took on the garage it was quite badly run down but I thought it had a lot of potential and over the years I worked hard and it looks a lot smarter. We had the petrol pumps fitted, painted and cleaned everywhere and bought more up-to-date equipment. So, as you can see, I'm not scared of a good challenge.

A few weeks ago, I took Liz and Mick to a Greek island called Zakinthos, probably better known as Zante, with two of our friends. We had a great time over the two weeks: we met lots of nice Greek people and partied most nights. About six months previous to this holiday, for a joke, I put an advert in the local paper: 'I want to learn Greek. Can anyone help me?' I put my mobile phone number in as well and waited. Weeks went by and I hadn't heard anything. Then, one day, I was driving to work and a lady phoned and said, "I have a book called 'Greek Language And People'. I taught myself enough to get by when I go over there. There are two tapes and a book, it's self-explanatory and quite easy."

I took her name and address and, later that day, I made my way to her house. She showed me the book, we agreed on a price and then I left with the goods. While I was driving back to the garage, I put the first tape in my cassette player and listened. It was English first then Greek. I must admit, it sounded impossible to start with. I heard a few words I recognised from previous holidays. So then what I started to do was, when I got home at night and everyone had gone to bed, I got the book out and, with Mick's personal tape player, secretly started listening. After a month, I could read it and understand a bit more. So I carried on. Sometimes I would be at it till three or four o'clock in the morning. I remember Liz coming down one morning to go to work. Luckily I heard the floorboards creak in the bedroom and managed to get everything under the settee and pretend to be asleep in the chair before she opened the door to the living room. I carried on reading, and learning, right up until we went on holiday. I never told anyone and by the time we arrived in Zante I could speak quite a bit. Luckily the first chapter was about food and drink and how to order it.

Anyway, on the first night we were there, we went for something to eat at one of Zante's amazing tavernas. After we found a table and were sitting down outside, I pretended to go to the toilet but in fact I went to see the waiter, who, I later found out, was called Costas. I explained to him that I wanted to play a trick on my friends and family, so would order the meal and drinks in Greek as best as I could. I quickly told him about my secret lessons and asked him to pretend he was an old friend. As I made my way back to my seat, I couldn't stop myself from smiling. I just couldn't imagine what the looks on their faces were going to be like.

After about five minutes, he came over to our table with his notepad and tray, dropped them on the chair and, as I stood up, he threw his arms around my neck. "How are you?" he said first, then went into his own language. I didn't have a clue what he was saying; I obviously hadn't got that far in my book. I answered him with some Greek and I could see him cringe, because I'd said 'with a bath' or 'without a bath'. This was in another chapter. But the rest of my party didn't know what I'd said. Costas picked up his pad and tray, laughing and, in Greek, said, "Ti tha fate." I knew what that meant.

I looked at Liz and she said, "What did he say?"

As I sat down, I explained, "He asked, 'what do you want to eat?'"

I heard Andrew, one of the friends we were with, say, "How do you know?" with a look of disbelief on his face.

It was the moment I had been waiting for. I quickly looked up at Costas and said, "Ton katalogo parakalau," (the menu please) to which he replied "Oriste" (here you are). So I asked, "Ti ehete?" (What do you have?). Then he started to reel off a long list of choices. I looked around at them all; you could have heard an olive bounce off the floor.

Four mouths dropped down to the table, then Costas said, "Ti tha parete."

Not a word had been spoken so I carried on. "Ena bookali grasi, tria byras, k ena bookali portokalatha," which means I ordered the drinks (a bottle of wine, three beers and a lemonade). Still nothing was said.

I thanked Costas and he said, "I will be back in a few moments to take your orders. Excuse me for just one moment."

I looked at Denise, Andrew's wife. She was the first to speak. "How, when, where did you learn?" She struggled for words.

Then Liz spoke. "Have you been here before without me?"

I started to laugh and Andrew said, "That's brilliant, you've even mastered the twang."

Mick was still looking up at me in disbelief. Then I told them the story. As you can imagine, they couldn't believe how well I had done in such a short time. Anyway, we had a good night; in fact, a very good holiday. I fell in love with the island and the people; their way of life is so relaxed and so different to ours. I would like to live there one day. Who knows, if I got caught playing my game, I might have to. Some people on Zante said I looked a bit Greek. They called me the man of the mountains, whatever that meant.

The girls I had in mind for my proposed birthday present were all good-looking and I'm sure none of them had been unfaithful before.

For these dates, or affairs, whatever they turned out to be, I needed to work out where to go, how to get there and how to get out of the house. It would only be for one night. The whole evening would have to be the best night out they'd had for a very long time and something they would remember forever. I didn't want it to be a quickie in the back of a car down some dark country lane in the middle of nowhere. I also needed some money; I had to have enough for the best of everything. It couldn't come from my wages, nor could it come out of the housekeeping, definitely not out of the garage account, so I would have to get it from some other means. I must also get fit, I thought: I would start running again in the mornings.

On the following Saturday I was going to a barbecue and some of the girls would be there. It was at our friend's house, the couple we went to Greece with, Andrew and Denise, who have no children because Andrew had a vasectomy some years ago.

It was Andrew's 40th birthday and they were having it in their back garden. The house is a big old Victorian house and the patio, which was built last year, is wooden. It starts from the back of the house and overhangs the first part of the garden that drops down like an American boardwalk, with a small fence all the way round the edge. There are two sets of steps, one at each end, leading down to the grass, tables and chairs with coloured canopies dotted about the lawn. There is a small stream that runs across the bottom of the garden, beneath a rickety old wooden bridge that leads into a large wooded field and just before the bridge on the left stands a large wooden shed. From there, back to the house, there are lamps on all the trees: it's very picturesque at night. Apparently they had recently had a big brick barbecue built that rises up out of the wooden patio—the same wooden patio that overlooks their private swimming pool. Quite impressive!

When I eventually arrived at the garage, I shuddered at the thought of being stopped by the police and breathalysed: I would definitely still be over the limit.

I ran up the stairs to my office, hiding the breakfast under my shirt. I heard someone shout, "Arrived, at last! It must have been a good one then."

I entered the office, sat down and devoured my cold breakfast before anyone could come up and catch me.

I started to do some paperwork but as I was sitting there, looking at pages and pages of numbers, they seemed to start moving around the paper. After about five minutes, I started to feel sick, so I dropped that idea. I stared aimlessly out of the window, thinking about the girls I wanted to take out.

Eventually I pulled myself together and decided to go home and help Liz clean the house.

When I'd left in the morning, it looked like we had been burgled. The mess was in every room; even the garage floor was covered in food and drink. The 'Happy 40th birthday' banner, which was tied up across the front of the house, had fallen down at one end. I glanced out of the kitchen window into the back garden. There were cans strewn all over the lawn, clothes in the pool and up the tree.

I locked the garage and drove home. As I pulled up on the drive, there were three people untying the banner from the bedroom windows with the help of a long ladder. All the doors were open, with more people walking in and out with bin bags. As I got out of the car, I could hear the vacuum being pushed and pulled, backwards and forwards, the chinking of plates being washed and dried. I began to feel better. Some friends from the party had come back to help Liz and it was nearly all done. I couldn't believe it. It was around four o'clock when everyone left and went home. We had a quiet night in by the telly, with a take-away Chinese meal, and were in bed for nine.

On the Sunday, I just messed about in the garden, pretending to be interested and nursing my bad head. We had lunch about two o'clock and I spent the rest of the day asleep on the settee.

During the next week, we were very quiet at the garage. There wasn't much work about, but I did sit in my office one day for a while and make a list of all the girls that I knew and would like to take out on a date. I crossed off some of the girls that would definitely say no, the ones that hadn't been married long enough and brought the list down to six possibles.

# Chapter 2

It was on the Monday morning when I realised the barbeque had been a raving success. Liz and I dropped Mick off at the babysitter's early on Saturday night and went on to the party at about eight o'clock to see if we could help in any way. Everything was ready so we lit the barbecue and started drinking. People began to arrive shortly afterwards. We couldn't have picked a better night; the weather was perfect. Everyone had summer clothes on, as the heat was tremendous from both the sun and the barbecue.

It was the first time Andrew had used this barbecue. There was a large spit that ran above the full length of the grill, allowing the pig to rotate slowly and, underneath, he'd had small ovens fitted to keep the food warm while everything else was being cooked. The shed at the bottom of the garden was filled with a stack of booze that got larger every time someone new appeared.

A few people I hadn't seen before brought some drugs. I don't think there was anything too hard. I saw plenty of brown stuff rolled into cigarettes and someone else I'd never seen brought some speed. In fact, I tried some of that; it certainly kept me awake.

The party went on all through the night. Some went home, others lay down on the grass where they'd been standing. There were even some that managed to find a bed in the house, Liz included. In the morning, about 7.00 a.m., I cooked breakfast for about twenty remaining people.

As the morning went on, a few people came back, collected a drink from the shed and carried on drinking. It was another sunny day and by about 11.00 a.m. there were quite a few gathered, so we had a second party. By this time, I had drunk myself sober. Liz came down about midday, and disappeared for a few hours to fetch Mick from the sitter's. She brought him back to play in the pool with the other kids that had appeared from somewhere.

At about nine o'clock, people started to leave and, by 10.30 p.m., there was only Denise and I left in the dark, sitting by the barbecue, with the flames flickering from the logs I'd thrown on when the coal had run out earlier. After talking about our holiday in Greece, we decided to ring the friends we'd met over there. They had a bar called 'The Hideaway' in Zante. After the fourth attempt, we got through and I heard Denise say, "Is that you, Stefano?" with a beam right across her face. Then, with one finger in her ear and the portable telephone on the other, she sat on my lap. I put my arm around her waist to stop her from falling off and she told Stefano quickly about the party. After five minutes or so, the phone was passed to me and I spoke a bit of Greek to him. I could tell she was impressed because she laid her head on my shoulder and kissed my cheek. I said goodbye to him and turned the phone off. Denise started crying and said how much she missed them all. I couldn't help myself. I kissed her on the lips, for a good couple of minutes, and she put her arms around my neck. Then all of a sudden, she jumped up.

"What if someone's looking?" she said, as she stepped back towards the fire.

"I don't think that anyone is awake but perhaps we should call it a night, in case," I said. I stood up and we walked to the back door of the house holding hands. We then stood by the door and kissed again. Denise went to wake Liz and Mick while I waited. I looked down the garden. I couldn't believe the mess: bottles, plastic cups, paper plates and napkins, chairs all over the floor and that's only what I could see from the patio and the lights down the garden. It must have been ten times worse than this in the daylight, I thought.

As I turned back to the house, Liz appeared at the door, carrying Mick in her arms.

"What happened to you?" I said quietly.

"Don't ask," she said, as she passed Mick to me asleep. "Just get me home."

We thanked Denise, who was in the doorway and, as I kissed her on the cheek, she winked and smiled. Liz had walked around the front and was probably already in the car, asleep. I carried Mick out and put him in the back, fastened his seat belt and watched his head fall to one side and his hands drop to his lap. I drove home very carefully, with both Mick and Liz fast asleep. When we arrived home, I had to carry them both to bed.

The next morning, not feeling too bad, I made my way to work. I thought about the few minutes Denise and I had spent alone together. It was something more than just a kiss in the garden, I could tell.

I went up to my office and was trying to work but it kept coming back to me, over and over. I kept thinking about her. I wanted to ring but I didn't know if Andrew would be at home.

Later that day, Liz rang me. "Denise and Andrew are coming round tonight, so can you bring some wine home?"

"Yes, I will. See you about seven o'clock," I said and put the phone down. It wasn't long after that when I started to go downhill. My head was throbbing and I felt tired. I sat there for ages, trying to work out a plan to get the money for these dates. I thought and thought but nothing sprang to mind—except to steal it.

Some years ago, I'd known a man that used the same bank as me. He walked from his offices to collect the wages with a big green cloth bag. When he walked back, it was always bulging and often I thought about robbing him. I made plans to go on Friday, to see if he still made his weekly visits, then I went to the shops to get some aspirins for my headache.

As I drove home that night, I felt a little better. Liz rang me on my car phone to remind me to bring some wine home, as Denise and Andrew wanted to chat about the party. I told her I hadn't forgotten, even though I had, and said that I would be home in ten minutes. As I put the phone down, I suddenly thought perhaps Andrew did see us from his bedroom or Denise told him. Maybe someone else saw us snogging and said something—that's all I needed. I thought about it for a while, then brushed it aside; maybe I was getting paranoid.

I collected the wine and got home just after seven. I quickly ran upstairs, got showered and changed, put Mick to bed with a story, ate my tea and sat waiting for them to arrive while watching the telly. They pulled up about 8.30. I remember thinking to myself, 'Here we go, I've been caught. I haven't started my game yet and I'm in trouble.' I opened the door and, luckily for me, Denise was first; Andrew was collecting the drinks from the back seat of his car.

I said hello and she kissed me on the cheek whispering in my ear, "Thank you for looking after me last night." I was relieved.

Andrew followed, loaded with bottles of wine.

"What's all this?" I asked.

He grinned and said, "There's loads left from the weekend, you might as well have some here." He carried the box through to the kitchen and placed it on the table. "How do you feel?" he asked. "I heard you haven't been to bed for two days."

"Just tired," I replied. "I had something to keep me awake. I think they called it speed. Someone rolled a ten-pound note into a tube and told me to sniff a line up my nose. I must admit, it worked. I never really felt tired till last night but it makes your eyes run for a while."

He pulled the cork from a bottle of Rioja and laughed. "The hair of the dog," he said, as he lifted his glass.

We took some glasses through to the lounge and sat drinking for a couple of hours, reminiscing about the barbecue. Denise and I kept glancing at each other, half smiling.

As they left to go home, Andrew said, "I didn't get a chance before." A cold shiver went down my spine. I thought, 'This is it'. "Thanks for all your help before the party."

"No problem," I said, relieved.

Denise kissed me again. "I will see you soon," she said, flicking her eyebrows up and down. That night I had a good long sleep.

The week went by and each day I felt a bit better. I'm convinced it takes longer to get over a session, the older you get.

On Friday lunchtime, I went to the bank to get the wages and popped round the corner to see if that man still collected his wages the same way.

I sat in a car park over the road from his bank for half an hour. I was sure it was about the right time but nothing. I was just about to go when I saw him marching up the stairs from the underpass, still with his green bag in his hand. He looked a little older than I remember but he went into the bank, collected the wages, the same as always, and left.

He was 45-50, five feet six, and about eleven stone. I had to work out how to get the bag from his hands without any harm or damage. I was surprised he hadn't been robbed before.

As I drove back to the garage, I started to plan the robbery.

# Chapter 3

Almost a month had passed. I had been very busy watching the man with the green bag, at the same time, every Friday. He took the same route to the bank, so there shouldn't be a problem with that. I worked out that if I could get the bag from his hand under the subway, on a motorbike, I could drive up the ramp on the other side, onto the road and along Fir Tree Lane to the canal in six and a half minutes. It would take the police at least nine minutes from the station in the nearest town, if the roads were clear. I timed it one night in my car. So, during the day, it should take longer.

'By the time he runs back to the bank, and phones the police,' I thought, 'I should have about, 15 to 20 minutes, unless there's a squad car in the area.' Then I'd drive down the embankment on the bike, dump it, jump into a speedboat and drive round to the next bridge, where my car would be parked.

I convinced myself it should be easy and decided to do it on the following Friday.

On the Monday, I bought myself a fast motorbike for £200 cash and gave the previous owner a false name and address so I could leave the bike and it wouldn't be traced to me. The boat was moored at the bottom of someone's garden, just by the side of the bridge. I just hoped that the bag was worth all this trouble.

I'd sat outside his offices and about thirty people worked there, so if my sums were right, at £150 per person, that should give me around four and a half grand. That was more than enough for what I wanted, I thought.

As the week went on, I got more and more nervous. I got up early every morning and, luckily, Liz had a few days off. I ran five miles, planning, thinking, trying to work out every last detail and what to do in the event of the police catching me. The more I thought, the faster I ran. I figured if I did get caught at least I could give the old bill a run for their money.

I couldn't sleep Thursday night. I tossed and turned till eventually I must have dropped off. The alarm woke me and I almost jumped out my skin. I couldn't remember my dream but I had a good idea what it was about.

I went for my run in the morning; it could have been my last. As I ran, I went over everything, worried in case I had overlooked anything. I was in such a trance, I nearly got run over twice. I checked my watch when I got back home to see how long it had taken me, as I did every time. I had run faster than I had ever done before, by three and a half minutes.

I took a shower, got changed and sat down to eat breakfast. I sat there, looking at the box of cereal and an empty bowl. I couldn't put them together, my stomach was churning. I just sat there thinking, 'Tonight, I will either be very happy and have enough money to take the girls out for this fantastic night or I will be sad and alone, in a cell'.

I went upstairs to say goodbye to Liz. She was brushing her teeth in the bathroom. I gave her a kiss and put my arms around her as she put her toothbrush back in the rack and wiped her mouth on the towel. I went to pull the door open and I heard her say, "What's the matter, aren't you coming back home?"

I turned and, with a forced smile on my face, said, "I will see you tonight," and walked down the stairs to the front door, where Mick was waiting for his lift to school. I dropped him off by the gate and, as he went to get out of the car, I put my arm over his shoulder, pulled him towards me and kissed his little cheek.

"Dad, everyone will be looking, get off!"

I smiled. "See you later, son," I said, as he slammed the door.

I drove back to the house, opened the garage door quietly and pushed the motorbike out on to the road, without Liz knowing. I put it on the frame at the back of the car that I'd had made especially by one of the lads at work. It fitted on the tow-bar and the bike sat in it across the width of the car. I tied it on then drove to the pub car park. I arrived there about nine twenty, went straight round the back of the pub, unloaded the bike, pushed it into the hedge and put a chain through the back wheel so that no one would steal it. The frame, I dismantled, put it in the car boot and then carried on to work. I stopped round the side of the workshop, removed the frame and put a full-face crash helmet and gloves in the boot before driving back round the front as normal.

"Good morning," I shouted to everyone and went up to my office to do some paperwork. I didn't want anyone to see how nervous I was.

I messed about trying to make myself busy and not think about the robbery. It was about midday when I told the lads I was going to get the wages and left.

I drove to the pub and parked the car next to the bike. As I got out of the car, I glanced around the car park to see if anyone was about. It was quiet and a very still day. There were a few cars scattered about, enough to shield me while I got dressed.

The overalls, that belonged to my mechanic Alan, I put on first, then the gloves and the helmet. I closed the boot, locked the car and hid the keys up the exhaust. Again, I quickly looked around the car park then unlocked the chain and pulled the bike out of the hedge.

I looked up into the blue sky and asked myself if I was mad as I fumbled with the key in the steering lock. It was either my nerves or the gloves. I couldn't take them off, because of my fingerprints, but eventually it turned. I kicked the engine over to start it but there was nothing. I kicked it again and again—still nothing. The visor on my helmet was steaming up and I was starting to panic. I checked everything and realised the petrol was off. A branch must have turned the knob as I'd pulled it out of the hedge. The bike burst into life as I kicked it again. It was so hot but I was shaking like a leaf. I tried to pull myself together as I headed off towards the bank. I drove past the bridge and glanced over the top rail. The boat was in place. I carried on to the car park opposite the bank. It was 12.50. From there, I would be able to see him come round the corner. At this stage, I was like a nervous wreck. I was still trembling and I had pains in my stomach. It was so hot in my overalls and helmet; the visor was steaming up again and I could hardly see anything. I waited and waited. The longer it took for him to walk round the corner, the more I thought of calling it off.

I had been there for about ten minutes and noticed some people were starting to look at me suspiciously. I kept saying to myself, 'One more minute.' If I gave up now, I'd never come back and try again.

I decided to drive a little way down the road, turn around and come back towards the bank. At least the fresh air might cool me down. I pulled out on to the road, lifted the visor on my helmet a little and drove off. All the time I was checking the rear view mirror. I could just see the top of the subway. I turned around and went back. As I indicated to turn into the car park, I saw him, bobbing up and down on the last few steps of the subway. With the bag in his hand, he went into the bank. I quickly pulled the visor back down and pulled up about three metres away from the door, with the engine still running. I waited with one foot on the floor. I couldn't see him from outside because there were too many posters on the window, so I put the stand down and got off. Then I pretended to look at my back wheel; I bent down by the side and looked in.

I could see him at the counter, talking to one of the cashiers as he put the money in his bag. My heart was pumping so fast, I thought it was going to explode. Through the window, I saw him throw his head back, laughing. He waved and turned to walk out. A cold shiver went straight though me as I pushed the bike forward off the stand. I sat back on the saddle and waited for him to walk outside. I checked my watch as he stepped onto the pavement, holding the door open for an elderly lady. Everything he did seemed to be in slow motion. As he turned towards the subway, I noticed the bag was in his left hand, which meant, as he walked through the subway, the bag would be between him and the wall. I was committed, I didn't have any choice at this stage. I waited until he got to the bottom of the steps and quickly looked again at my watch: it was ten past one exactly.

I revved the bike up and took off. I didn't have time to stop and think about it any more. Bumping down the stairs, I could vaguely see him; everything was a blur until I got to the bottom. I looked up at him in front of me. He hadn't turned round yet and I was about ten metres behind him. There were about five people that could see me coming and they were moving to the sides.

As I approached him, he turned his head round first, then his whole body seemed to follow. His arms started to go up over his scared expression and the bag was right in front of me. I grabbed it in my left hand, which was lucky because I had to work the throttle with my right. I carried on dodging the people that were screaming and shouting. I turned left and drove up the ramp to the pavement at the top. The noise from the bike was echoing off the walls.

All I had to do now was to get to the bridge as fast as possible—every second counted.

I turned right along the pavement, still weaving my way through the people, dropped down onto the road and took off like a scalded cat, up Holy Lane to the roundabout.

By now, I had tucked the bag inside my overalls. As I approached the island, there were about six cars waiting to pull away. I managed to get past three on the inside but the next car was too close to the kerb so I jumped up the pavement, went past them and pulled away with a screech of tyres. I heard someone sound their horn but I couldn't turn round to look. I drove up towards the traffic lights on Fir Tree Lane and checked my watch again; it had taken me five and a half minutes so far. I had to pull up for the lights that were on red. I weaved my way to the front of the traffic queue. I was so close; from this point I could see the bridge and I could only wait. I sat there looking up at the lights for what seemed ages, revving the bike, pushing forward all the time, inch by inch. I heard someone sound their horn again; it was obviously the same person I'd upset at the island. The adrenalin was pumping around my body faster than ever. I had half a mile to go and, if the police were coming, I had to hit that bridge soon.

The lights changed. I was the first to pull away, concentrating on every car coming over the bridge towards me. I bounced up the kerb to my left and went across the grass, skidding and sliding into the bushes and brambles. The engine cut out and I leaped off the bike, throwing it to the side; it carried on sliding down the embankment and stopped on the towpath with an almighty crash. I slid the rest of the way down, on my backside, to the stone.

I'd planted the key that I'd made to fit the boat and a knife for the rope under it the week before. I kicked them into the canal and had to fish them out. Then I ran back under the bridge to the boat. With one stroke, I cut the rope and threw the knife into the canal. I jumped into the boat and turned the key. It was a bit awkward with gloves on but it started almost straight away. I pushed the throttle lever forward, turned the steering wheel and took off. As I went under the bridge, I noticed the bike had caught fire and was giving off thick black smoke that was drifting over the road above. I looked back to the rails up on the bridge and some people were looking down at me as I sped off. All I had to do was to get around the bend to the next bridge and the horrendous ordeal would be all over.

As I approached the bend, I wondered what was happening at the bank and if the police had arrived yet. I eased the throttle forward a bit more and pushed the visor up on the helmet. The cool breeze on my face was welcome. Every item of clothing I had on was soaking wet with sweat. As I turned the corner, I could see the bridge getting nearer—it was almost over. I pulled my helmet off and threw it into the canal, turned the engine off and threw the key in after it. I aimed the boat at the embankment and got myself ready to jump off and leave the boat unmoored. I stood on the side, then jumped onto the towpath and the boat carried on under the bridge, slowly.

As fast as my legs would carry me, I ran up the grass bank to the road, careful to cover my face as some cars went by. Then I hurriedly crossed over and went into the car park behind the pub, to my car. I bent down to get my keys from the exhaust, opened the boot and quickly took my gloves and overalls off. It was so hot; I thought that I would melt. I unzipped the overalls and felt for the bag of money.

A blank expression came over my face when I realised it wasn't there. All I could think was that I had done all that for nothing. I must have dropped it somewhere by the bike when I'd jumped off. My head dropped and I covered my eyes with my hands. I stood there for a second longer, then suddenly realised I had to hurry, bag or no bag. It wouldn't take the police long to get round to the bridge by car. I threw everything into the boot and slammed the lid. I was still shaking, with either anger or fear, when I dropped the keys on the floor and had to stoop to pick them up. It was then I saw the bag on the ground under the rear bumper. A smile beamed right across my face as I quickly picked it up and got in the car. I opened the glove box and threw it in, then speedily drove off towards work.

I was so relieved that it was over. I opened the sunroof and all the windows to let some fresh air into the car. I knew I could never do it again. I had never been so scared in all my life.

I'd been driving for a couple of miles when I found a lay-by, so I pulled in and sat for five minutes with my head on the headrest and my eyes closed, thinking about what I had done.

I opened the glove box and stared at the green bag, scared to open it in case I had done all that for a few pounds. I finally plucked up the courage. Gingerly, I pulled it out and put it on my lap. It certainly felt heavy and lumpy. I opened the top and peered in. There was a load of notes inside. I smiled to myself as I pushed the top back together and placed the bag back in the glove box. Then I carried on to the garage and pulled up on the forecourt.

I hadn't got out of the door when one of the lads came running out of the workshop, excited, shouting, "Have you been listening to the radio? There's been a robbery in Helden. Someone on a motor bike drove down the subway, grabbed a bag full of money off some bloke and drove off!" I looked up at him and casually said, "No, I've been listening to my Greek tape." I locked my car door as he walked back inside. As I squeezed the handle of my briefcase, my hands were still shaking. I went up to my office quickly, sat down at my desk and let out a loud sigh. It was all over.

Still trembling, I rang one of the lads in the workshop and asked him to bring me a coffee up, while I tried to calm down and concentrate on some paperwork.

# Chapter 4

A COUPLE OF weeks passed and, from what I heard from the radio and the television, the police had found the boat, checked it for fingerprints, found none and returned it back to the owner. The man was just a little shook up but he was all right. The bike was just a mass of melted metal by the time they'd managed to put the fire out. So, hopefully, I'd got away with it.

The money was upstairs in my safe. I burnt the green bag and counted the money on the Saturday morning while I was on my own. It came to a grand total of £4796.90p. I thought that would be enough, so all I had to do was to ask Denise out, my first date, the girl from the barbecue. Denise was English, tall and slim and stood just short of six feet. She had dark skin and long Afro hair. Her father was a black American pilot, who died just after the war. Denise had a very good figure and was an airhostess for one of the world's biggest airlines. She worked long-haul, which meant she travelled long distance from Heathrow Airport, all over the world; some journeys were three to four days long, some could be up to fifteen days, depending on where she was sent.

Denise had been to India and returned to England on Wednesday night. Andrew, her husband, rang me on the Thursday morning at work to ask me if we would like to go round that night because there was nothing in the fridge, as usual, and, "As Denise is too tired to go shopping, we thought about a take away."

"Yes," I said, "but I'll ring Liz to make sure."

"No need," he replied. "I've already spoken to her and she said she wasn't working, so I will see you then." We said our goodbyes.

On the Thursday night, I went home a little bit earlier than normal, got changed and Mick, Liz and I collected some wine on the way to Denise and Andrew's. When we arrived, Andrew opened the door and Denise was behind him in the hall. As we walked through to the kitchen, I asked Denise if she'd had a good trip and she briefly said yes but that it was long and tiring; she was glad to be home. Andrew poured the drinks and we all went through to the lounge and chatted a bit about India.

Andrew hadn't said a great deal by this time and he looked vacant, as if there was something on his mind. I asked him if anything was wrong.

"No! Can we go and get the food? I'm starving."

We left the girls talking on the settee and Mick playing with the dog in the corner.

As we drove off in my car along the country lanes, he asked me if I was busy at work. I explained to him it was not too bad. "How about you, have you got plenty of trees to chop down?" I asked and then I found out what was wrong.

He looked at me and said with a straight face, "Could you be unfaithful to Liz?"

I couldn't believe it. All sorts of things went through my mind. I was dumbfounded, lost for words. I thought, what does he know that I don't?

I carried on driving, hoping and praying he would say something else to give me a clue, instead of looking absently out of the car window. Then he said, still looking through window, "I went to this house today, to chop this big oak tree down, and the lady that owns the house asked me and the lads if we would like a coffee." Just then, he turned towards me and said, "Why are you smiling?"

I laughed aloud; it was relief more than anything else. I pretended to know what he was going to say. Then he carried on. "So, in all innocence, I said, 'Yes please, two without and one with please. I'll come up soon'. So I climbed down the tree while the others were sweeping the broken branches from the grass and went to the back door, expecting three coffees to be ready. All of a sudden, the door flew open and she said, 'They're in here'. So, not wanting to get the floor dirty, I asked her if she could pass them out. I heard her say, 'No, you will have to come in'. I stuck my head round the door and you will never guess what she had on!" At this point I was all ears. "Nothing, not a bloody button!"

I started laughing again. I just about composed myself enough to say, "What did you do?"

"Well, what could I do? After I had had a look, and I mean it was a good look—she was beautiful; long brown wavy hair—I said, 'No, I can't, I'm married.'"

"Didn't you fancy it then?" I said, still laughing.

"Yes, of course I fancied it, but what could I do? There were three blokes outside waiting for their coffee, it would have been cold." He burst out laughing then and we carried on to the Chinese take-away.

While we waited for our order, I asked Andrew, "Did you finish the job or do you have to go back to this house?"

"Not bloody likely," he said. "We rushed to finish it and I didn't tell the others till we were on our way home. You can imagine the abuse they threw at me."

We collected the take-away and made our way back to the house. As Andrew opened the front door, he said, "I haven't said anything to Denise. I've only told you, so mum's the word."

"OK," I said, smiling to myself.

We went into the kitchen, served the dinner onto plates and ate it on our laps in the lounge as we talked. We had a good night and left about 10 30. Nothing was said about the date but I did hear Denise tell Liz that she was going to New York on Monday, returning to England on Wednesday, staying in London for one night and then off to Washington the next day, so maybe that could be the night. She'd be staying there on her own. There'd be no point in Denise travelling all the way home for a few hours and going back again the next day.

On the Saturday dinnertime after work, I went to Sharley to buy myself some new clothes. I parked my car in the car park and, as I got out to lock it, I just happened to glance across to the shops on the other side of the road. There was Denise, looking in a dress shop window. I quickly ran over, crept up behind her, put my hands over her eyes and, with a Greek accent, said, "I love you, what's your name please?"

She put her hands on mine, turned and said, "Denise," with a huge smile on her face. "I saw you pull up, I was hoping you would come over."

We chatted for a few minutes, then I explained to her that my cousin had rang me a couple of weeks ago, to see if I could sell his car for him, and I had to go down to London to collect it some time in the near future. Then I said, "I overheard you say that you might be there for one night this week."

That naughty smile appeared on her face again. Then I couldn't believe it when she said, "Can we spend the whole night together?" A strange feeling ran through me. At first I thought she was joking until she said, "I've been thinking of a way to ask you out for ages."

I kissed her on the cheek. "Can I take you out to dinner first?" I asked.

She nodded as I turned to go back to my car, then I heard her say, "See you Wednesday night then."

I was so excited as I drove home.

As I walked into the house, Liz shouted from upstairs, "What did you buy yourself then, anything nice?"

My mind went blank instantly. I had forgotten to go to the shops. "I . . . didn't see anything I . . . fancied," I shouted and went straight into the lounge.

On the Sunday, I needed an excuse to ring Denise to make arrangements, so I phoned Andrew to ask him if he fancied a beer, hoping Denise would answer. And she did.

"Hello, is Andrew there? If he is, just listen-" I said, without drawing a breath.

She interrupted me. "No, he's down the garden."

"Good, what night will you be in London?"

"Wednesday, about tea-time I land, so I'll ring you on your mobile phone," she replied.

"Where do you stay?"

She gave me the name of the hotel and the address and said, "I'll look forward to seeing you then."

Just before I put the phone down, I said, "Ask Andrew if he fancies a beer."

"I don't think so, he's covered in mud," she said.

"Well, tell him I rang, OK? And I'll see you Wednesday night. I hope you won't be delayed."

On the Monday, I phoned my cousin and made the arrangements to collect the car on Wednesday afternoon, took some money out of the safe and drove into town to buy myself some clothes for the night. I bought shoes, a shirt, tie and a black dinner suit, so I wouldn't have to take any clothes from home. Then, in the afternoon, I got the mechanic to check the truck over and filled it with diesel.

Tuesday, I did a bit of paperwork but couldn't concentrate. I told Liz when I got home that I was going to London the next day to collect a car.

I woke at 6 a.m. on Wednesday and went for a run, got back home, showered and went straight to work. Everything was OK there, so I left for London about one o'clock.

I hit a small amount of traffic on the motorway as I approached the M4 and arrived in Wimbledon about 4.15. I found the massive house almost straight away and loaded the Rolls Royce onto the back of the truck.

It was just the car for a night out in London. I'd been asked to sell it from my forecourt, as my cousin was a very rich man and he didn't use it any more. It had been abandoned in one of his many garages for the past six months—he was driving a red Ferrari now.

I had a coffee with him and he explained the history of the car to me. To be quite honest, I wasn't listening. I was too busy thinking about the night out with Denise in the Rolls—it's a black 1984 Shadow with cream leather interior and white-wall tyres.

We chatted for a bit about the families and, as always, his parting words were, "Remember, if ever you need anything or anybody done, just give me a call."

We said goodbye about 5.30 and I made my way through the traffic to Heathrow Airport. While I was stuck in a traffic jam, I rang Liz and explained that the roads were blocked solid and I would probably be home very late or first thing in the morning. "If it takes me too long to get out of London, I'll probably get my head down in the truck for a few hours." She wasn't very happy because it was the first night off she'd had for a week.

I found a car park close to the airport—it was more like wasteland with rope around the perimeter—and parked the truck. I unloaded the Rolls and got changed into my suit about 6.30. All I had to do then was wait for the phone call.

The car park attendant, in his cap and yellow coat, came over from his hut while I was waiting and said, with a cockney accent, "Do you want me to look after your truck, guv?"

"Yes, please," I said. "I might not be back till early in the morning and I'll need to get off straight away." I slipped him a tenner and said, "Will this help?"

"Thanks very much, guv, that's fine. I'll make sure the path is clear when you arrive."

I thought to myself, I bet when they see a Rolls Royce these attendants must love it: 'I'll tap him up for a few bob.'

Just then my phone rang. It was Denise. She told me she had landed and would be at the hotel for seven. My pulse rate went up and I started to shake with excitement. As I drove out of the car park, the attendant touched his cap and waved.

I drove to the hotel, parked around the back and waited. I loaded a tape in the player and stared out of the window. Eventually, the phone rang. Smiling, I answered it in a smooth voice. "Hello."

"What time do you think you will be home then? Is it worth me waiting up or shall I go to bed?"

Pulling and I've been caught already' smile, I went hot all over. I almost followed with, "Is that you Denise?" Luckily Liz had spoken first. "Go to bed, I'm still stuck on the motorway trying to get out of London."

"All right, I'll see you in the morning then."

As I turned the phone off, it rang again. "Where are you?" this quiet voice said.

"I'm in the car park, why are you whispering?"

"I'm in the foyer. I'll meet you by the front revolving doors. What car are you in?" she asked, still very faintly.

"A black Rolls Royce."

"A what?"

Then the phone went dead.

I drove round to the front with a nervous smile on my face and she came running down the stairs, opened the door and jumped in.

"This is nice, where did you get this?" she said as she was looking all around the inside.

I pulled away quickly, glancing at Denise and noticing how gorgeous she looked. As I looked back up to the road ahead, there was a man about two metres in front of me. I swerved and heard him say something. I don't know whether my mind was playing tricks on me but he looked like Andrew. I didn't say anything to Denise; luckily she was too busy trying to find the seat-belt buckle.

I told her about my cousin selling the car as we drove towards London looking for a quiet restaurant. You could tell we were both nervous because we didn't speak much after that.

I drove about three miles and came across a nice place, laid back off the road, behind some trees. We pulled into the car park and drove slowly past the front door. It looked expensive.

A doorman suddenly came running down the steps. I opened the window, expecting him to say, "You can't park here, mate", like they do in our town, but in fact he said, with a soft Irish voice, "Can I park your car for you, sir?" and he opened the door.

Not being used to this treatment, I got out and he jumped in. Another doorman appeared and opened the door for Denise. I waited at the bottom of the steps and Denise came over clutching her purse. I put my arm around her shoulders and we walked up the steps.

As the car drove off, I said, "You look beautiful tonight."

She smiled as we approached the door and said, "So do you. Do you always drive a truck dressed like that?"

"Yes," I said, "It's called a truxedo."

We laughed, just as the door flew open and the waiter said, "Can I take your coat, madam?"

We stopped at the reception desk, while she slipped out of a black lace jacket.

The restaurant was a mass of greenery and waterfalls. The waiter showed us to a table, pulling the seat out for Denise, and we sat down opposite each other. "Shall I give you a few moments, sir, or would you like a drink while you browse through the menu?" I ordered a bottle of Shiraz and he left us a menu on the table.

"How do you feel?" I asked Denise.

"Nervous . . . and excited," she replied. "I feel like I'm on my first date."

In the background, we could hear faint music and the trickle of water from the waterfall. It was a very romantic setting for, hopefully, a very romantic night.

Denise put her one hand on the table as she picked up the menu with the other. I placed my hand on top of hers and said, "Can we forget everything else and enjoy each other till dawn?"

She looked up at me, smiled and said, "Sorry, I'm just a bit . . ." and paused. "You know, I've never done anything like this before."

Just then the waiter appeared. "Would you like to taste the wine, sir?"

"Yes, thank you." I held my glass up and he poured a bit in the bottom. Trying to look impressive, I smelt it first, then tipped the glass to my lips, swilled the wine around my mouth for a few seconds, put the glass down and nodded. "Yes, that's quite nice, thank you." He filled both our glasses and asked if we were ready to order.

Denise put one finger in the air and said, "Could you give us just a minute longer? There's so much on the menu, I can't make up my mind." With that, he bowed and left, walking backwards from the table.

Still holding hands, we started to talk more and calm down. The restaurant was empty really; there were only two other couples eating. It was nice because we didn't have to rush. We ate our meals, and a dessert from the trolley, drank a couple of liqueur coffees and were ready to leave by about ten o'clock.

After I'd paid the bill, the waiter brought Denise her jacket, and me the car keys, and said, "Your car is waiting for you at the bottom of the stairs."

As we walked towards the door, the manager said, "Goodnight and thank you for your custom, we hope you enjoyed your meal."

Denise said, "Yes, it was lovely, thank you," and we left. Sure enough, the Rolls was there and the two doormen held the car doors open for us. I said thank you and we drove away from what, so far, had been a successful evening.

We drove back towards the hotel, holding hands across the centre console and listening to music.

When we arrived at the hotel, Denise said, "I'll go in first and meet you at the bar. I'll just check to make sure no one is there from the flight and then I'll come over."

I watched her walk through the revolving door, then parked the car. I hung back and followed her in. Looking around quickly, I made my way into the lounge and up to the bar as instructed. I sat on a stool and ordered myself a large whiskey—Dutch courage perhaps—and waited.

After about five minutes, Denise came over and said, "I'll have to go up to the room, there's a stewardess over there from the flight and she's been on a trip once, when I took Andrew to New York. Give me ten minutes and come up. It's on the second floor, room number 206." With that, she turned and left.

I ordered another whiskey and sat stirring the ice with the straw, looking at myself in the mirror, behind the bottles of different spirits hanging up on the wall in front of me. I suddenly realised the night was going too fast. I came down to London, collected the car, picked up Denise, and ate a meal, now it was time to have my first affair. I hadn't noticed what she was wearing, what colour her shoes were. I hadn't even noticed how much the bill was for the meal, or whether I gave the doormen a tip. I had been in a daze for hours and it passed with the click of a finger. And here I was, going up to a room in a hotel, with my best friend's wife.

It didn't take long for me to realise there was no turning back. I downed the last mouthful in my glass, stood up by the stool and the barman came over. "Are you all right, sir?"

"Yes, thank you. Could you send a bottle of champagne up to room 206 please?"

"Certainly, sir," the waiter said as he took my glass away and wiped the bar.

I paid him and made my way over to the lift. The door opened and I stepped in nervously. "Two, please," I said to the elderly, smartly dressed man, in his blue jacket with gold braiding down the sleeves.

On the second ping, the doors opened. I thanked the lift attendant and stepped forward looking at the room numbers: 201, 202, 203, 204, 205, 206. I stood by the door, staring at the gold numbers. My mind was saying, "Don't go in," but my one-eyed trouser-snake was saying, "Knock on the door". I couldn't decide what to do. I clenched my fist and held it up to the door, about two inches away, still looking at the numbers. Then all of a sudden the lift pinged again and made me jump. I was trembling and so nervous that my knuckle hit the door. It clicked open, so I gingerly pushed it and looked though the three-inch gap. As I pushed it open more, I looked up and down the corridor to see if any one was there, and went in.

I closed the door and looked around the room for Denise, with one hand behind me, still on the doorknob, holding it tightly, still very nervous and undecided. Then, all of a sudden, Denise walked into the room, wearing a see-through black nightie. The light from the bathroom shone behind, showing off her perfectly shaped body. All the doubts, fears and inhibitions went straight out of the window dropped two storeys and smashed on the car park floor. I let go of the doorknob and began to loosen my tie, when all of a sudden there was a loud knock on the door. A cold shiver went down my spine and, for a split second, I thought to myself, it's Andrew—he was in the car park when I pulled away earlier.

Denise ran back into the bathroom and closed the door. I pushed my tie back up and quickly opened the door.

"Your champagne, sir." It was the man from the lift. I was so relieved; I reached in my pocket and pulled out a note. As I held it out and took the tray, I realised it was a £20 note. "Thank you, sir, can I get you anything else?" he asked with a big grin on his face.

Reluctantly, I said, "No, that will be all, thank you."

He put the note in his back pocket with one hand, as he turned the 'do not disturb' sign round on the door handle with the other, and said, "Have a good night, sir," as he turned to go.

I whispered, "Orange juice at seven a.m. would be nice."

He smiled again and replied, "No problem, sir. With a red rose, no doubt."

I pushed the door to and quietly said to myself, "Goodnight, smart arse."

I put the tray down on the side, carried the ice bucket and two glasses over to the bed, put them on the table and opened the bathroom door. Denise was standing there with a towel draped in front of her. "Who was it?"

I half smiled and said, "I ordered Champers."

With a sigh of relief, she placed the towel back on the rail and said, "I thought it was-"

I placed my finger on her lips before she could say anything else and whispered, "Don't say any more." I put my arms around her and we kissed, for the first time, in the doorway.

Denise undid my tie and dropped it on the floor. I took off my jacket while I was kicking off my shoes and sat on the bed to slip my socks off. I pulled Denise on top of me. We kissed, more and more, and, holding her as close as possible, my hands glided all over her negligee. We rolled over each other and she lay on her back, looking up at the mirrored ceiling. Laying by her side, I unfastened the pink bow that held the top together and peeled off her skimpy see-through lace undies, then placed my hand on her knee and slowly worked my way up the inside of her tanned, smooth thighs until I felt a little tuft of hair. I slowly stroked it until Denise parted her legs. She was moist and warm.

I opened my eyes and she said, "Now, I must have it now." Her hand slid into the front of my pants, she stroked and pulled me out in one movement.

We made love for ages, slowly and passionately.

After a while, we sat up on the bed. I poured two glasses of champagne. The ice had melted in the bucket but it was still cold and we drank it holding hands, in between kissing. I asked Denise what time she had to be at the airport.

Sipping her drink, she said, "Eight o'clock," so I leaned over and put the radio on very low. Louis Armstrong was singing 'We have all the time in the world'. I turned and put my glass on the table next to the bed and asked if she wanted to dance. I stood up; Denise pulled the sheet up to her waist and slid over to my side. I held my hand out and she stood up, wrapping the sheet around us both. With a cold glass in the small of my back, and nothing on, we slowly moved from side to side, our cheeks touching each other. We were all alone, slowly dancing, saying nothing, thinking nothing, just listening to the words. Then afterwards, we kissed again.

Denise placed her empty glass on the table, picked up two silk pillows and dropped them onto the floor. As I filled the glasses again, she dropped to her knees and pulled me down towards her. I gently peeled off the sheet, picked up my champagne and, lying next to her, I poured a few drops slowly over her stomach. Placing the glass on the floor, I gently massaged it in to her perfectly round nipples and then licked them dry, kissing and caressing my way up under her chin to her wet lips. We licked each other vigorously, until she said quietly, "You make me feel so sexy. Can you do it to me once more?" It had been a long time since I had made love twice in one night. We fondled each other softly and slowly and eventually it happened.

Afterwards, we lay on the bed and fell asleep holding each other, as if we were locked together.

I woke up as Denise was trying to untangle herself. The alarm was beeping. I looked at the clock by the bed as she kissed me and said, "I must have a shower, its 5.30."

Half awake, and worn out, I got up and sat on the bed as Denise slipped her panties on and went into the bathroom. I rubbed my eyes, trying to get them to focus, and thought about last night. I sat with my head in my hands when I heard the shower blasting, then I realised that in a couple of hours it would be all over. A cold shiver went through me. I lifted my head and noticed steam coming from the bathroom door that was ajar. I stood up and pushed the door open a little more. I could just see through the steam. Denise was rubbing soap all over her body with a yellow sponge, behind the frosted-glass door. I went into the bathroom, pulled it open and stepped in.

Denise wiped some foam on my nose and said, "I hope you weren't peeping out there," with a wanton smile on her face.

I put my arms around her waist and moved under the water jet. "I need a shower too, you know."

She grabbed my hands and sat back on the bench in the cubicle and I fell to my knees. She sat there covered in foam, with her legs apart. As I thrust myself into her, she dropped the sponge and stuck her nails into my buttocks, pulling me further and further in.

It was all over. I'd never experienced an orgasm so quick and so explosive as that before. I just knelt there, holding Denise, not wanting to let go. With the shower still spraying on my back, I dropped down onto the wet floor and Denise stood up and said, "I must have a shower and get ready, or I'll be late."

I rinsed myself down and wrapped a white towel around my waist. Dripping wet, I went back into the bedroom. I was drying myself off when there was a knock at the door. I went over, with the towel still around my waist and peered around the door as I opened it. The orange juice had arrived, with the red rose on the tray. I took it, thanked the waiter, and closed the door. Then I went over to the champagne and made two Buck's Fizz drinks with what was left from last night, just as Denise came out of the bathroom in a bathrobe. She looked up at me holding the rose between my teeth, with the drinks in my hands. She took a glass with one hand, the rose with the other and put it to her nose.

I looked into her big eyes, tipped my glass and said, "I will never forget how gorgeous you are," and kissed her cheek.

We got dressed, Denise packed her case, and left about 7.30. We kissed once more by the door and, as she opened it, with a tear in her eye, she said, "I'll see you at the weekend," and left first. I glanced round the room to see if we had left anything and followed her down in the lift.

As I walked across the foyer, I could see Denise talking to someone with the same uniform by the desk, so I walked past her and gently touched her hand with my finger, but kept on walking, didn't turn back, just carried on through the door and out into the car park. I found the car, got in and drove towards the exit, past the coach parked on the front, and made my way back to my lorry. I got changed in the cab, loaded the Rolls onto the truck, tied it on securely and made my way towards the motorway.

I pulled up at a road island to let some cars go by and the same coach stopped beside me. I looked along the coach and saw Denise sitting halfway along by the window. She lifted her hand, waved her fingers discreetly and smiled. A lump came up into my throat and the coach pulled away with Denise looking back at me. I quickly turned the radio up louder, trying to distract myself, and pulled away. The traffic wasn't too bad and all the way home I relived every second of the time we had spent together. The journey seemed to pass quickly and I arrived back at the garage by mid-morning.

# Chapter 5

A COUPLE OF days went by and, luckily, I didn't see Andrew, so the guilt was wearing off. I'd told Liz that I was still stuck in the traffic at eight o'clock, so I'd found a little cafe, had a bite to eat, fallen asleep in the truck till five o'clock in the morning and got back to the garage about nine.

On the Saturday morning, the phone rang. I was cleaning the Rolls when one of the lads said, "It's for you."

I took the call and a voice said, "Hello, it's me, how are you?" I was surprised; it was Denise. She said, "I'm on the motorway coming home. Is everything OK?"

"Yes, fine, hold on while I run upstairs." I went up to my office, and picked up the receiver. "I've missed you."

"Not as much as I've missed you," Denise said. "I've tried to ring Andrew but there's no reply. Have you seen him?"

"No, he's probably working, I haven't spoke to him yet. Does he know what time you'll be home?"

"Yes, he always-" The phone went dead.

I replaced the receiver and waited. After a while, I phoned Denise's car phone and a posh voice said, "Sorry, the number you are calling is not responding. It may respond if you try again." It was probably because she was in a built-up area and had lost the signal.

I went back down the stairs. When I got to the bottom, the phone rang again. I answered it in the workshop and Denise said, "These phones are bloody useless." I laughed and she said, "He must be working. It's funny because he usually rings me. Never mind, I'll speak to you later, when I-" The line went dead again.

I finished cleaning the car and left for home. As I turned into my road, the phone rang. I pulled over to the kerb to answer it. It was Denise again.

"Have you found him yet?" I jokingly said.

She sounded worried. "No, I'm home and there's no sign, or note. I've phoned everywhere I thought he might be and no one has seen him. It's not like Andrew, he always rings me."

I mentioned a few places he could be and Denise told me she had tried them all. I started to worry as Denise started crying. "Don't worry, I'm nearly home now. I'll ring a few people as well and call you back." As I pulled away the same thought entered my mind as when I was in the room in London: perhaps he was in the car park.

I turned onto my drive. I could see his car in the corner. I was so relieved as I quickly phoned Denise back. "It's OK, he's here, or at least his car is."

"I never thought of ringing Liz," she replied. "See you later."

I parked the car and, as I entered the house, Liz was talking on the phone in the kitchen and Andrew was in the garden, playing Swing ball with Mick.

I opened two cans of beer, went outside and sat on the chair while they finished their game. Andrew came over and sat next to me, sweat pouring from his brow.

"How are you?" I said first.

"Worn out . . . your son . . . has had me running round like an idiot."

Then Mick came over. "Hello, Dad, do you want a game?"

"Not yet, son, perhaps later."

Just then, Liz came out with a glass of white wine in her hand and said, "Denise is looking for you."

Andrew stood up quickly and said, "I forgot—what time is it?"

"Don't worry, she's coming round for a quick drink, as it's so warm and sunny."

I sat waiting for the doorbell to chime, so that I could be the one to open the door. Mick got changed and dived into the pool to cool off and Andrew followed him, so I went into the kitchen to fetch some more beers. Just as I opened the door to the fridge, I heard a car pull onto the drive. I got to the front door before Denise had time to ring the bell.

"Hello, how are you?" I asked, kissing her cheek.

"Better now. I thought Andrew had found out about us and left me. I'm very tired; I've not slept much in the last few days. While I was in Washington, I couldn't stop thinking about you."

I closed the door and, as we walked in to the kitchen, she said, "It must never happen again but thanks for a lovely night. I think it would be better if we didn't mention it again, for obvious reasons."

I rescued a couple of beers from the fridge and poured Denise a glass of red wine. As I handed her the glass I said, "Perhaps we could go for a drink one day."

"No, what we did was nice, but wrong."

Just then Andrew walked in. "Hello, have you had a good trip?"

"Yes, it was nice. I was worried when I couldn't find you anywhere."

Andrew apologised and said he was too busy playing with Mick, then we all went out into the garden and sat there till about seven, drinking and talking.

A few days passed; I didn't speak to Denise at all. Andrew rang me to tell me that he had booked a squash court for Thursday night. So I went home early and met him at the courts. We trashed the little green ball up against the wall for twenty minutes or so and then went for a beer in our local.

While we were talking about work and things, he asked me if we would like to go for a meal in a couple of weeks. The table was booked for eight people. It was a new restaurant, in Lyddington, and the food was supposedly very nice. We had another drink and I went home.

Liz was in bed, so the following day she rang me when she finished work and I told her about the meal. "I know," she said. "It will be nice. I will probably be working, but I'll swap my shift with someone. Can you organise a minibus so we can all go together?"

"Leave it with me, I'll do it now." I said goodbye and drove up the road to see a friend who hired them out. I went into his office and booked it.

"The only problem is, no one but you can drive it, so you will have to stay sober," he said, laughing.

I filled the forms out, thinking to myself, I will anyway because Denise will be there, and Julie—hopefully my next date—and I don't want to say anything wrong.

On my way back to the garage, I had a phone call telling me that there was someone looking at the Rolls Royce. I told them I'd be about five minutes and hung up. As I approached, I could see someone sitting in the car on the forecourt. I drove past to park my car at the other end and, as I looked at him, I could tell he was, what we call in the trade, a time waster or a dreamer. If someone wants to buy a car of this class, they don't bring the three kids and let them climb all over the back seats.

After about ten minutes of him looking under the bonnet, inside the boot, kicking the tyres and revving the engine, trying to seem like he knew what to look for, I started to get a little angry. He asked questions like, "How many miles will it do to the gallon?" and "Are the tyres expensive?" Straight away, I could tell he couldn't afford it. Then I really lost interest when he said, "Will you take £4,000 in cash?" It was £3,000 less than I wanted.

I closed the bonnet, shut the boot, took the keys out and locked the doors. As I walked away, I couldn't help myself. I said, "I bet you drive a mini."

The man said, "There's no need to be like that, I didn't come here to be insulted."

I replied, "Your type can probably go anywhere for that." I walked away and went up to my office shaking with anger.

The following week, I sold the car to an Arabic-looking man, from Liventry. Apparently, he'd passed the garage a few times on his way to work and had fallen in love with the car. It was just what he had been looking for. He paid me the asking price, with a cheque, and, when it cleared at the bank, I rang him and he collected the car, after we completely valeted inside and out. I would have liked it myself but, with business not so good, I couldn't justify it.

As it drove off down the road, I thought about my first date with Denise. I had made a small profit, so I was quite pleased with myself. I rang my cousin, told him and arranged for the money to be sent down to London by registered post to save me the journey; not that I would mind if Denise was going to be down there again.

On the Friday, I made a quick phone call to make sure everything was OK with the minibus and arranged to collect it on the way home.

I arrived home about six o'clock to see Liz walking round the house in curlers and a dressing gown. Mick was watching telly with his overnight bag ready by his side, eating sweets and dropping wrappers all over the floor with one leg dangling over the arm of the chair. I went upstairs and got in the bath after a quick chat with him about school.

As I lay there, soaking in the steamy bathroom, I tried to think of ways to ask Julie out. Maybe while we were dancing, or outside; perhaps I could get her to sit in the front of the minibus? None of them seemed a good idea, in case someone overheard me.

I got myself ready in a dinner suit that I'd hired. I thought it best not to wear my own, which was at the garage; Liz would have asked me questions.

Liz wore a tightly fitted, long red dress, with long sleeves and a row of pearls around her neck that I hadn't seen before. She looked lovely. It was probably the first time we'd been out together in ages.

We climbed into the bus and dropped Mick off at his Nan's on the way. There was no school the next day, so we didn't have to worry about collecting him till the morning.

We were the first to arrive at Denise and Andrew's. It was decided we'd all meet there because the location was in the middle of everyone's house and not far from the motorway. They could all have a drink before we made our way to the restaurant.

First to appear were Sandra and Henry. Sandra was a lovely girl but I hadn't included her in my game because I knew she would definitely say no. They were only married about two years ago. I could remember that wedding like it was yesterday. It was one of those weddings you never forget; even the stag night was a good one. If I remember, it was on the Thursday night; Sandra wanted Henry to be sober on the wedding day and have Friday off to help with the organising.

We went to a few bars and clubs in the city centre, getting a little more drunk at each one. By the end, Henry was so drunk he couldn't stand on his own. Three of us had to carry him out of the last place, so we took all his money off him and put him on a train to Scotland. It was about ten in the morning when someone found him and woke him up. He had to reverse the charges and ring Sandra, who wasn't very pleased at all with any of us, and her father had to pay to get him back. He arrived home about seven o'clock that night, still covered in sick and piss.

The wedding was much the same; the car broke down and was late to start with. Then it went to the wrong church, the organ music was out of key and, to top it all, the vicar was pissed and forgot his words. The bride started crying, the groom was trying to console her outside the church. The best man put his arm around Sandra's mum because she started as well and he was accused by Sandra's dad of trying to get off with her.

Anyway, it all calmed down in the end and the photographs said it all: most people had red sore eyes through crying or laughing.

I laughed through most of it. In fact I was in pain at one stage. We still talked about it at parties.

As I was standing talking to Henry, the doorbell rang. It was Simon and Julie. Andrew opened the door and my heart came up into my mouth; Julie looked like a film star. Her hair was shorter than I remembered. I couldn't stop myself staring; she looked sexier than ever. I hadn't seen her since the barbecue. Her auburn hair was layered just over her shoulders and her blue eyes looked piercing as she smiled at me. She was wearing a black short skirt to just above her knees and a black shiny top. She had lost some weight and looked absolutely stunning.

After I stopped myself dribbling, I went over and kissed her on the cheek and said hello. I wanted to throw her on the carpet and have her, there and then.

We all stood in the kitchen and talked for a while and Henry opened the champagne that he'd brought with him. I was standing by the fridge, still looking at Julie, when the cork popped. Out of the corner of my eye, I could see Denise peering over her fluted crystal glass. She winked, which reminded me of London, then she smiled and turned away.

When everyone had finished their drinks, I loaded them into the bus. I put the men at the back and the girls towards the front, so when I looked in the rear-view mirror, I could see Julie and Denise while I was driving.

We arrived at the restaurant just after eight. The waiters took our coats and showed us to the long table that was laid out well. The girls sat one side and the men the other. I sat opposite Julie, on the end, and by her side was Denise, so I could look at them both all night.

Denise looked extremely sexy with her dark hair and short, pleated white skirt. In fact, we all looked like millionaires and so did some of the other people that were in there. The diamonds on some of the women were massive. And gold—I'd never seen so much in one room.

We ordered some wine. I had a glass while we were waiting for the menu. We talked a bit and the waiter came over with a menu for each of us and we ordered some more wine with our meals. Some of the people who had already eaten were dancing on the other side of the room to a five-piece soft jazz band. The restaurant was quite large inside and full of people. The decor was very modern; lots of chrome and glass everywhere.

While we were waiting for the food to arrive, I asked Denise if she would like to dance. She placed her glass on the table and said, "Yes, please, I thought you would never ask." She stood up and I could hear the others on our table clapping as we walked towards the dance floor.

There was a big round pillar in the middle of the room, so I wanted to dance with that between our table, and us so no one could see what we where up too. We stepped onto the dance floor. Denise put her arms on my shoulders, and I put mine around her waist. She looked deep into my eyes, tipped her head slightly to one side and said, "I love you." Then she pulled my head towards hers and kissed me, long and slowly. We started to move from side to side gently, still kissing each other passionately as a clarinet introduced the next tune softly.

I lifted my head and looked around. A few other couples were dancing close together around us. After a while the rhythm changed. It was more upbeat. We danced lambada-style in the middle of the dance floor, with all the others watching us. Everyone started clapping and cheering as the beat got faster and faster.

After the music finished, we walked back to the table. Simon followed us. As we sat down, he asked what was happening. "I couldn't see from the side, there were too many people standing around the edge of the dance floor."

I told him that there was a couple dancing and they were very good, just as the waiter appeared with our food. I had a steak in white wine sauce. It was nice but very small; I had to move the ten peas and one potato to find it—they call it nervous cuisine, I think.

When I finished, I looked over at Julie and hoped I might have a dance with her later. While I was sipping the last of my red wine, I noticed that Liz was having a deep conversation with Andrew at the other end of the table and Henry and Sandra got up and went for a dance. I talked to Julie, hoping Simon would ask Denise for a dance so I could ask her out, but he started talking to her instead, so I asked Julie for a dance. She stood up and dabbed her mouth with the table napkin and held my hand as we walked through the tables to the dance floor.

We held each other closely as we danced, but I couldn't bring myself to say the words, then Henry came over with Sandra and said, "It's my turn to dance with Julie, can we swap?"

I agreed and danced with Sandra for the rest of the song but every time I looked at Julie as we faced each other, she seemed as if she wanted to say something.

After that we all sat down. Some of the girls had sweets, Simon ordered more wine and I had boring lemonade. Simon and Andrew had started to look a little worse for wear by this time and Liz didn't look too good either. I looked at my watch; it was almost 11.30.

Denise said, "I've had enough now, take me home." Henry called the waiter over and asked for the bill.

Liz was just starting to nod off, slumped back in the chair, so Andrew tapped her arm. She opened her eyes and just said, "Home," and closed them again.

The bill came and Andrew paid it with his credit card and said something like, "Short it out tomorrow." Another waiter came over with the coats, and we made our way out to the car park. Andrew helped Liz most of the way, then she came round as the fresh air hit her. The others were swaying a bit and I was as sober as some judges.

I opened the minibus's side door and everyone piled in. As we pulled away, Simon started to sing and, by the time we got to the motorway, they were all joining in.

We pulled up on Andrew's drive and I heard him shout, "Let's get the driver pished, everybody into our houshe!"

I locked the van and we all went in. Liz walked in the front door, turned left and straight up the stairs to bed. Andrew poured some more drinks and Simon put the music on. I had a few drinks, a dance or two and fell asleep next to Henry on the settee.

When I awoke in the morning, Henry had gone. Simon was snoring in the chair across the room, so I went into the kitchen and made some coffees.

I was banging the cups so someone would hear me and come down. Liz was first, with make-up all over her cheeks, trying to focus on anything. "Are you all right?" I asked with my arm around her shoulder.

"I think so," she said as she yawned.

"Drink this then and we'll go and fetch Mick."

"I don't want anything, just my bed."

I put some cold water in my coffee to cool it down and left the rest ready for when the others awoke. I drank mine quickly, poured Liz's down the sink and we left. We picked Mick up and I dropped them both off at home, took the bus back, then made my way to work.

# Chapter 6

THE NEXT WEEK passed quickly; we had a lot of work at the garage for a change. On Friday night, I stopped at the Wooden Cross pub for a drink. I'd often do this on my way home from work. There would usually be a crowd of my friends who meet there once a week, telling stories and jokes. There were financial consultants, salesmen, truck drivers, and accountants, Simon, Andrew and sometimes Henry. It was the end of the week and we'd wind down and have a laugh and a joke before going home.

Simon came in late, bought himself a drink and came over to join us. Apparently, Julie's car had broken down and he'd had to stop and fix it. We talked about this and that and then he said, "I'm looking forward to the party tomorrow night—are you?"

I shook my head and said, "What party?"

"I told you the other night in Lyddington, it's Ken's 40th birthday party at the Greek restaurant in Applers Green. I did tell you."

"Well, who's been invited?" I asked discreetly.

"There're loads of us, all the crowd from last Saturday."

I didn't hear any more. I went into a trance because Julie would be there—that's when I would ask her out.

I finished my drink and carefully made my way home. As I went in, Liz was just finishing her tea sitting by the telly. I kissed her on the head and carried on into the kitchen to get my tea out of the oven. Liz walked in behind me and put her plate in the sink. I asked her if she had remembered about tomorrow night at the Greek restaurant.

"Yes, I can't come because I'm working Sunday morning and Denise isn't here. She had to go to India, so you and Andrew will have to go on your own."

It was getting better. I pretended to be upset but at the back of my mind I was thinking, we can play up and hopefully get drunk. I took my dinner through to the lounge on a tray, sat and watched some telly for a while and Liz went upstairs and got into bed.

I awoke next morning on the settee with the tray still on my lap. Liz had gone to work, so Mick and I had some breakfast and I took him to work with me. We messed about, washed my car, cleaned the truck and did some of the jobs I never usually got time to do in the week.

It was about midday when the phone rang. It was Simon panicking. "Julie has broken down on the motorway travelling back from her Nan's and I need someone to fetch her and the car. I've just spoken to Andrew and he said you might be able to help me with your truck."

"Slow down," I said. "Tell me where she is first."

"Sorry, she's by the M54 somewhere in Telford," he explained. "She was ringing from a callbox—I've got the number, have you got a pen?"

I wrote it down on my notepad. "Do you want to come with me or do you want to meet me there?"

"That's my other problem, I've only got three hours to paint this car I'm working on before it's collected. I haven't got time," he went on to say.

It suddenly hit me—Julie all alone, in the middle of nowhere, sitting, waiting for me to collect her like a knight in shining armour; tired, scared, not knowing what was happening. I could not believe it; I was beside myself. I tried to act calmly and said, "Yes, I'll go, but you'll owe me a few pints tonight." He couldn't thank me enough. It was me that should be thanking him.

I quickly rang Liz and asked her to get my suit ready and explained briefly that I wouldn't be back till late and that if I came in then to get changed, I would probably wake her. I would be home soon to drop Mick off and would have a shower before going to collect the car, then I could go straight to the party afterwards.

I put the phone down and rang Julie. I could hardly hear; it was a terrible line. I could just make out that someone was there. I found myself shouting. "Is that you, Julie?" It was no good. I dialled the number again. It was a bit better but it wasn't Julie. It was a woman's voice. I asked, "Is there someone by you?"

She said, "No."

"Is there a car close to you with the bonnet up?" She said no again, so I said, "Where are you?"

She replied, "Here, talking to you on the phone."

So I tried once more. "Where is the phone?"

I couldn't believe it when she said, "In my hand." I put the phone down smiling but I was starting to worry a bit; it sounded like she had broken down in a nut-home.

I sat by the phone for five minutes, hoping Simon had told her I was on my way to fetch her. Then, as I was about to lock up, the phone rang. It was Julie. "Are you all right?" I said first.

"Yes, I'm on a different phone number to what Simon gave you, I found somewhere to wait."

"OK, I will be there as soon as possible." She gave me a rough idea where she was and the new phone number, then I said, "I'll ring you from the truck when I'm a bit closer."

I put the phone down and turned the computer off that Mick had been playing games on. We locked the office door and drove home in the truck, leaving my car at work.

When we got home, I had a quick shower, put my clothes in the truck and set out. As I pulled on to the M6, my phone rang in the cab. It was Julie.

She said, "It's really nice of you to come all this way to fetch me."

"It's my pleasure," I replied excitedly. "I'll be with you in about two hours, are you all right where you are?"

"Yes, no problem. I booked myself into a hotel in case anything went wrong and I couldn't get home tonight."

It's too good to be true, I thought to myself. I told her I would be there as soon as possible and her exact words were, "I can't wait."

I put the phone down and my foot to the floor and thought, neither can I.

The traffic was slowing down on the inside lane just before the turn off. I crawled on to the junction, pulled up on the side of the road, rang Julie and she gave me directions to the hotel.

When I eventually pulled up, she came running out of the front door. I opened the truck door for her and she leapt up into the cab, sat on my lap, flung her arms around me and gave me a kiss straight on the lips. She wasn't the only thing that jumped up in the truck.

After a couple of minutes, she said, "I don't believe we are here together all alone. Will we be in time for the party tonight?"

With a smirk on my face, I carefully said, "That's up to you, we could turn up late."

After all she had been through, she still looked beautiful. She thought for a second and looked up at me and said, with a beaming smile, "It would be a shame to waste the room." She kissed me again, with her hand slowly falling down my cheek.

We climbed out of the cab and I followed Julie, past the reception, up the stairs to the third floor, running and holding hands. As she unlocked her door, we kissed again briefly and then she pulled me in. As soon as the door was closed, she pushed me back against it and unzipped my trousers, licking my lips and tongue with the tip of hers, as if we only had the room for minutes. She flicked my trouser clip open and they fell to the floor, followed by my pants. We continued to lick each other.

I put my hands up under each side of her skirt, felt for the thin sidepieces of her panties and ripped them off. As they dropped to the floor, she kicked them away. I put my hands under each of her legs and, pulling them apart, I lifted her off the ground, turning round and pushing her back against the door. I felt myself enter Julie in one thrust. She shouted, "More, more, faster, faster!"

It wasn't long before it was all over. I found it hard to control myself, I couldn't stop. I opened my eyes to see Julie's lovely face in front of me. Her head was resting against the door and she had beads of sweat on her forehead.

She opened her eyes and said, "I've being waiting for that to happen for years and years."

I gently placed her back on the floor and we kissed some more, holding each other.

Still standing in the room, I glanced at my watch over her shoulder and quietly said, "It's 6.30, shall we make a move?"

Looking up at me with big blue eyes, she said, "Can we stay a little longer? It might never happen again."

"I wanted to ask you last week in Lyddington about going out for a night but I couldn't ask you when we were dancing. I was just scared in case you said no and then

Henry butted in and I lost my chance. I would like to spend the whole night with you."

"I'd love that," she replied.

"So if I arrange something in the next week and let you know?"

"Just give me a few days' notice and I'm sure I could work it," she said and kissed me on the nose.

We collected our things together, got dressed and made our way down the stairs to the reception desk. I took Julie's bag out, climbed into the truck and Julie followed a few minutes later.

She rummaged through her bag as we pulled off the drive and found a pair of panties to put on.

"The others are still in the room," she said.

"Don't worry, they wouldn't fit you now anyway," I jokingly said. We laughed as we drove off to fetch her broken-down car.

Julie gave me directions and we found the car on the side of the road. She stayed in the cab while I loaded it on the back of the truck and strapped it down tight. We started back. On the way she told me how she'd taken a taxi to the hotel. I told her about the funny phone call I had trying to reach her and how surprised I was when Simon phoned.

We arrived back at the garage about nine o'clock. I left the car on the back of the truck, locked in the yard, and we drove quickly back to Julie's house. I got changed downstairs while she had a bath and we were at the restaurant 45 minutes later.

As we walked though the door of the restaurant, Simon came running over and kissed Julie. She looked a bit guilty and dropped her head as he shook my hand and said, “Thanks for doing that.”

Smiling to myself, I mumbled that it was a pleasure.

Everyone looked as if they were having a good time singing and dancing, so Julie and I went and sat down to have something to eat. Everyone else had already eaten. We were so hungry. Simon went up to the bar to get us a drink, while we sat waiting to order. I held Julie’s hand under the table and she squeezed it hard and said, “Thank you for bringing me home.”

I whispered in her ear, “You can thank me again next week. Can you come up with a good excuse to stay out all night?”

“Yes, I’ll just say I’m going to see my aunt or something like that.”

“No, you can’t say that, it must be somewhere that Simon can’t ring you. Have you got a friend that lives far away? Someone you can go and visit? And then you can ring Simon and say you had one drink too many and you’re going to stay the night and you’ll be back in the morning.”

I looked across the room and Simon was bringing the drinks over. As he put them on the table, he said, “I’ve had trouble trying to get you something to eat; the kitchens were just closing but I explained what has happened and why you were late and the manager is sending a waiter over.”

Julie took a mouthful of wine and said, “Good, I haven’t eaten all day.”

Simon sat next to me and thanked me again and asked if I'd found it OK. I told him everything went to plan and he said, "Good, I thought Julie might have to pay for the hotel."

A cold shiver went straight through me. I didn't know what he was going to say next; I wasn't sure how much he knew. Then Julie interrupted. "I gave them my credit card at the desk and, while I was waiting, I went up to the room and lay on the bed for a bit—they charged me for it, I'm sure. As I left, I signed the slip but I was so glad to be coming home, I didn't look to see how much it was."

"Never mind, at least you're here now". Then he stood up as the waiter came to the table and said, "I'll get you another drink to have with your meal, you have some catching up to do."

We ordered starters and a main course. We could see the waiter wasn't very happy; he probably thought he had finished for the night. I was disappointed he didn't look or sound Greek, so that I could show off.

Julie grabbed my hand again and said, "That was close, I had to tell him that because he'll see the bill when it comes in."

"I know I was worried about that too."

We talked for a while and the food arrived. It was a different waiter. He put the tray down on the table and said with a Greek accent, "I hear you broken down with your car, I am so happy for you to make in time for the meal. I was closing the kitchens as you came. It would have been a shame for you to miss such a beautiful meal, so enjoy."

Julie said thank you as he placed a salad in front of her and, as he turned to me, I said, "Efharist'o garson" (thank you waiter).

His ears pricked up and he smiled and said, "You can speak the Greek?"

I told him, just a little, and asked him, "Ti kanei?s" (How are you?)

He replied, "Kalla, esis ti canis?" (Well, and how are you?)

I replied with, "As ta lene kala" (can't complain). I began to eat my starter, as if to say, no more talking, I'm hungry, and he said something else that I didn't understand. I nodded and said, "I will speak with you after my dinner, at the bar."

He smiled and said, "A little ouzo later, perhaps," and left.

I had the calamari; that's squid in batter. It was very nice. For the main dish, I had beef stifardo. Julie had fish. The food was excellent.

When we'd finished at the table, Julie had a dance and I went to speak with the waiter. I had a couple of ouzos (my favourite drink) and talked to him for a while. The party came to an end just after midnight and most of us went back to Ken's house by taxi and carried on. I had a couple of dances with Julie and left about 2.30 and arrived home an hour before Liz got up for work. I fell asleep on the settee downstairs and when she left I went and got into bed.

Mick woke me up at ten o'clock by jumping on my head, shouting, "Dad, can we go over the park?" We had a pillow fight first, then went to the park and played football for a while. When Liz came home, she took me to collect my car from the Greek restaurant.

* * *

On the Monday, I got up early and went for a run. Liz had a day off. I made my way to work after dropping Mick at school. The traffic was quite bad, so I went the back way, past Lucy's house. Lucy is number three on my list of dates. She is five feet six, with blonde shoulder-length hair and slim with a gorgeous big bust.

As I passed her house, I saw her crossing the road, so stopped and chatted for a while. Lucy told me that her husband Ivor was away again on business and how bored she was staying in on her own night after night, so I told her to ring Liz and arrange a night out; Liz hadn't seen Lucy for ages.

"That would be nice," she said. "We've been so busy lately with one thing and another. The roof has had to be done, the next door's windows, it's been a nightmare. I won't go into it now but when Ivor is back, you and Liz will have to come round for a meal and I will explain how much work Ivor caused us while he was on the roof one day."

"It sounds fascinating, I can't wait. Give Liz a ring and sort something out soon then."

I said goodbye and drove off to work. Lucy would be harder to ask out; she was not really the unfaithful type.

I was almost at work when my mobile rang. It was Julie. I asked her if she was all right and she said, "Yes, the kids have gone to school, Simon's gone to work and I thought you might pop round to see me, the house is empty."

"No!" I said and explained that we had to be very careful about this. "If any one of your neighbours saw me going into your house in the day, they could say something to Simon. I'll arrange something this week and call you back."

With a sad voice she said, "I want to see you, I can't wait that long."

"I'll ring you back, I promise." I turned the phone off as I pulled up at work.

When I got out of the car, Roger reminded me that I should have collected a car on the way in. I had completely forgotten about it.

Later that day, I had a good idea. I phoned my friend down the road, to see if he could recommend someone that would hire out a chauffeur-driven limo. He gave me a number to try and, when I eventually got through, I explained that I wanted to take someone out on a very special date.

"That's our speciality," he said. "We have a fully stretched white Lincoln limousine, with full air conditioning, colour TV, drinks compartment and leather seats." He gave me the price with a chauffeur and I booked it for Friday night. I quickly phoned Julie, to tell her, and said that I would ring her later in the week. One of Julie's favourite films was The Bodyguard with Kevin Costner and Whitney Houston.

Julie was a very romantic girl, so the limo would be a good start to a very exotic evening.

# Chapter 7

IT WAS ON the Monday afternoon when I drove over to Bletchminster, found a quiet restaurant and booked a table for two. Then I went into the town and came across a club that looked like fun but it was closed till six o'clock. I went across to the Chateau Etoile and booked the honeymoon suite in the name of Houston and on Tuesday I drove over to see the limo and paid for that.

I was very excited about this date. I phoned Julie on the Wednesday to make the final arrangements but Simon answered the phone. I was stumbling and fumbling for words; I was surprised when he said hello. I asked him if he'd found out what was wrong with the car.

". . . Yes," he said eventually. "You're lucky to catch me in."

I interrupted him and said, "I haven't got your work number in my truck and all week I've been meaning to ring you. I've just done another recovery and it reminded me and I thought Julie could tell me. I was just curious. When I get back to the garage, I'll probably forget again . . ." I suddenly thought to myself, I bet I'm nervously going on a bit, then he went into a long conversation about the car and what the problem was—I didn't really want to know.

I hung up eventually and rang Julie back later. I told her how to get to the restaurant and that the table was booked for 7.30, the rest would be a surprise. Then Julie told me that she'd told Simon she was going to a hen party in Worcester and he was all right with that.

On the Thursday night, while we were having dinner, I told Liz a group of us where going up to Yorkshire in one car on Friday afternoon, to a car auction. We would stay the night and get up early ready for when it opened, so that way we could have a good look at all the cars first on the Saturday morning and bring them home Saturday afternoon; apparently they are a lot cheaper up there, or so I told her.

"That's a good idea," she said. "I'm off at the weekend, so I can look after Mick. Is Andrew going with you? I know Denise is away."

"No, I didn't ask him, there won't be enough room in the car."

On the Friday morning, I got up early and went for a run as usual and left for work with some clean clothes in the car and my overnight bag. I dropped Mick off at school. As we stopped up by the gates, I noticed a woman dropping her daughter off at the same time. She was tall and slim with long dark hair and sunglasses holding her fringe up. I kissed Mick, and told him I would see him the following night. Even he passed a comment on how nice she was. As I pulled away, she was just locking the door to her BMW and I had to slow down. She looked at me with one of the sexiest smiles I've ever seen. I carried on to work.

There wasn't much going on, so I spent the day making the wages up, then stashed them in the drawer before an early finish. I stopped off at the dry cleaners to collect my tux, then carried on to the Chateau.

I used the room to get changed. It was an amazing place. I had a quick shower, which was more like a massage, put my suit on and went to wait for the limo.

As I stood by the entrance, mesmerised by all the paintings on the walls, I heard someone's voice in the background. "Mr Houston, your car is here." At first I took no notice, then it suddenly hit me, that's me. I turned around to see half a dozen people staring. I moved closer to the door; the long white limo was parked there at the bottom of the steps. The driver was holding the rear door open as the doorman escorted me outside.

As I approached, the driver took his cap off and said, "Good evening sir." I sat in the back and looked out of the side window as the door shut. I could see people trying to look inside, but they couldn't see me through the dark glass.

Everything in the car was cream leather and walnut. The television was on as we pulled away. The driver adjusted his mirror and said, "I've got the music you requested, shall I put it on yet?"

"No, can you put it on when we come out of the restaurant after the meal? Julie will be with me then, it's a surprise for her," I said excitedly.

The driver opened the door for me again when we arrived at the restaurant. As I stood up from the back seat, I arranged to meet him at nine and then I asked him, "Could you do me a favour? I tried to book everything in advance, but I couldn't pay for the club called the Manor, it was shut. If I give you some money, can you go there now, pay for it and ask if we can go straight in? We don't want to wait outside, it will spoil the night."

The driver winked and said, "Leave it with me, I know one of the doormen."

As I walked towards the restaurant, I had a quick glance around the car park to see if Julie's car was there but I couldn't see it. My stomach was churning over; I didn't know if it was because I was hungry or scared.

"I have a table booked for two," I said to the waiter who greeted me just inside the door.

"Yes, sir, if you would like to step this way. Your guest is already here."

That's odd, I thought, she doesn't know what name I booked it under. I followed him to the table and, as I approached, I could see it wasn't Julie. I explained that he must have got us mixed up and he was very apologetic. I did say to him that if my guest didn't turn up, she would do, and he laughed.

I sat at the table, nervously waiting, and ordered myself a large whiskey and lemonade with ice. The excitement was starting to wear off as it approached eight o'clock. Then the door flew open and Julie was standing looking around the room as she took her coat off and passed it to the waiter. I stood up so that she could see me. With a big smile on her lovely face she waved. I was so relieved. Julie looked fantastic as she walked towards me; she was dressed in a short black shiny dress, with diamonds around her neck, and her auburn hair had drooped over the sides of her face. We kissed and sat down together. She apologized for being late, as she pushed her hair behind her ears. I told her I was worried the car had broken down again but she reassured me with a smile that everything was all right on that front.

The waiter appeared and gave us two menus and then he asked Julie if she wanted a drink. She looked at him and indecisively said, "Can . . . I . . . have, err . . . gin and tonic, please, I am dying of thirst."

"I'll have another one of these, please," I asked as he walked to the bar.

Julie explained that she'd left the motorway at the wrong junction and had to go all the way down a long dual carriageway before she could get back onto the right road.

The waiter was already back with the drinks and asked if we were ready to order. After Julie took a sip from her glass, she said, "Two minutes, I must have a look and choose something nice."

We talked for a while browsed through the menu and ordered our meals with a bottle of wine. I had a steak and Julie had chicken in a white wine sauce. After that, we had two sweets from the trolley, coffee and brandies and sat talking till the waiter came over and said, "Your car is here, sir."

Julie looked up and grinned. "What car?"

"It's a surprise." We stood up and walked over to the door and Julie put her coat on. We said thank you and walked outside. I looked at Julie's face as she stared at the limo. She was ecstatic. She grabbed my arm with both hands and, squeezing it tightly, she said, "That's the car from The Bodyguard."

I laughed and said, "Wait till you see what else I've got planned for this night of ours."

The driver opened the rear door and, as we got nearer to the car, we could hear Whitney singing her heart out. The driver touched his hat with his finger and thumb and said good evening. Still with a smile on her face, we climbed into the back and the chauffeur walked round the rear of the car and got in.

Julie put her arm through mine and kissed me on my cheek. I looked at her as the car pulled away and she had tears in her eyes. "This is so romantic," she said. We sat there, holding hands and listening to the music. The driver told me everything was arranged at the other end. As we turned the last corner before the Manor club, I could see a queue of people outside waiting to go in. The car pulled up, the driver got out and opened the door for us. I got out first, still holding Julie's hand, and we stood together by the car. Every one in the queue turned to look at us; they must have thought we were film stars.

A doorman came down the steps and said, "Would you like to follow me?" and held my arm.

I heard the driver shout; "I will see you at 11.30." I turned and thanked him as we went up to the entrance, past everyone else who was waiting, and in through the door.

The manager came over and shook Julie's hand first and then mine and said, "I hope you have a pleasant evening."

We carried on up to the bar first. I stood leaning on the bar, with Julie in front of me, and my arm around her waist. After I ordered the drinks, she kissed me again. We looked around the room; all the lights were flashing and the music was very loud. I paid for the drinks and shouted in Julie's ear, "Shall we sit down over there?" She nodded and we walked over to one side, where it was a bit quieter and more secluded. We sat for a while, danced two or three times, had a few more drinks and eventually, when the music slowed down, we had a few close dances. I couldn't stop myself thinking about the rest of the night in the hotel.

At about 11 o'clock we sat back down. I left Julie for a moment, to visit the Gents. When I came out, there was a scruffy man sitting next to Julie. He was leaning all over her. I hurried back to our table and, as I approached, I heard him say to Julie, "Who the fuck are you, then?"

As I stood in front of him, he lifted his head up and tried to focus on me. He was about 35-40, and looked paralytic. Julie seemed upset, so I grabbed her hand and pulled her onto the dance floor. I asked her if she was all right.

"I was scared more than anything." I held her close and we danced for a while, hoping he had collapsed somewhere in a corner.

A few minutes went by, then, out the corner of my eye, I could see him staggering on to the dance floor towards us, knocking people out of the way. I quickly looked around the room to see if there was a bouncer handy. As he got nearer, he shouted, "I was talking to her, mate."

I turned my back on him and tried to take no notice, but he started poking me in the back. I turned quickly and grabbed him by the throat at arm's length, with one hand. He looked horrified. I shouted calmly, "Look, ginger, I'm here with this lady and I don't need aggro from some pissed up arsehole like you."

Just then I noticed a big bouncer appear like a genie from a lamp, grab his arm and drag him along the floor to the exit. I turned back to see if Julie was OK and she buried her head in my chest. I held her in my arms for a few moments to try to calm her down; she was shaking like a leaf. Then I took her back to our table, sat her down and said, "He's gone now, don't worry," and put my arm over her shoulders.

As I looked up, the bouncer knelt down on one knee in front of us and said in a deep voice, "Is the lady OK?"

"Yes," I said. "Just a bit shook up."

"The manager sends his apologies and has asked me to get you both a drink from the bar."

"No, it's all right."

Then he interrupted me. "The manager insists." He stood up, clicked his fingers and a waitress came over. He ordered two glasses of champagne and explained to us that the drunk was in the queue outside when we walked in and while he was paying the cashier, he'd said, "What have they got that I haven't?"

"We thought something might happen, so we were watching him." The waitress came over with our drinks on a tray and put them on the table next to us. "We've thrown him out now, so don't worry, enjoy yourselves." I thanked him for his help, and he walked off.

Julie looked up and said, "I'm all right now".

I looked at my watch; it was 11.25. "Shall we go? The car will be here in five minutes." We both had a mouthful of champagne and walked out to the door.

As we were waiting, the manager came over and apologised once again and asked if we were leaving because of the trouble. "No," Julie said. "Our car's picking us up at 11.30, we had a lovely time and there was no need for the free drinks."

"As long as you've enjoyed yourselves," he said as he shook my hand.

The driver walked through the door bang on time. As he took his hat off and tucked it under his arm, he said, "Are you ready to leave?"

I nodded and shook hands with the bouncer that had looked after us and I walked towards the door. As I looked through the glass, I could see the drunk standing by the back of the car. Not wanting to upset Julie any more, I had to think quickly, so I whispered in the driver's ear, "There's someone pissing on your limo." He went through the door like a rocket, jumped on the drunk and threw him to the ground. The bouncer ran out, so I quickly said to Julie, "Let's go." I grabbed her hand and, as I pulled her, she banged her foot on the doorframe. I looked up and the driver was holding the car door open while the bouncer was holding the drunk down on the floor. Julie had stopped to rub her ankle, so I picked her up in my arms and ran down the steps quickly to the car. I placed her in the back seat carefully, pushed her over to the far side and got in as the door slammed behind me. I put my arm around her as the driver jumped in his seat.

I shouted, "Drive off quickly before the police come," and he took off like it was a formula one racing car. "That's the last thing we need now," I said to Julie, who was laughing. "Are you all right?" I asked.

She nodded as if to say yes. We cuddled up in the back with the music still playing, when all of a sudden she looked up at me and said, "Did you help write the script for The Bodyguard?" I laughed, and in the mirror I could see the driver chuckling to himself.

The car drove through the entrance of the Chateau Etoile and along the massive drive. Julie didn't say a word, she just stared out of the side window all the way. We eventually pulled up in front of the hotel. Julie couldn't believe her eyes.

"Are we staying here tonight?" she said staring at the magnificent floodlit building.

The driver opened the door for the last time. Julie got out first. She thanked the driver and, as I stood up, I shook his hand and thanked him too.

He said, "I've got £25 left; you gave me too much for the club."

I shook his hand again and said, "Keep it, you earned it tonight."

He touched his hat again, nodded his head, and said, "Thank you, sir, that's very nice."

I put my arm around Julie's shoulders and she put her arm around my waist. We walked up the steps into the hotel slowly, through the doors and up to the reception desk. "Can I have the key for room 416, please, in the name of Houston?"

Julie looked at me and said, "Whitney."

I kissed her quickly to stop her saying any more and said quietly, "Shhhhh," as the man got the key and placed it on the desk. I asked if we could have an alarm call at six a.m., then we said goodnight and walked towards the lift. There was music playing very faintly in the background as we waited for the lift doors to open. On entering the lift, we were finally alone, so we kissed and messed with each other all the way up to our floor; there was only one thing on our minds now.

As the door opened, we stepped out and found our room. I nervously unlocked the door, with Julie pushing me and whispering, "Hurry up, Kevin, I want you."

We went in and I locked the door while Julie went over to the bed. As I turned around, she was holding up a bunch of flowers. She looked and smelt them and said, "You are so romantic."

I thought for a moment, undecided whether to pretend they were from me. As she pulled the card out I said, "Unfortunately, I didn't send them."

She unpicked the envelope and said, "They're from the hotel management, and this bottle of champagne. The card says 'Best wishes Mr and Mrs Houston on your wedding day'." She placed them on the side and I walked over, put my arms around her and kissed her. "Not yet, you naughty Mr Houston," she said and went into the bathroom.

I casually glanced around the room. It was amazing. Everything was silk; I hadn't really noticed earlier. The carpet was white and the giant four-poster bed was in black, with drapes all around it. I felt it to see how soft it was and wasn't surprised to find it was a water-bed. I lifted the champagne out of the bucket, slowly unwound the wire from the cork, then unscrewed the cork so it wouldn't make a loud pop. I poured some into the first glass. I was so nervous, it went all over the table. I grabbed a towel, soaked it up and poured the second one with a little more skill.

As I put the towel back, Julie opened the door and walked into the room, wearing a short see-through nightie, suspenders and white stockings, with no panties on. I didn't know how to speak, never mind what to say. I sat on the bed and she'd taken my breath away.

"What do you think?" she said in a sexy voice. I pulled her on to the bed and looked at her lying next to me. All I could see was Julie's face looking up at me, those gorgeous eyes with slight creases at the side as she smiled. Her hair was thinly spread over part of her face and her lips were moist as she ran her tongue over them slowly. I kissed them softly and slowly for a while; I wanted to remember every second of this night. Then I couldn't control myself anymore. I stood up quickly, tore off my jacket and shirt in one; some of the buttons fell on to the bed as they became unattached. I threw my clothes across the floor. As I bent down to take my shoes and socks off and undo my trousers, Julie picked up the buttons and started flicking them at me, so I jumped back on to the bed. It was like jumping into a rubber dinghy, the way it swayed with the water.

I pulled her over to me and slapped her bottom and said, "You naughty girl."

With a cheeky look on her face, she said, "Not half as naughty as I'm going to be." She put her hand in my pants and started stroking me, very slowly. I gently peeled off her nightie and threw it to the floor. I glanced down at her tanned body, with her white stockings and suspenders fastened together, a thin strip of brown hair in the middle that disappeared between her legs, and slowly started kissing her face. Then we climbed into the bed between the black silk sheets. I lay in the middle of the bed, and Julie climbed on top, forcing me in with her fingers. She sat straddled over my lap, with her shiny hair falling down over her face, slowly gliding up and down, with her bottom lip between her teeth. I sat up and she wrapped her legs around my waist. We kissed and licked each other's tongue until I came inside her.

We stayed in that position for a few moments holding each other tight. I pushed her hair off her face with my fingers gently, so I could see those big blue eyes looking down at me. Julie reached for a glass off the side and took a sip of champagne, as she flicked her hair back behind her ear with one thumb. Still breathing heavily, she said, "It's been a long time since I had it like this."

I lay back on the pillow, still inside Julie, and she offered me the glass. As I held my hand out to take it, she shook her head from side to side slowly, teasing me, and downed the last drop. She leaned over and put it back, then kissed me, passing the cold champagne into my mouth and licking my lips. Some ran out the corner of my mouth and down my chin. I swallowed as Julie lifted her head. I licked her pink nipples as she ran her fingers through my hair, chanting, "Again, again." She pulled my head into her chest and held me there. We rolled over together, with me staying inside her. I slowly moved in and out. Julie grabbed the top of the headboard behind her with both hands and shouted, "Harder, do it to me harder!" I thrust myself in as far as possible and Julie stuck her nails in my back. Again I came and she let out a long sigh. Then we lay there trying to get our breath back.

I rolled over onto my back and reached for my drink. "You want some?"

She whispered, "Just a little, please."

I poured some into her glass as she sat up and straightened the sheets. We both lay with our heads resting against the headboard, sipping our drinks. We didn't say anything for a few minutes, then Julie said, "Tonight was wonderful: the meal, the car, the dance . . ."

I interrupted her and said, "Apart from the drunk."

She smiled and carried on. "The hotel—I don't think I've ever been in a place like this before—and the sex; it's been a long time since I was treated like this."

I put my arm around her shoulders and she gently kissed my cheek. I put both the glasses down by the side of the bed; we slid under the silk sheets and lay there, naked, holding each other till we fell asleep.

I awoke as the phone buzzed and picked up the receiver. A voice said, "Good morning, this is your alarm call." I thanked him and put it down, then rolled over to look at Julie. She looked like Sleeping Beauty, so I kissed her on the lips gently. Her eyes opened slowly and, with a sleepy sexy voice, she said, "I was too scared to open my eyes then in case I was dreaming."

"It's just after six, would you like me to ring room service for anything?"

"No, I don't think so," she said with a yawn at the end. I kissed her on the forehead and, as I stroked her hair, she said, "I want to stay here for ever."

I smiled. "So do I but it's not possible, is it?"

"How long have we got?" Julie asked, pretending to burst into tears.

"How long do we need?"

Then she smiled and said, "Have you seen the size of the bath? It's big enough for two."

I jumped up, went into the bathroom, turned the taps on and found some bubble bath in a sachet. Ripping it open with my teeth, I emptied the whole sachet and a bit more from another packet. It was a big bath, white with gold taps; in fact the whole bathroom was white with gold fittings. I checked to make sure it wasn't too hot, turned the water off and went back into the bedroom, walked round the bed and ripped off the sheet Julie was holding around her neck. She started laughing when I tickled her. I picked her up in my arms and carried her. She put one arm around my neck and kissed me as she unfastened her suspender belt and slid her stockings off with the other hand. We entered the bathroom and I kicked the door shut with my foot. Then I gently placed her in the bubbles. She was totally covered, except for her face. I knelt down by the side of the bath and kissed her. She had a dirty look on her face, as she bit my bottom lip and, holding it between her teeth, said, "Get in now."

As I went to step in, Julie stood up covered in foam and moved forwards and I sat behind her and laid back, so she could sit on my lap. She lifted her legs and drooped them over the sides of the bath. With a firm grip she played with me for a while and I played with her, until she pushed me into her and sat forward. I rubbed soap up and down the inside of both thighs and all over her nipples. She lay back on my chest, slowly gliding up and down my solid erection. The water was spilling onto the floor from the bath as she got faster and faster, until I came. Then she sat forward with her back arched again, holding her hair up behind her head with both hands, groaning, trying to get every inch of me inside her.

Letting go of her hair, Julie stood up and turned around, then sat at the other end of the bath. We lay there for a while, splashing each other in turn. Then Julie said, "I'm hungry now, I need something to eat."

"I'll ring room service. What do you fancy?"

"A coffee and toast with marmalade."

I washed myself down, wrapped a towel around my waist and went into the bedroom, rang reception and ordered breakfast.

After about ten minutes, there was a knock at the door. I opened it and took the tray from the boy, just as Julie came out of the bathroom in a bathrobe. After we'd eaten, we talked about our night out and, eventually, got dressed to leave.

As I went to open the door, Julie said, "I will never forget last night, it was the best night I've ever had."

I smiled, put my arms around her waist and kissed her once more, trying to stretch every second we had left together.

We collected our things and went down to the reception desk. When the manager came over to us, I shook his hand and thanked him.

He asked Julie if everything had been OK. "It was lovely, thank you."

"It's been a pleasure having you and we wish you every happiness in the future," he said as he rubbed his hands together.

I thanked him again before leaving. I drove back to the restaurant to get Julie's car, holding hands with her all the way. We stood in the car park kissing for a while, then Julie said, with tears running down her cheeks and dripping off the bottom of her chin, "I'll see you then." She stepped back and got in her car. I couldn't speak; there was a big lump in my throat.

I followed her some of the way back, as she turned off the motorway a few junctions before me. I pulled up alongside her car and blew her a kiss, then carried on to work.

I rang Julie later that day to check that she'd got home safely and she thanked me again.

# Chapter 8

A WEEK PASSED, work was a bit scarce and the bills were starting to pile up on my desk. During that week, Liz rang me at work to tell me that we had been invited to Lucy and Ivor's for a meal. It had been a long time since I'd spoken to Ivor. He was very high up in the company he worked for and travelled abroad quite a lot. I'd known him since school days; we went to nightclubs together and raced round the streets in our first cars. We were very close in those days, then he got married, had two children and we lost contact for a while. We bumped into each other at a party some years ago and now we tried to see each other as often as possible.

On the Thursday morning, I sent a bunch of flowers round to their house; I thought they might give me a head start. I left work about five o'clock and dashed home to get ready. We were there by seven. As we walked in to the front room, Lucy stood up, kissed me on the cheek and said, "Thank you for the lovely flowers."

Ivor laughed and said, "She thought they were from me."

I looked at Liz as she nudged me in the ribs, with a 'you're in trouble' look and Ivor went into the kitchen to get us all a drink.

Lucy took us through to the dining room, where the table was laid out. The food was excellent that night and we carried on drinking after the meal.

"This is one of the advantages of working away," said Ivor as he opened the drinks cabinet. There was every conceivable drink you could wish for. "What would you like?" he proudly said, as he moved the front bottles on to the floor below the cabinet. We all had a brandy and he sat down.

"Have you told them about the escapade on the roof yet?" asked Lucy.

I could tell he was embarrassed. "No," he said. His head dropped. "I wasn't going to tell anyone about that," he said, then he looked at me. "It was nothing, take no notice of her."

"Come on, I'm all ears," I said, as I put my brandy down on the table in front of me.

"Well, I was cleaning the dormer window on the side of the roof a few months back. It was a lovely day and, while I was up there, I just happened to look up at the chimney and growing out of the side was a small weed. So I thought the best thing to do, while I was up there, was to shuffle along the apex of the roof and take it out. So carefully, hanging on for dear life, I pulled myself along on my bum slowly, with one leg over each side to keep my balance. As I got nearer, I could see three or four sticking out the back." Ivor took a large swig from his glass and went on. "This is where it all went tits up. I stood up nervously, gripping the chimney as tight as I could, trying not to look down, and plucked them out. As I pulled the last one, which was a little more stubborn, a brick became dislodged and fell from the chimney, on to the next-door neighbours' roof slates and slid all the way down, taking 15 tiles with it. Then it hit the gutter, ripped that clean off the wall and dropped into the garden with a clatter." At this point, I started laughing. "That's not all," he said with a straight face. "I quickly shuffled back to the dormer window, panicking, and, trying to get back in, put my foot straight through the glass I'd just cleaned. I climbed down the ladder, ran down the stairs and out into the back garden to see what damage I'd done. The brick had fallen onto a stone ornamental statue and demolished that into a thousand bits." By now the tears were running down my face. "Then," he said, still without a smile, "knowing the neighbours were out, I quickly rang about six roofers from the phone book, to try and find one that would come out straight away. Eventually one said yes, and he would come round in ten minutes, so I thought, while I'm waiting, I'll clean up the broken glass in the bedroom. Eventually the roofer arrived and I showed him the damage and explained that I wanted all the broken tiles taken off the neighbours' roof and replaced with mine before they came home, as they were the same. 'No problem,' the roofer said." Ivor stopped to take a gulp of brandy again and I had to dry my face on my napkin. Then he carried on. "By this time, it had started to rain. The roofer untied his roof ladder on the pick-up truck, him and his mate carried it over and stood it up to the roof on the front of our house. Then the roofer said to his mate, 'Just put your foot on it while I get my fags out the cab.' As he walked towards the truck, his mate stood by the bottom of the ladder and searched in his pockets for his hat. When he couldn't find it, he turned to the roofer and shouted, 'Look in the cab for my hat, Lofty.' With that, a gust of wind blew the ladder sidewards and it went straight through the same neighbours' double-glazed bay window, that was fitted two weeks previously."

I was in bits, I couldn't breathe. My eyes were streaming and my chest was hurting. Ivor still hadn't smiled once. Liz and Lucy were doubled up as well. Ivor stood up to get some more drinks and asked me if I wanted something different. I couldn't speak, I could only just, nod.

After about five minutes, I calmed down a bit and Ivor sat back down, with his two hands cupped around the brandy glass. It almost went quiet then he said, "And to top it all, not only had all this gone on outside the house but a brick had fallen down the inside of the chimney into their open fireplace and there was black soot all over their furniture and walls."

I was off again, nothing was going to stop me laughing. I could just imagine this going on and the look on his face, as everything got worse.

Eventually I pulled myself together and Lucy said, "I left him to it and went out to a friend's house down the road. Everything he touched that day went wrong; when the insurance man came out he couldn't believe it."

I couldn't resist it, I had to ask: "What did the people next door say when they got home?"

Ivor looked at me and said, "They weren't very happy as you can imagine. When their house was rebuilt, they put it on the market and moved into the country, with no neighbours for miles.

We sat and drank some more, talking about old times. Liz went up to the bathroom and Lucy asked Ivor to check the kids were still asleep. Lucy and I were sitting at the table on our own and both quite tipsy by this time, so I asked her, "Would you like to come out with me one dinner-time for a drink, the next time Ivor's away?"

She looked up at me and said, "Yes, that would be nice. I'll ask Ivor if that's all right, and-"

"No! If we go out it will have to be our secret."

"Oh yeah, what have you got in mind, then?" she said with a suspicious look on her face.

"Well, we can't talk here tonight. I'll stop on my way to work in the morning and explain. In the meantime, just think about it."

With that, Ivor walked in, Liz behind him laughing, and said, "They're all fast asleep." Lucy looked like she was deep in thought.

It was around midnight when Liz asked Ivor for our coats. We left, thanking them for a very memorable night. As I shook his hand, I added, "That must be one of the funniest stories I've heard for a long time." All the way home I kept thinking about Ivor on the roof and bursting out with laughter.

* * *

The next morning, I drove past Lucy's house; she was walking across the road with the kids. I waited at the bottom of her drive while she dropped them off at school and when she came out, she stood by my door and tapped on the glass. I dropped the window and then she said inquisitively, "What did you mean last night?"

I couldn't think of anything else to say except, "I mean an affair."

"With me?" she said with a surprised look on her face.

"Yes, with you."

"No, I couldn't, we would be seen by someone. It's not the thing to do, Ivor is your friend and Liz is my friend. It's impossible, we couldn't."

I asked her to sit in the passenger seat. She looked up and down the road as she walked round the car and got in, leaving the door open and one foot on the pavement. "It wouldn't work," she went on to say. "If we were seen by someone, we would both be in trouble."

"We wouldn't be seen by anyone."

"How do you know that?"

"Because we wouldn't be around here, we'd be miles away. I thought we could go somewhere quiet, have a drink or two and maybe spend the night together."

She started shaking her head from side to side slowly. "No, I don't think I could."

"Well, why don't you think about it and I will ring you later in the week. I'd love to take you out somewhere really nice."

She looked at me with a blank expression on her face and said, "I've heard of people doing this sort of thing but you've really surprised me. I didn't think you were like that. Ring me then but don't hold any hopes." She kissed me on the cheek and got out, shutting the door behind her. I carried on to work, thinking to myself at least she didn't say no.

It was the following afternoon when Lucy rang me at work. "Hello," she said. "I've thought about it."

"What's your answer?" I asked, with my fingers crossed.

"No one will know, will they?"

"No, it's strictly between you and me. Don't say anything to anyone, not even your best friend."

"The answer is yes then," she said apprehensively. "I've been a good housewife up to now."

"Don't worry, it's going to be lovely," I added, trying to reassure her. "I'll think of somewhere nice and ring you back—when is Ivor away next?"

"Tomorrow for four days, next week for five and a week on Wednesday my mum's having the kids for a couple of days to give me a break."

"I will aim for then, that will give me plenty of time to arrange something really special." I put the phone down and went down the stairs to see a customer, with a big grin stretched across my face.

A few days later, I had to go out to someone that had broken down on the motorway in their car. They were travelling to the airport to go to Ireland for a week. I tried to repair it but the cam belt was broken, so I loaded the car onto the truck and explained that it was a big job and that I would repair it while they were away.

I dropped them off at the airport and told them it would be ready for when they got back. They were very grateful and on the way to the airport we talked about Ireland. It suddenly struck me—that would be a great place to take Lucy. I dropped them off by the entrance to the main terminal and got the luggage out of the boot of their car. From the amount they had, anyone would think they were going for a year. I gave the man a phone number to call me on his return and left.

On the way back, I was day-dreaming about a romantic night in Ireland. I unloaded the car and went up to my office and found an old map. I glanced at it for a while, wondering where to go. I phoned the airport information desk and the girl told me that Ryan Airways flew twice a day to Dublin, so we could go Wednesday morning and fly back Thursday afternoon, just in time for Lucy to collect her kids from school. We didn't need a passport so we could have a nice night in a little Irish village and no one would know we'd been.

Later that day, I made my way down to the travel agents and picked up a few brochures for short breaks in Ireland. I sat in my car for a while looking at all the lovely places and the golden sandy beaches, then drove back to work, took them up to my office and studied them carefully, page by page. There were too many nice places to choose from; there were castles, hotel rooms of all shapes and sizes, but eventually I found the one. It was a castle at the base of a mountain, overlooking a huge lake. It looked amazing. I rang to see if they had a room for one night.

A woman answered, with a very soft Irish accent, and said, "Of course, we have large rooms and some smaller ones. What would you be fancying?" I explained I wanted a double room, with a view of the lake and told her I was bringing my wife; it was an anniversary present for her. She went on to tell me the price and I told her I would ring back later. The flight was no problem apparently, so I quickly rang Lucy and told her it was all arranged for Wednesday morning and that we would be back home on Thursday afternoon. When she asked me where we were going, I told her it was a surprise and she would need an overnight bag. She asked me if it would definitely be all right and I told her that no one would know, as long as she kept quiet. Then I told her I would ring a bit nearer the time and put the phone down.

A couple of days passed and Lucy rang me at work. "I can't do it," she said. "I've sat in the kitchen for ages thinking about it and I convinced myself I could but it just doesn't seem right. Can I think about it and let you know later? I'm flattered that you asked me but basically I'm scared."

I tried to explain that there wasn't anything to worry about but, after a long conversation, we decided to wait a little longer. I hadn't paid for anything, so it wasn't a problem; I knew that taking Lucy out would be the hardest one of all.

A few weeks had gone by and I hadn't heard from Lucy at all. I thought I had frightened her off.

I was starting to worry about work; we hadn't had a lot of work and things didn't look too good for the rest of the year. The bills were mounting up on my desk and I hadn't got any money to pay them. It was hard not to spend the money I was saving for my dates. The wages were getting harder to find each week and the Inland Revenue was sending me demands.

I sold a couple of cars for a lot less than they were worth, just to get some money in, and I hadn't had time to think about the game. Until one day in November, Lucy phoned and said, "I haven't forgotten about our date. I've been too busy lately, with Christmas coming. I think I might be all right now, so perhaps I could ring you soon." I was so pleased to hear her voice. I told her to leave it till after the New Year. She reminded me about New Year's Eve and said if we didn't see each other over Christmas, she would see me then.

I thought for a moment and said, "Why don't we go out into the country, have a drink and a chat somewhere one dinner-time in the next few days?"

"That would be nice, perhaps tomorrow, as long as I'm back to collect the lads from school at 3.30."

"OK, I'll see you at the White Swan in Denton, it's just off the M6 junction 4, at one o'clock".

Lucy sounded like a different person from when I'd last spoken to her.

The following day, I left work about twelve o'clock, drove to the White Swan, parked around the back and waited in the car. After a while, I decided to go in and get myself a drink. I locked the car door and, as I walked across the car park, I heard a loud screech of tyres. I looked up thinking it was Lucy but it wasn't. A red transit van went hurtling off down the road. I went in and sat by the bar and ordered myself a drink. After about five minutes, Lucy walked in through the door in a black leather suit and a white see-through blouse. It was open at the neck, showing off the top of her cleavage. She looked stunning as she sat on the stool next to me. I couldn't help but look her up and down three or four times before I spoke a word. My mouth was wide open and I was probably dribbling again.

"You look absolutely beautiful and I don't know what to say."

Lucy just smiled and said, "When I walked in, your face said it all. Now can I have a drink before the bar shuts?"

I ordered two more drinks and we sat there for a while, talking and joking and left about three o'clock and went out in to the car park. The cars were side by side and, as we approached them, Lucy grabbed my hand and said, "Thanks for being patient with me. I needed to do this because I'm still very nervous."

We stopped by the cars and kissed for the first time. The smell of leather was all around us as we held each other close and kissed some more. After about 20 minutes, we said goodbye and I said I would phone after the New Year about our date. I told her I was looking forward to the party on New Year's Eve and perhaps I could arrange something and talk to her about it then. We kissed once more and parted company. As I pulled out on to the road, I could see that same red transit, parked up by a gateway. I took no notice and carried on back to work thinking about Lucy and how she had changed.

Christmas came and went as quickly as it usually did. We had the family for dinner, then a few friends round for drinks on the evening till about midnight.

Boxing day, Mick and I played with his presents all day. We bought him a radio-controlled car and a number of games. The toys he had were great; they kept us amused all day long.

But before I knew it, I was back at work, opening more bills. I just added them to the pile I had already.

On New Year's Eve, I finished work at dinnertime. I was looking forward to the party. There were 12 of us going for a meal and a dance. Denise, Julie and Lucy would be there, among others, so midnight should be good fun. I shaved and showered, got myself dressed into a hired dinner suit and Liz wore a long cream dress. The taxi picked us up and we dropped Mick off at the sitter's on the way.

We arrived about eight o'clock, and were directed to our seats by the doorman. A few couples had beaten us and by about 8.30 we were all seated and ready to party. We sat around a big oval table, with wine bottles in the centre and Christmas crackers on our plates. There were tubs of exploding streamers, balloons everywhere you looked and two cans of silly-string that were almost empty. The contents were all over the table and resting on everybody's hair within minutes. I glanced around the room. There were about 200 people doing the same thing. Party poppers were banging and some of the balloons were bursting.

In the next room, there was music playing and Denise asked me if I wanted to dance. Choking on my red wine, I said yes and we went through onto the floor. We had a nice slow dance but I thought it was far too early to start anything yet. When we got back to the table, the starters were there. I ate mine, and as soon as Julie finished hers, she asked me for a dance. So again, I went through to the dance floor. By this time, everyone was warming up, including Julie; she wanted to go over the other side of the room, out of sight for a kiss. So, not wanting to upset her, we did. As we were dancing, a hand grabbed my shoulder and pulled it. My life passed before me in a flash as I turned round slowly and this loud voice said, "It is, how are you? I haven't seen you for three years."

With a long look, I realised it was John and, with a sigh of relief, I shook his hand and said, "Hello, mate."

He was a friend from another garage I used to deal with. We started talking about old times and Julie said, "I'll see you back at the table."

John said straight away, "That's not your wife," with a grin on his face.

"No," I quickly added. "I'm in a party of twelve. It's Simon's wife. You remember Simon, he works at Bill's garage in town."

"But you were a bit friendly."

"So, it's New Year's Eve, isn't it?"

We laughed and then John said, "Have you met my wife, Debbie?" He turned around to a girl that was facing the other way and grabbed her arm. As she turned towards me, I went weak. My legs turned to jelly, then the whole world disappeared, the music faded and in front of me was the mother I saw getting into her BMW outside Mick's school.

She smiled at me in the same way she had done by the gate. I was speechless. She spoke to me and I hopelessly said, "We've met somewhere before."

She smiled again and said, "You're Mick's dad, I've seen you dropping him off outside the school."

In the distance, I faintly heard John say something about a drink. I said, "Yes, please," half thinking about a drink because my mouth was dry and half thinking about screwing his wife. He walked off over to the bar. I stayed and spoke with Debbie. "How long have you been married, then?" I asked first. She went on to tell me that she had been married to John for 11 years, they had one child, a girl who went to Mick's school, and they only moved into the area about six months ago for a fresh start. With a puzzled look on my face, I asked, "For a fresh start?" She started to tell me that she had some problems with John but unfortunately he came back with the drinks. I carried on talking to them and suddenly remembered my dinner would probably be on the table so I said I would see them later and left.

I strutted across the floor with that feeling again and I said to myself, "She must go on my list."

When I got back to the table, Liz asked me who I had been speaking to and I explained briefly as my dinner was placed in front of me. By about eleven o'clock, almost everyone was well oiled and looking forward to midnight. We ordered some bottles of champagne and left them in the ice buckets on the table. I danced with Liz and, at 11.55; we all stood around the table with a glass of champagne and waited. Then every one in the room started shouting the countdown: "5-4-3-2-1—HAPPY NEW YEAR!" It was great, then we all kissed each other. After Liz, Denise grabbed me and kissed me, then Lucy—she whispered in my ear, "I'm ready when you are,"—then a couple of the other friends from our table and then I looked up and the ever beautiful Julie was waiting with her arms stretched out.

I went over and she hugged me first, then she said in my ear, "Can we go out again sometime?"

I smiled, kissed her and said, "I would like that, Happy New Year."

I suddenly thought about Debbie and wondered what she was doing. I slowly made my way into the other room and headed for the bar to see if I could find her. Everybody was kissing each other and I couldn't see her anywhere. I turned to walk away disappointed then a hand came from nowhere and grabbed my jacket. I turned quickly; it was Debbie. "Are you looking for me or John?" she asked.

"You—I don't want to kiss John."

She moved forwards and kissed me softly on the lips, staring into my eyes. Then she said, "Will you dance with me? John's collapsed over by the bar as usual. I knew he wouldn't be any good tonight." We moved down onto the dance floor and she held me tight. We danced for a while and she whispered to me, "Can we go outside and dance on our own in the car park?"

I wasn't expecting that. I thought for a second. No, this was not a good idea but as I went to say no, I opened my mouth and it came out wrong. "Yes." I couldn't believe I'd said it.

"I'll see you outside in five minutes, then."

I nodded and walked back towards my table. Lucy was dancing with Ivor and Andrew was dancing with Liz, so I carried on towards the door and Denise walked in with Simon. I carried on and up to the table. There were a couple asleep and a few others talking, so I picked up a half-full bottle of champagne, slipped it under my jacket and walked out of the front door.

As I passed a doorman, he said, "Goodnight, sir." I explained that I was going out for some fresh air and I would be back in five minutes.

I walked around the back and into the car park. Debbie was over the other side, under a tree, sitting down on a bench. It was a cold night, with a thin layer of snow on the ground, so I hurried over to her. As I got nearer she stood up. She had a big thick white fur coat on, with the collar pulled up half over her face. She started to unbutton her coat from the bottom and, just before I got to her, it opened. She was wearing nothing but knee-length leather boots.

I quickly put the bottle down on the ground, grabbed each half of her coat and pulled it together. "You'll freeze out here," I said with steam coming from my mouth. I fastened one button near the top and put my hands inside her coat, and gingerly touched her body. It was warm and soft. I slowly slid my hands down to her hips and back up to the side of her breasts. We licked and kissed each other passionately, then I started to fasten her buttons slowly.

She looked at me and said, "Don't you want me, then?"

As I fastened the last one, I said, "You don't know how I have had to stop myself. I want you more than anything but not in a car park, in the cold; I want you for a whole night, all to myself in the warm."

With her hands on my cheeks, she whispered, "Any time."

I picked up the champagne and took a swig, then I passed it to Debbie. She looked at me, licked her lips slowly and tipped the bottle up to her mouth and licked her lips again. Debbie held the bottle and we slowly walked back to the front door, through all the parked cars.

As we walked, I asked if I could take her away for a night and she nodded as she took another drink from the bottle. Then she said, "Soon." I told her I would see her the on the first day of the kid's new school term, then I waited on the corner while she went in first.

As I walked through the door, Denise was standing there and said, "Are you all right? I've been looking everywhere for you. I wanted a dance. Andrew and Liz are kissing on the dance floor."

I smiled and said, "I wanted some fresh air." We walked over and put the bottle down on the table, then we went into the other room. I could see them dancing together, so I took no notice and danced with Denise on the other side of the room. We walked passed Ivor and Lucy. It looked as if he was holding her up. Simon and a couple of others were wandering round, still trying to get New Year kisses from anyone in a skirt.

By about two o'clock, people were starting to drift away from the party and, not long after, we all left in taxis. I was in one with Julie next to me with Liz and Andrew. Julie had a coat on her lap and we held hands all the way back to Sandra and Henry's house. By this time, a few had sobered up a bit and Henry asked us in for a last drink. As we climbed out, two other taxis pulled up behind us and we all went in and carried on till about five in the morning.

I only just managed to order a taxi and we left to go home, shattered. I woke up about eleven o'clock and left Liz in bed asleep, made myself a coffee and went to collect Mick from the sitter's house. He told me about the fun they'd had and how he'd stayed up till one o'clock, so I made him get into bed and have a sleep while I was sitting downstairs on my own, nursing my bad head.

About midday, I decided to go for another drink, to see if it would help. So I made my way down to the Wooden Cross and met a couple of other friends there. We swapped stories about New Year's Eve and, after about three pints,

I decided to go home because my idea wasn't working; in fact, it made it worse.

By the time I got back home, Liz was up and walking round like a zombie and Mick was snoring his head off. We tried to watch the telly but by three o'clock I fell asleep in the chair and didn't wake till late that evening. That's when I gave up and went to bed. Liz was already in there.

* * *

I got up the next day not feeling too bad and made my way to work. I started to feel more human in the afternoon and, after a couple of days, I was much better; in fact, a week later I was better still because Mick was going back to school and hopefully I would see Debbie.

I woke on the morning very excited. Mick got dressed for school and we left about 8.40. I dropped him off as usual and hung around by his classroom as long as I could without looking too conspicuous but she never turned up. I walked slowly across the playground to the gate. She still didn't appear so I walked back to my car and got in—still nothing. I couldn't hang on any longer so I left. But, as I pulled away, I saw her car pulling off the drive. I waved as I passed and she waved back discreetly. I started thinking about New Year's Eve in the car park and, as I got to the T-junction at the bottom of the road, I pulled up behind some cars and waited. As each one pulled away, I moved forward slowly and, just as I got to the part when she unfastened her white fur coat, the car in front of me went to pull away. As I moved forward again, it stopped—I drove into the back of a Metro. My front bumper hit the rear lights, smashing them into bits and denting the bumper. I got out, apologised and told the woman I would take her car to work one day soon and mend it for her. She was a nice lady, luckily for me, so I carried on to work, thinking of somewhere nice to take Debbie.

I stopped at a travel agent and asked the girl for something up north with a log cabin. She recommended a little village called Stanton and told me that she went last year, with her ex-boyfriend, and how romantic it was. I laughed aloud and said, "It couldn't have been that romantic."

She looked at me and said with a frown, "It was but he decided to take someone else there this year."

I said how sorry I was and left with the brochure.

As I approached the garage and parked my car, I could see a man standing on the forecourt with a black suit and an orange folder under his arm. I locked the car and walked over to him.

"Can I help?" I hoped it was a customer.

"Mr Vaughan?" he asked in a strong voice.

"Yes," I replied. "What can I do for you?"

"I'm from the Inland Revenue. Are you the proprietor of this garage?"

I looked at him and thought for a second, how can I get out of this? I had to say yes. He opened his folder and pulled out a piece of paper. "Have you got somewhere we can talk?"

I walked up the stairs to my office, with him walking behind me mumbling on about fines if you don't pay your bills on time. It was easy for him to go on; he didn't have to pay them. We walked in to the office and I told him I was going to send the money today.

With a look of disbelief he said, "I need a cheque for three thousand, two hundred and fifty-seven pounds, sixty-six pence."

I nervously wrote the cheque out, knowing full well I hadn't got it in the bank. I just wanted to get rid of him. He took the cheque and slipped it in between the flaps of the folder and left, thanking me. I spent the rest of the day phoning my account customers and insurance companies trying to collect money that was owed to the garage.

I left work about eight o'clock that evening, tired. It was a cold, wet and windy night. When I got home, I was just pouring myself a large whiskey, when I heard Liz shout from upstairs, "There's a letter on the side for you about the mortgage. I've had one as well, it says we are in arrears."

I drank the whiskey in one, and shouted back, "It must be a mistake, I'll ring them in the morning."

Then I heard her say, "I hope so, I don't want to lose this house."

I quickly poured myself another shot and opened the letter; it was the perfect ending to a crap day.

When I awoke the next morning, Liz had already gone to work. I got Mick ready and took him to school. I went with him into the classroom and, as I walked out, I could see Debbie in the corridor, hanging up her little girl's coat on the hook. She looked stunning. I didn't say anything to her. I walked outside and pretended to fasten my shoelaces, keeping my eyes on the door for when she came out. As she pushed the door open, I looked down at my shoes and realised they were slip-ons. As she walked towards me, I stood up and we chatted as we walked towards the cars. I asked her if she would be able to stay out one night, some time next week. She said it wouldn't be a problem because she often travelled down to London on the train with her job.

"Great," I said and told her I would let her know one of the mornings. Then she told me she couldn't wait and I drove off to work very happy.

I went up to my office with the mail threw it on the desk and browsed through the brochure. I found a lovely place in Deerwood Hill. I phoned it and the woman told me she had some rooms vacant and that the weather was quite bad up there. I rang a friend down the road and asked him if I could borrow his Range Rover for a couple of days because I had to fetch a car on the trailer. He said yes, so long as I was careful, and remarked on how bad the weather was up north. I phoned the woman back, provisionally booked a room for Wednesday night and sat down to open the mail. The first one was a cheque, the second a bill, the third was a bill and the fourth another cheque, so it was a better start to the day.

I sat in my office upstairs for a couple of hours and attacked some of the paperwork that was mounting up. The more I did, the more I realised how much I was in debt.

It was about four o'clock when the unleaded petrol ran out. So the day ended the same as usual.

I went home and the first thing Liz asked me was about the mortgage; I'd forgotten all about it. I just said that I'd spoken to the building society and that they were looking in to it and would let me know as soon as possible. She soon went up to bed, so I ate my tea in silence and, as usual, fell asleep in the chair till morning.

After breakfast, I dropped Mick off at school and spoke to Debbie. I told her we would go away early next Wednesday, and I would meet her at the train station at 7.00 a.m.

She smiled at me and said, "Isn't it exciting? I've never done this before!"

# Chapter 9

Over the next few days, I sold another car and some more cheques came in. Things were starting to look a little better. On the Monday I took some money out of the garage account, paid the mortgage, then explained to Liz that night that there wasn't enough in our personal account and so the bank hadn't paid it. I told her I'd asked the bank manager to send me a statement, so I could find out what was wrong.

Liz looked at me with a blank expression on her face, and turned away. I told her I was going up to Scotland to fetch a car back on Wednesday, knowing full well she had a few days off from work. She asked if it was going to be for long and I explained it would probably be for just one night but that the weather up there was not too good at the moment.

That night, I noticed that she was very quiet and obviously had something on her mind since I mentioned the bank statement but I was too scared to ask. It wasn't long before my eyelids closed and I was fast asleep again. I woke about two o'clock and went to bed.

When I woke next morning, I left for work as usual, forgetting how quiet Liz was. I dropped Mick off at school, only seeing Debbie for a split second to check that everything was still on. She couldn't say a lot because she was talking with another mum. She nodded and winked as she smiled at me. I carried on to work, thrilled about the trip.

During the day, I collected the Range Rover and phoned to make sure we still had a room booked. I asked the lady about the weather and she explained that the snow was about eight inches thick, the sun was shining, it was very cold and they'd forecast a bit more later in the week. Just right, I thought to myself, Debbie will have to wear her fur coat.

I took the Range Rover home, so I could make an early start. As I opened the front door, Liz came out in a rush, shouting, "I'll see you later. I'm going out with a friend I haven't seen for a while, I should have been there at eight." She jumped in her car and drove off down the road.

I went in and Mick told me that someone had rang earlier and Mum had quickly got changed. I sat on the settee next to him and we watched the telly and talked about school. After about ten minutes the phone rang. I picked it up, but there was no one there. I decided to go upstairs and pack my overnight bag. Then, after that, I put Mick to bed and had a long relaxing soak in the bath, almost falling off to sleep. I ate my dinner and got into bed with a glass of whiskey, the telly on and waited for Liz to come home.

The next thing I heard was the sound of the alarm. I looked at the empty pillow next to me and jumped out of bed. I ran into Mick's room and then into the spare room. Liz was just stirring. As she turned to me, she said, "I didn't want to wake you, so I slept in here. What time is it?"

"I set the alarm for six, so it's just after. Did you have a good night? It was a bit sudden. If you'd told me earlier, I would have come home."

Half asleep, she said, "I tried twice but I couldn't get through," then she mumbled something about an old friend from school.

I got dressed and Liz went back to sleep. I kissed her and Mike on the head and said, "See you tomorrow."

I left with my bag and a flask of coffee and drove past Debbie's house first. The car had gone so that was a good sign, then I carried on to the station. I arrived there about ten minutes late. As I pulled into the car park, I could see the back of her BMW. I pulled up behind it, flashed my headlights and the door opened. Debbie got out with a smile and the fur coat on. She had a black case with her and waved as she locked the car and set the alarm. I waited in the warm while she opened the rear side door and put her case on the back seat then climbed in the front. She kissed me on the lips as she fastened her seat belt. We pulled out on to the road and started the long journey up north.

There was very little snow on the ground as we drove on to the motorway but it was cold and dark. The clouds looked like they were full of it but we didn't mind as the heater was on full and I had my thoughts of the night to keep me warm. I asked what excuse she had used to get away for the two days and she said she was going on the train to Manchester on a refresher course, to do with her job. I asked what her job was and she told me she was a solicitor's secretary. I was surprised. If I had known that, I probably wouldn't have asked her out.

The snow got gradually thicker as we carried on up the motorway. The further we went, the deeper it looked. The motorway wasn't too bad because of the traffic but the countryside was like a large sheet of white paper. The wipers were on all the time and the traffic slowed down to about forty miles an hour. It was wonderful.

It was about midday by the time the snow had almost stopped. The traffic was still ploughing through the sludge in between each lane. Every sign above the motorway was lit up with different instructions and most of the blue information signs were blanked out with snow. We just carried on regardless. The Range Rover was sailing along in the outside lane that not many people used because the sludge was a bit thicker and some cars could get stuck. We decided to stop at the next service area and have a warm drink and a bite to eat, so I slowly eased my way over into the slow lane and pulled off.

I parked the Range Rover and we held hands as we went inside. It was quite crowded. While we were eating, I looked on the next table and the truck driver, Nigel, from home was there. My insides turned over as he put his paper down and looked at me. He was as speechless as I was. I laughed with a look of disbelief on my face.

"What on earth are you doing here?" he said.

"I'm going to fetch a car back from Penrith."

"In this weather?" he said. "And who is this, then?"

"A hitchhiker, she broke down on the motorway in the snow, so I offered her a lift. I don't think anyone will be able to help her in this weather, do you?"

"No," he replied. "I wish I could find hitchhikers this gorgeous." Debbie blushed and dropped her head.

I asked Nigel where he was going and he said he was on his way back home from Scotland. He told me how bad the weather was up there and how long the journey had taken him.

As we walked out into the car park, Nigel called me back and said, "What's going on here, then?"

Pretending I didn't know what he was on about, I said, "What?"

"Come on," he said. "You can tell me, I won't breathe a word to anyone."

I acted a bit vague and said, "There's nothing going on. I picked her up because she was wet and gorgeous, that's all. If I get my leg over for doing that, I will be very happy but, apart from that, I will drop her off at the next junction."

He smiled and lifted his eyebrows up and down and looked at me as if to say, 'you sly old bastard'.

I shouted, "I'll see you on Friday night," and he turned and waved.

We climbed back into the Range Rover, drove back onto the motorway and got back into the outside lane. After a while, we didn't know how far we had travelled up the motorway because we didn't stop talking. The radio was on very faintly and we never heard one traffic message; we didn't even know how bad the weather was further on apart from what Nigel said. We just carried on clocking up the miles until the traffic slowed down again and we came to a halt. Nothing moved for about twenty minutes, except a couple of police Range Rovers squeezing through the middle of every one with the lights flashing and sirens blasting. I turned the radio up to see if I could hear anything about the hold up and we waited with the engine running to keep us warm. We kissed a few times and the snow slowly started again, as the traffic did. We slowly crawled along and when we got to the next junction, the police directed us off the motorway. As we passed the cold policeman stamping his feet, covered in snow, I dropped the window and asked what the problem was.

He shouted, "There's been a pile-up further on and no one can get through so you will have to make your own way back on to the motorway at the next junction but my advice to you is, even though you're in a Range Rover, I would seek somewhere to stay for the night as soon as you get off the motorway." I closed the window and followed the other car off, realising how cold it was.

We slowly crawled along the road and noticed cars just abandoned almost in the middle of the road. There were gritting wagons on the side, if you could work out where the side was, full of grit and with no one in them. The grass, the pavement and the road were all one level. No one could work out where the road started and stopped. Some of the cars banged into the gutter, fern trees were draped over the road with the weight of the snow and some trees had fallen almost across the road and blocked it off.

We managed to pass some cars as they skidded backwards and forwards, trying to get their tyres to grip on something. We carried on as best as we could. I asked Debbie if she was all right. She just looked stunned. "I've never seen anything like this," she said, still looking outside.

"Do you think we should stop somewhere soon?" I asked.

"It's up to you, if you think we can go on." The snow was getting worse and I was a bit doubtful as to how far I could push the Range Rover. We passed most of the cars and it looked like a pretty straight road so we decided to carry on a bit further, at least until we found a village or a house of some description. It was just open countryside; the road fell away into ditches and it looked treacherous.

We crawled along and, out the corner of my eye, I saw the tail-lights of a car in the ditch. They were very faint and I couldn't even tell what car it was. I pulled up, stepped into the deep snow, then ran over to see if anyone was in there. I forced open the driver's door and Debbie shouted, "Can you see anything?"

"Yes," I shouted back. "Close the door and turn the heater up to full." The car had hit a tree and the front was badly damaged. I turned the key and the engine just about started. I checked the heater was on, and looked at the driver; his lips were blue and he was dithering so I closed the door to keep whatever heat there was in, opened the back door, unfastened the two children from their seat-belts and pulled them out of the car. I carried them, one under each arm, up the embankment to the Range Rover and put them in the back. Debbie climbed over the front seats and sat in the middle of them. I shouted, "Give me your fur coat, take their hats, gloves and damp coats off to let the warm onto their bodies and cuddle them close to yours."

I slammed the door shut and slid back down the bank to the front passenger door. I just managed to open it, leaned over the woman and wrapped the man up in the fur coat. He looked like he was about to pass out. I unbuckled the woman and pulled her out; her whole body was shivering and her teeth were chattering. I looked at her face. It was as white as the snow and her lips were blue as well. I threw her over my shoulder, slammed the door shut and carefully climbed back up to the car, hanging and pulling on twigs that were sticking out of the snow. The damaged car was still running. I could only hope it was getting a bit warmer inside. My leg muscles were pulling with every step I took up the bank. I just made it to the top and opened the back door again. The children were crying; I thought that was a good sign. Debbie stood up and moved the children to one side and started to undress the woman as I placed her on the back seat. I shut the door again and went back down to the car for the man. I tried the door but it wouldn't open. I wiped the snow off the window to see if the man was OK and he started moving his head from side to side, as if to say no. I looked at the door lock and it was pushed down; he had locked himself in. I quickly looked around and felt in the snow for something to smash the window, but the snow was too deep and too cold. I moved to the back door and punched it. I was so filled with adrenalin and anger at the man for giving up, my fist went straight through. I reached forward and pulled the lock up and opened his door. As I grabbed him and started to pull him out, I heard him say very faintly, "Leave me, just get the others to hospital."

I grabbed him and—only God knows where I got the strength from—I picked him up in my arms and ran up the bank to the top in what seemed a split second. I took him round to the front of the Range Rover and put him in the front passenger seat, undressed him as quickly as I could and both Debbie and I rubbed him all over as she climbed back into the driver's seat. The woman looked a bit better in the back and the children were still crying as they moved over and clung onto the woman's arm. The man started to come round a little but he still looked dreadful. I told Debbie to sit on his lap and I would drive and try to find a hospital. As I shut the door she moved over. I quickly ran round the car pulling my wet jumper off, and as I climbed back in I threw it in the back and drove off as fast as possible, shivering myself from the cold and wet clothes I wore.

We ploughed through the snow and devastation. I didn't have a clue where we were heading. I looked at the man and his eyes were closing; I didn't know where to go.

I shook his arm to wake him and said, "Help me, I don't know where the hospital is." He almost opened his eyes and then closed them again. Debbie slapped him across the face hard and he came round and tried to focus.

The woman in the back started crying and shouted, "He's dying!"

I fumbled for my phone to ring 999 and the man opened his eyes again and mumbled, "Go straight into the town and turn left." He was almost unconscious and he closed his eyes again. I tried to drive as fast as I could but it was almost impossible. In the distance, I could see some lights on. I skidded and slipped all the way into the town and, as instructed, turned left and found the hospital. There were ambulance men outside shovelling snow from the tyres and others trying to push the ambulances up the road. I drove straight up to the front entrance and, as I jumped out, I shouted, "Can you give me a hand? I found a family freezing to death in a car down the road."

About five ambulance men came running over and opened all the doors and one by one they carried them into the hospital. We followed them in. There were lots of people in the waiting room. Most of them had blankets wrapped round them and were drinking hot drinks; they must have abandoned their cars and walked.

Debbie got me a blanket and wrapped it around my shoulders and asked the nurse for a hot drink. I sat down and Debbie sat next to me, rubbing my arms to try and stop me shivering. The nurse brought me a drink and I sat there with my hands gripping the mug of hot chocolate. Doctors and nurses were running around and disappearing behind curtains; other people were still arriving, freezing from the weather.

After about 15 minutes I started to feel a lot better, but we hadn't heard how the people were who we'd brought in. I started to walk round the waiting room and a nurse came out from behind a curtain. I asked her if she could tell me how they were and she smiled and said, "The mum is fine and the children are OK."

"What about the man, is he OK?"

"Yes, he will be. He suffered a bang on the head as well as being cold. The doctors are with him now."

I walked back over to Debbie and sat down. She asked me if everything was all right and I quickly explained. I asked her if she wanted a hot drink and she shook her head. "No, I'm fine, thanks. How do you feel?"

"I am much better now," I said. "We'll go as soon as I find out how they are." Debbie grabbed my hand and we sat for a while watching everything that was going on. The same nurse that I'd spoken to earlier came over and said, "I hear you two saved their lives."

I felt Debbie squeeze my hand; I was speechless. I looked at the big clock on the wall above the information desk. It was just after five. Then the nurse said, "Will you come with me?"

We stood up and followed her and she pulled back the curtain. The children were sitting on the bottom of the dad's bed and the mum was sitting by the side holding his hand in a white dressing gown. With Debbie behind me, we walked to the other side of the bed and the woman stood up. She grabbed my hand and kissed it and said, "I don't know how to thank you both. If it wasn't-"

I had to interrupt her; she was going to have me in tears. I said, "As long as you are all going to be all right that's the main thing."

She kissed Debbie's hand and the dad sat up and said, "I personally want to thank you for not listening to me in the car." I could feel myself filling up. "I was that cold I wanted to . . ."

His wife put her hand over his mouth and said, "Don't say any more."

I turned to find Debbie's hand and the dad said, "We will never forget what you did for us, God bless you both."

With the lump in my throat increasing in size, I tried to tell them that we were travelling up north and that we were diverted off the motorway and that we still had a short distance to go. Now that we knew they were all OK, we said we would have to be on our way.

They pleaded with us to stay a little longer but we decided to go on. Debbie and I shook hands with them again and we made our way towards the main door. I opened it for Debbie and, just as we went to go out, the two little girls ran up to us and said, "Thank you," and kissed us both on our cheeks.

With tears in our eyes, we ran and climbed into the Range Rover and carefully drove off.

I couldn't speak for a while; it was the quietest we had been all day. Debbie held my hand and eventually said, "What you did today, I will never forget for the rest of my life."

"It wasn't only me; you kept them going and warm."

"No," she said. "The way you-"

"We both should be very proud of what we did today but can we drop it and talk about something else? Let's talk about where we are, for instance." I looked across at Debbie and she smiled and leaned over and kissed me on the cheek.

We eventually found a sign that said 'Motorway 2 miles', so we followed it and pulled onto the slow lane. The traffic on the other side of the motorway was at a standstill. We drove for about another hour and found a sign that said 'Deerwood 3 miles'. I was so glad and so shattered. We pulled off and followed the signs to the village. The snow was still bad but at least it had stopped for the time being.

I phoned the place where we were staying and the lady said she honestly didn't think we were coming. I asked for directions and we found it straight away. I did notice a little country pub as we pulled into the road, so once we'd checked in we walked over and had a few drinks and something to eat. Debbie kept calling me her hero. We talked for a while and then made our way back to the cabin.

As I opened the door, we were pleasantly surprised to see a real open log fire burning in the hearth. I went back out to the car and got the champagne I'd brought from home. As I walked back in, Debbie still had her fur coat on and was standing in front of the fire. I placed the bottle in the freezer compartment of the fridge and said, "You'll melt in that, you can't still be cold?"

She undid one button and it fell to the floor. She was naked. The flames from the fire flickered around the room as I turned the light off. I quickly took my clothes off and Debbie lay down on the white fur rug. Her body was one of a Greek goddess. I didn't see one blemish on her entire body; it was perfect in every sense of the word.

I lay down next to her and softly stroked every inch of her and kissed every curve on her body. Then we kissed each other, until Debbie sat up and tossed her hair over her left shoulder and pushed me onto my back. I looked up at the dancing patterns on the ceiling from the firelight. Debbie sat over my legs and slowly ran her fingers through the hair on my chest. Her hand slowly moved down and she gently touched the base of my erect penis, then, with her thumb and forefinger either side, she massaged her way to the top. By this time I had closed my eyes and was lying there in ecstasy. She sat up and moved further down my legs. She half clenched her hand and ran it up and down slowly. Then stopped, as if she knew I was ready. Then with the other hand she gently touched the inside of my thighs. Still with a soft grip she slowly placed me in her mouth. I could hardly control myself. I sat up quickly. Debbie looked up and lifted her left leg over and knelt by the side of me. We kissed more as she moved and sat next to me in the opposite direction. She lay back in my arms across my lap. Still kissing, we held each other for a while and then she stood up and said, "Don't go away, I'll be back," and went into the bathroom.

I lay there with my hands under my head, looking up at the ceiling again. The door opened and she came back into the room with a short see-through black nightie. We knelt in front of each other on the rug and kissed some more. Then we made love, very tenderly and passionately.

We lay on the rug for a while, then I stood up and went into wash myself down in the shower. When I got to the door, I turned and said, "There's a bottle of champagne in the freezer, why don't you open it, I won't be long." I quickly showered and went back into the room soaking wet and covered in foam. Debbie was facing the other way pouring the champagne into the glasses. I crept up behind her and rubbed lather all over her nipples. She threw her head back onto my shoulder and put the bottle on the table. I put my arms around her and she held them tight on her chest, then she slowly rubbed her back on my chest and her buttocks on my clean, half erect penis that was rapidly growing again. She shuffled her feet along the wooden floor till her legs were apart and she fell forward, with her dark hair touching the fur rug and her hands clasping her legs just above her ankles. Her cheeks were backed on to me and, without any help, I slid inside her. I placed my hands on her hips and slipped in and out as she groaned continually with every thrust.

I noticed a wooden chair next to me, so I sat down and Debbie stood up and turned round. She put her arms around my neck, opened her legs and sat on me, slowly gliding all the way down to the bottom of my now fully erect penis. We sat there, kissing and licking each other.

My hands were all over her nipples as she moved her hips in a circular movement on my lap for a while and I came inside her for the second time.

We held each other tight for a while and Debbie took a sip from her glass and passed me the other one. Then she stood up, walked slowly into the bedroom and brought out four pillows, placed them on the fur rug and sat down in front of them. "Sit by me," she said, tapping her hand on the floor and staring into the fire.

I picked up my glass and the bottle and sat down. As I placed the bottle on the floor she grabbed my hand, still looking into the flames. "Are you all right?" I asked. "You've gone quiet all of a sudden." She looked at me and I could see the reflection of the fire in the tear that sat in the corner of her eye, just before it rolled down her cheek. "What's the matter?" I put the glass down and draped my arm over her shoulder.

She sniffed and wiped her cheek and said, "Nothing, it's me being silly. You are a lovely guy, you care about people and everything you do is wonderful. I bet you haven't got a nasty bone in your entire body."

"What's brought all this on?" I asked.

"It's just things at home aren't so good and I have had a lovely time tonight. Sometimes it gets me down, you know, it just makes me think." She took a sip from her glass, but it was empty, so I filled them both as she carried on. "John's got a drink problem and it's hard work trying to cope." She moved the pillows and lay back on them, so I did too. She talked about how she had to hide all the bottles in the house and how when they go out, like on New Year's Eve, he would drink too much and pass out in a corner and how embarrassing it was.

I sat up and threw some more logs on the fire from the pile on the side and said, "Has he talked to anyone about his problem?"

"No, he doesn't think he's got one. He tells me he won't drink for a week and the next night he comes home from work staggering, saying 'I'll start tomorrow.'" I sat down again and leaned back on the pillows as she carried on. "Dawn, our daughter, isn't mine."

"Isn't yours?" I asked with a surprised look on my face.

"I'm sorry," she said. "I shouldn't be spoiling our night."

"It's all right, we've got something to drink, it's warm and there's plenty of time." She obviously wanted to talk and I was too intrigued to let it go. "How do you mean, Dawn's not yours?"

She sat up, took a sip from her glass and as she put it back down, she wrapped her arms round her knees and stared into the fire again. "About eight years ago, John had an affair with a girl called Jenny. She became pregnant and said he was the father, so they decided she would have the baby and bring it up together. She was about six months into the pregnancy and, in a drunken state, he told me he was going to leave me for her. I didn't know about the baby. So he moved out of our house and they lived in a flat above a shop somewhere. He never sent me any money towards the bills, so I had to track him down at his work to see why. It was then I found out about the baby. His boss said he was having a couple of days off to look after his new little girl. Devastated at the news, I drove home, crying all the way. It hurt me more, I think, because I can't have children." The tears started to appear in her eyes again as she carried on. "He was happy, he got what he wanted and I had nothing but an empty house that I could hardly afford."

As she wiped the tears from her cheeks with the back of her clenched fist, I asked why she couldn't have any children. "I was in a car accident. John was driving stupidly, showing off, just after we got married, and I damaged my insides as I went through the screen." The tears were running down my cheeks now and I tried very hard not show them. "I was in hospital for a while, with cuts and bruises, and that day the doctor told us we could never have children. I can't explain the feeling; it was awful. We both wept for days. It was the word never, It's such a final word, you can't argue with it. Anyway, about a year later, Jenny was out with Dawn in the park. She crossed the road to go home and a van came screaming round the corner. As it approached them both, Jenny pushed the pram to the side of the road and was killed instantly. Luckily, someone caught the baby after the pram hit the kerb. John tried to bring Dawn up on his own but found it really hard. I helped him as much as I could and eventually he moved back in with me and we tried again, with Dawn. That's when the drinking started. It wasn't too bad to begin with, then it got heavier and heavier."

"Has he ever hit you when he drinks too much?"

"Not at first but he does now, but only when he drinks."

I couldn't believe it; she was such a lovely girl. I put my arm around her shoulder and she said, "I'm sorry, I shouldn't be telling you all this."

Debbie lay back on the pillow, as I threw another log on the fire and said, "I would like to help you when we get back."

"No," she said as she sat back up again. "If he finds out, he will kill me!"

I sat down by her side and stroked her hair. "It can't keep going on, someone must do something for you. Have you told anyone else?"

"Not really, I don't think anyone can help. It's not like a cold where a couple of tablets will take the pain away."

We lay back down on the pillows together. I looked up at the ceiling and said, "I will help you." I couldn't stop thinking about it for hours.

I awoke as the beam of sunlight shone through the split in the middle of the curtains, still in the same position as we fell asleep. I quickly glanced all the way down Debbie's naked body before I woke her with a kiss. As her eyes opened, I asked her if she was OK and she smiled and said in a sleepy voice, "I was just dreaming about you." I kissed her again as she lay there with her hands under the pillows and one knee in the air swaying from side to side. I stood up and went over to the curtains and yanked them apart. The sunshine was so powerful it almost blinded me. Debbie rolled over on to her front and placed a pillow over her head shouting, "Close them, I've got a headache."

I looked round the room so my eyes would get used to the light. I looked out of the window onto a magnificent sight. The snow had covered everything. There wasn't a footprint in sight, just a blue line where the snow finished and the sky started. I could see for miles and miles; we could have been a million miles from anywhere.

I told Debbie to come and have a look and she muttered something into the pillow and slowly stood up, wrapping the fur rug around her body, and walked over squinting with one hand over her eyes. She slowly peeped between her fingers with one eye, then she dropped her hand, grabbed the rug and said, "That's lovely." She opened the rug and wrapped it around me as well. We stood there for a while, just looking out of the window, then she said, "I'm sorry about last night, I must have had too much to drink."

I turned and kissed her nose and said, "Don't think about it till we get home," then kissed her lips and the rug fell to the floor as she put her arms around me. I picked her up and carried her in to the bedroom and we made love again on the bed.

I finally got myself showered and changed and waited by the fire while Debbie got ready. Then we went out for a walk in the snow. It was a bitterly cold day even though the sun was shining.

We walked into the village and stopped to look in some shop windows, with our arms around each other's waist. It was a quaint little village and very quiet. There were a number of thatched cottages on the main road and a small garage with two pumps that was closed due to the weather. We found a little pub, went in and had a brandy to keep us warm; we were the only ones in there apart from the landlord and his wife. We talked for a while and, after a couple more brandies, we left and walked across the fields, throwing snow balls at each other, like two children. Our feet sank into the snow as we stepped over fence posts that were only just sticking up and carried on till we found a small stream still flowing rapidly. We walked along it for a while, talking about what she had told me the previous night.

I glanced at my watch and noticed it was just after 11.30, so we slowly made our way back to the cabin and collected our things to start the journey home.

We made it straight on to the motorway and headed south. I phoned Liz and told her I would be home around eight, expecting the traffic to be quite heavy but it wasn't bad at all; in fact, we made very good time.

Just as we were about to pull off the motorway, Debbie went quiet again. I asked if she was all right and she looked at me and said, "I have really enjoyed myself; it's been lovely and so nice to be treated like a lady again but it's nearly over, isn't it? You go back to your wife and I go home to that pig of a husband of mine."

I pulled over on the slip-road and held her hand and said, "I've been thinking about John. I will help you if you will let me but I need him to tell me, or catch him doing something wrong. I promise I won't let on that I know and we will pretend that we haven't seen each other since

New Year's Eve. I'll ring him on Friday and ask him out for a drink on the night, with me and Liz, so he'll ask you to come with him to make up a foursome."

"No," Debbie quickly said. "I couldn't face Liz after the night we've just had together."

"It will be OK. Then when we leave you, ask if we want to come back for a nightcap. I'll say yes before Liz has a chance to say anything and, when I'm in your house, I'll drop my keys down the side of the chair. Then, when we leave and I realise I can't get into my car, I'll come back. When we were walking by the river, you said that's the time when he is worst."

"I don't know, do you think it will work?" she said as she shook her head in disbelief.

"Of course it will." I pulled away and carried on. I could see Debbie out the corner of my eye thinking about it.

When I pulled up at the train station, Debbie leaned over and kissed me. "Thanks for a wonderful time."

I smiled and said, "I'm going to miss you tonight."

Debbie smiled back, opened the door and stepped out. She opened the back door to get her things and said, "Not half as much as I'm going to miss you." As she closed the back door, she put her bag down and slipped her fur coat on. I couldn't stop myself. I opened my door and walked round to her and held her in my arms tight for the last time. We kissed again and we wouldn't let go of each other. I was falling for this girl and it was something I hadn't planned on happening. Debbie picked up her bag looking into my eyes, and said, "I'll see you at school."

She made her way over to her car. As she unlocked it, I stood and watched her. I wanted to shout over and spend another night with her but she climbed in and started the engine. I waited for the reversing lights to come on, hoping she was thinking the same thing. Then it hit me—I must go home—and I turned back to the Range Rover. I drove forward a few metres and looked in the rear-view mirror. I watched her reverse out of the space and pull up behind me, so I pulled away. It was about six o'clock and I thought about Debbie all the way home.

# Chapter 10

Reality struck me as I pulled up on the drive. It looked as if Denise and Andrew had come round. I climbed out of the Range Rover and opened the front door. Mick ran down the stairs and gave me a big hug, told me how much he'd missed me and Liz opened the kitchen door looking flushed.

"I didn't expect you for a while, I'm just cooking something for dinner. Andrew's here."

I went into the kitchen, put my keys on the side and Andrew was pouring me a drink from an almost empty bottle of red wine. I picked it up and said to Liz it was no wonder she looked flushed. She gave out a shallow laugh and said, "I'm not working tomorrow, I thought I would get pissed."

Andrew asked how I was, if I'd had a good trip and we chatted while I opened a bottle of whiskey and poured myself a large one with loads of ice. I ate my dinner and we carried on talking and drinking till late in the lounge.

When I woke the next morning, I was still sitting in the chair in the lounge. Andrew had gone home and Liz was in bed. I must have fallen asleep talking to Andrew.

I woke Mick and got him ready for school. We ate breakfast quickly and said goodbye to Liz. I was in a hurry because I wanted to see Debbie at the school.

As we pulled up, I could see her getting out of her BMW just behind us. I waited and when she walked past the car we followed her across the playground. I said goodbye to Mick by the school and slowly walked back, waiting for Debbie to catch me up. I opened the back door of the Range Rover and pretended to look in a book that was on the back seat. I could see her walking towards me; I had this strange feeling of excitement, as she got closer.

"Good morning," she said with that lovely smile on her face. I wanted to kiss her in the road.

"I did miss you last night," I said as I closed the door. "Was everything OK when you got home?"

"Yes, I was quite surprised. I thought about what you said last night, and I'll give it a go if you still think it might work."

"I'll ring him today then and ask him out tonight."

She smiled again and said, "I'll see you later then." She walked away and got into her car and we drove off in different directions.

I arrived at work just after nine o'clock. One of the mechanics said, "You had some funny phone calls yesterday. I put the list on your desk next to the phone." I went up to my office and looked at the list. There were two from the bank manager and three from a Mr Wiseman.

I spoke to the bank manager first: he told me that the cheque I banked—and had express cleared—for £3,267 wouldn't clear. I asked him if there was any other money available. He replied with a very unsympathetic voice, "I'm sorry, the other cheques you put in won't be cleared till next week." I explained that I needed to draw wages and he said, "There's nothing I can do, my hands are tied."

I thought to myself, it should be your balls, in a knot. I pleaded, grovelled, asked, shouted, all to no avail, and then I slammed the phone down and ran downstairs to the safe. There was enough in there from the petrol money for the wages but not the rent, so I would be all right till Monday and some customers were due to pay me for work that was done in the week.

Then I phoned Mr Wiseman. He was from a company called Halsted demanding money. I agreed to put a cheque in the post. I went back downstairs to find out if anything had happened while I was away. They told me the petrol was delivered and they'd given the driver one of the cheques that I had left signed.

I went back upstairs and phoned the trader that gave me the cheque that wouldn't clear but there was no answer. I jumped in the car and drove round to his workshop. He was in his office with a customer that was buying a car from him. I stood by the door and peeped through the crack in the glass. They paid him in cash for the car. As soon as he saw me I could hear him stuttering. As the customer left, I burst into his office and he apologised about the cheque and started to write me another one. I put my hand on his cheque book looked straight into his eyes and said that cash would do. He looked up at me and reached for his briefcase. He could tell I was not in a mood to be messed about. I left with it all in cash and went straight down to the bank. I was hoping to bump into the bank manager so I could stick my fingers up at him.

As I was driving back, I suddenly realised I'd never rung John. I made a slight detour, dropped in to see him and arranged to meet him and Debbie at eight o'clock in the White Swan; it's just down the road from their house.

I became very excited at the thought of seeing Debbie again. I left work at six o'clock and went home. We had dinner, I got changed and Liz and I dropped Mick off, at the sitter's, on the way.

We were standing by the bar ordering our drinks when I caught a glimpse of Debbie walking towards me. John was behind her. I introduced them to Liz. I could see Debbie was a little embarrassed. I ordered a couple more drinks and we sat down in the corner. I couldn't stop myself from staring at Debbie; she looked lovely. We had to be very careful not to do, or say, something that would get us in trouble. We all drank quite a bit and had a good time. John was up and down to the bar every 15 minutes and I noticed he was drinking shorts while he was waiting for the other drinks to be poured.

As the lights flashed for last orders, Debbie said, "Would you like to come back for a night cap? I think I could find some whiskey." I noticed John give Debbie a look of contempt and his eyes blinked very slowly as he looked round the room. He stood up to go to the toilet and he staggered across the floor. Debbie looked at me and dropped her head in shame, so I tried to make a joke of it and said he must have had a head start. Debbie smiled with her cheeks, but not her eyes as she normally did. I felt sorry for her as she stood up and lifted her handbag off the back of her chair and placed it over her shoulder. John staggered back and downed the last dregs of his beer. Liz looked at me with a frown, as if to say, 'I don't want to go back to their house'.

I quickly said, "We'll come back for one, I'll take you home in my car." I'd only drunk shandy and I felt very sober.

We all left together and arrived at their house. Debbie opened the front door and John staggered down the drive, behind Liz and in front of me. He walked into his speedboat, which was on a trailer parked in front of the garage by the side of their house, and stumbled in the door clutching his leg, then made his way into the kitchen. Debbie poured the drinks and John went up the stairs to the toilet. I found the armchair and pushed my car keys down the side of the pillow, while Debbie showed Liz around the house.

By the time we'd finished our drinks and stood up to go, John was slumped in the chair opposite me and his eyes had almost closed. I pretended to kick his chair by accident as I walked past. I didn't want him to fall asleep after all this. He looked up and said something like, "I'll she you mate," with his eyes still blinking very slowly, trying to focus.

Liz went up to the bathroom and Debbie whispered to me as we stood by the front door, "He's in a foul mood, don't leave me too long with him." Then John came out, walking like Andy Pandy, and Liz came down the stairs.

We said goodnight and left. I walked up the drive and felt for my keys and said to Liz that I must have put them down in the house. Liz waited by the car and I went back and knocked on the door. I waited and knocked again louder.

As it opened, Debbie was standing there crying and her sleeve was ripped. I burst into the house and into the kitchen. I didn't need to ask what was happening; John was leaning on the sink with a knife in his hand, shouting, "Come here, bitch!"

I put my hands up in front of me, trying to calm him down, and asked him, "What are you doing?"

He lifted his head and said, "Piss off, it's nothing to do with you."

I grabbed the hand with the knife in it and opened his fingers. He dropped it on the floor, then he went to grab another from the drawer that was still open but he pulled out a spoon. I opened the back door and pushed him out and he fell on the ground. I followed him out and slammed the door.

"What are you trying to do?" I said angrily as he rolled up into a ball.

"Leave me here," he said. "You don't know what it's like."

I grabbed his arm and pulled him up and sat him on a bench in the garden. He struggled a bit but he was in no state to start fighting. "I don't know what, what is like?" I asked, as he put his head in his hands.

"It's that bitch in there, she keeps hiding all my bottles of whiskey and I can't find them."

"I know why," I said. "You have got a serious drink problem." He looked up at me and I asked him, "Have you hit Debbie before?" His head drooped again and he nodded. "You will have to get some help, you can't carry on like this."

He interrupted me and shouted, "I think she's got another bloke," with dribble coming out of his mouth.

"I wouldn't blame her if you beat her up every time you get pissed. What makes you think that, anyway?"

"She goes away on courses, or that's what she says. She's just been on one this week and I don't believe her. We don't sleep together, we argue all the time."

I wanted him to say something about his girlfriend, so I asked, "Have you ever had an affair?"

He nodded again. "I met a girl just after we got married and when I found out she was pregnant I left Debbie and moved in with her. Sometime after the baby was born, she got knocked down in the street and I moved back here."

I was still mad and too cold to talk outside anymore, so I said, "It sounds to me like you're the problem," and I walked towards the back door. As I opened it, I looked back at him. He was trying to stand up. I opened the door and Liz was standing next to Debbie by the cooker. As I went in, they both looked at me. Debbie was still crying. She wiped her eyes and asked how John was. I was just about to say that he'd calmed down a bit, when I heard him behind me by the back door. I turned to see him support himself by his hand on the door frame and, with a cough, he threw up all over the doorstep.

I looked at Debbie with one hand over her eyes. She shook her head from side to side and said, "The dirty bastard's done it again."

Liz said, "Shall we stop and help you clean up the mess?"

"No, it's all right, I'm used to it now. You get off, thanks for all your help."

Liz walked out into the hall. I looked at John still by the door and said, "You lay one more finger on her and I will give you a beating like you've never had before."

He wiped his arm over his mouth and, still trying to focus, turned and went back outside. Debbie walked us to the door and thanked us again. As I walked up the drive, I suddenly remembered my keys. "Can I just look for my keys? I've lost them somewhere." I went into the front room and Debbie followed me. I put my hand under the pillow to get them and she said, "Thanks, I'll see you in the morning."

"Will you be all right?"

"Yes," she said. "He can sleep outside for all I care. I'm leaving him, I can't stand it any more."

I kissed her on the cheek and said, "I'll see you tomorrow, then."

As we drove home, Liz said, "It's a good job you lost your keys, he would have killed her." I just agreed as we pulled on to the drive.

We went in the house and Liz went straight up to bed. I poured a large whiskey and sat watching the telly for a while, thinking about Debbie. When I'd finished my drink, I went to bed; Liz was already snoring.

The next morning I got up early. I hadn't slept very well; I kept thinking about Debbie. I was still thinking about her when I went for a run. I collected Mick from the sitter's and we had breakfast together. I picked up a letter from the carpet. It looked like the bank statement I'd been waiting for. I put it in the car and took Mick to school. On Saturdays, the teachers ran a swimming club for a couple of hours and Mick loved to go. It was handy for all the mothers and fathers that had to work weekends.

Debbie's car was parked by the gate, so I took Mick to the main doors as usual. Debbie came out and we walked back together. "How did you get on last night?" I asked.

She looked very tired and said, "After you went, I cleaned up and went to bed. I left John outside, hoping he would freeze to death. Unfortunately, he came in, sometime in the night, and slept on the settee. I left early to collect Dawn from my friend's house and he'd gone by the time I got back."

"What are you going to do?"

"I don't know," she admitted. "I lay in bed last night with all sorts of things going through my head. If I walk out on him, what happens to Dawn? He's in no fit state to look after her, is he? I wish he was dead, at least I could get on with my life and not have to worry about being battered every time he comes home. I'm having the day off. I'll have a serious think today and sort something out."

As we got to her car, I said, "If you want to talk to someone, I'll be at work till about two; just ring me if you want."

She looked at me with a sad face and said with a tear in each corner of her eye, "Why couldn't I have met you . . ." She opened her car door and got in, reaching for a hanky from the glove box. I slowly walked away and drove to work wondering what I could do to help her. She was in such a state and obviously hated him.

I pulled up on the forecourt none the wiser; nothing sprang into my mind. I went into the workshop to see what was happening and everyone was working hard. I made myself a coffee and went upstairs to my office with the mail. I opened three out of the six letters and they were bills, so I left the rest until Monday.

I left work about one o'clock and stopped at the Railway pub for a drink on the way home. Roger, one of the lads that worked for me was already in there drinking by the bar. I had a couple of beers with him and walked out with fifteen pounds extra that I won from the fruit machine.

I was just about to pull out of the car park as my phone rang. It was Liz, panicking: "Mick has fallen off his bike onto the kerb. I think he has broken his leg, shall I take him to the hospital, or call an ambulance?"

"Is he in much pain?" I asked as I pulled away in a hurry.

"He's laid out on the settee and he won't move his leg. He's as white as a sheet—what shall I do?"

"Take him in your car, and I'll meet you there." I put my foot to the floor and drove as fast as I could to the hospital.

As I screeched around bends and raced along the country lanes, I began to think the worst. The more I thought, the faster I drove. I didn't stop at any of the traffic lights, I went straight through them, overtook other cars on the inside, pulled out at junctions without stopping and skidded to a halt in the car park, just as Liz was pulling up by the accident unit's main entrance. I opened the car door, jumped out and two policemen grabbed my arms. I looked up and noticed six police cars around me all with their roof lights flashing.

One of the policemen said, "Just hold on there, can you tell me why you were speeding, sir?"

I glanced over to see Liz with a horrified look on her face as she was trying to lift Mick out of the car. "My wife phoned me to tell me my son has had an accident and I was worried about him. Can somebody help her get him into the hospital?"

Then I heard Liz shout, "He's fainted."

I tried to struggle free but they wouldn't let me go. A couple of policemen ran over to help Liz and she looked back at me helplessly as she went through the electronic doors, holding Mick's head up and stroking his hair.

The two policemen let my arms go and one bent down to pick his hat up off the floor. As he stood up, he said, "Have you been drinking, sir?" I couldn't deny it. I explained that I'd popped into the pub on my way home from work, had two drinks and that afterwards was when I'd got the phone call from Liz. "I was worried and I drove here as fast as I could."

"We followed you for two and a half miles and you were travelling at speeds in excess of 98 miles an hour," pointed out one of the policemen. In the distance, I could hear another policeman talking on his radio, checking the registration number on my car. I told them how sorry I was and how worried I'd been and they asked me if I would mind taking a breathalyser test. I followed them to their car and sat in the back. While I was waiting, I noticed two of the other cars pulling away and the two policemen that had helped Liz carry Mick into the hospital walking towards us.

One of them opened the car door and said, "Your son is with the doctor now."

"Is he OK?"

"We don't know. They took him straight in on a stretcher."

Just then one of the policemen in the front seat turned and said, "Can you breathe into the mouthpiece with one long continuous breath and stop when I say." I took the device, placed it to my lips and blew into it as instructed. I was beginning to feel a bit nervous now; I was cold and shivering. As I blew harder, one policeman was looking through his paperwork and the other was looking at his watch. I thought I was going to run out of breath and he said, "OK, that will do." I passed it back and they took it in turns to inspect it carefully. I sat patiently in the back seat, while they passed it from one to the other, and then the driver turned and said, "You're OK, I can tell you have had a drink or two but you're just under the limit."

I smiled to myself and let out a sigh of relief. Then the other policeman said, "Unfortunately, I have to caution you. Anything you say will be taken down and used against you in a court of law. You don't have to say anything but if you do, it could be used as evidence against you. Do you understand?" I nodded and he carried on, "We had to report to the station that we were chasing you along the road at 76 miles per hour and you will probably have to go to court. But, as we said before, you were travelling a lot faster than that, so I will write 76 mph in my report. Off the record, your driving was impeccable but you were driving too fast."

I nodded my head and said, "Thank you and I am sorry."

The driver turned his head and said with a smile on his face, "I quite enjoyed it. I love a good car chase now and again."

Then the other one gave me a small slip of paper with writing on and said, "You will have to produce your driving licence, MOT certificate and insurance certificate to your local police station."

I took the piece of paper and the driver let me out of the back. As I stood up, he said, "I hope your son will be all right."

I smiled and said, "Thanks again," and ran into the hospital to join my family.

I asked the nurse at the reception desk how Mick was. She flicked through some papers on her desk and asked, "When was he admitted?"

"About twenty minutes ago, with a suspected broken leg."

"Ah, the little blond boy, he's with the doctor. Are you a relative?"

"I'm his father," I said anxiously.

"If you go through those doors there, ask for the nurse and she will take you to him."

I thanked her and dashed off down the ward. When I reached Mick, he was laying back on the bed with his hands behind his head and a big smile on his face, Liz by his side and an attractive nurse bandaging his ankle. "How is he?" I asked Liz.

"He's only sprained it and when he came in I thought he'd fainted, but he's fine now."

"It's nothing that a couple of weeks off school won't cure," added the nurse. Mick smiled even more.

"What happened to you with the police?" asked Liz.

I explained quickly then Mick sat up; he thought it was great. "What happened then, Dad?" he said, all excited.

"I'll tell you later when we get home."

We left shortly after. Mick hobbled all the way out of the hospital; he wouldn't let me carry him. He wanted everyone to see him with his leg out in front of him and a big bandage on his foot. All the nurses waved as he went through the door. Liz drove him home and I went to get some fish and chips for tea and a bottle of wine.

While we were eating, I told Mick about the police chasing me to the hospital—I exaggerated a bit and he loved it.

Sunday, Liz and I ran around all day, fetching drinks and sweets for Mick as he lay on the settee. One or two of his mates popped in to see his bad ankle and, later in the day, Denise and Andrew came round. We had a few drinks and Mick went up to bed.

Andrew popped out to get something more to drink and Liz went with him to get some crisps and nuts. I poured some more drinks in the kitchen and, after a couple of minutes, Denise came out to see if she could give me a hand. As I uncorked the last bottle of red wine, she said, "I want to go out with you again."

I looked at her with a blank expression and she kissed me. I put the corkscrew down and placed my arms around her waist. "What's brought this on?" I asked.

She looked up at me, put her arms around my neck and said, "I love you and I want to be with you." Then she licked her finger and gently stroked my lips. We kissed again for a few minutes, until I heard the key in the front door. I quickly turned and picked up the corkscrew and placed it back in the drawer, as the kitchen door opened. Andrew placed the carrier bag on the cupboard top and pulled out some bottles of wine, then Liz followed him in with the crisps. Denise pretended she was getting some bowls to put them in and I nearly had a heart attack. With my hands nervously shaking, I drank straight from the bottle. I was burning up inside, I was too frightened to turn and look at them, in case I was as red as a beetroot.

Liz went out of the kitchen first, followed by Denise, then I heard Andrew say, "Are you keeping that one to yourself?"

I turned and looked at him over the top of the bottle and realised I was drinking it like a pint of beer. I put the bottle down on the side; it was half empty.

Andrew laughed and said, "Are you on a mission?"

"No," I said with half a smile, still embarrassed, and followed him through to the lounge. As I walked in, still thinking about what Denise had said in the kitchen, I caught the look in her big brown eyes as I sat down opposite her in the chair. I was still stunned; I couldn't take in what she had said to me.

Liz asked me to put some music on, quietly in the background, so I put my glass down on the carpet, found a cassette in the cupboard and put it on. After about half an hour, Denise went to the bathroom. I gave her a few moments then said to Liz that I would check on Mick and I followed her upstairs. As I got to the top, Denise came out of the bathroom. "What were you on about earlier?" I whispered.

"I want to go out with you again," she whispered back. I put my head round Mick's door to make sure he was asleep and pulled it to.

"You'll have to ring me next week then and we'll sort something out," I said a little louder.

Denise winked as she started to walk quietly down the stairs holding the rail for support. I stood at the top of the stairs for a few seconds before joining her. I grabbed another bottle of wine from the kitchen on the way. Liz was dancing with Andrew, arm in arm, at the other end of the room. So I put the bottle down on the table and danced with Denise.

I ordered a taxi for Denise and Andrew at about midnight, when we'd run out of wine, and they left holding each other up. Liz went straight to bed. I threw the bottles away, collected the glasses and put them in the kitchen, ready to wash up in the morning. I poured myself a little night cap, whiskey with ice, and plonked myself in an armchair. I thought for ages about Denise and what she'd said.

Mick didn't go to school the next day because of his ankle; so on my way to work, I drove slowly past the school, hoping I would catch a glimpse of Debbie, to find out if she had decided what to do with John but I couldn't even see her car by the gate. As I drove, I kept hoping she would ring my car-phone. I arrived at work, still not knowing, so I collected the mail and went upstairs. It didn't take me long to forget about Denise and Debbie as I opened the letters, one by one. More and more bills, one court summons, two small cheques and a letter from the bank. Same shit, different day, I said to myself as I threw them in the tray with the others.

* * *

The first three days of the week were much the same. I had even mastered the art of disguising my voice when I answered the phone, so I could tell everyone I wasn't available. I hadn't seen or spoken to Debbie and I was starting to worry that she might have done something stupid. I couldn't ring her in case John answered the phone.

It was Thursday morning when Mick decided he wanted to go back to school, so Liz and I checked his ankle. The swelling had gone down considerably so we made him promise he wouldn't play outside at break-times and we left it wrapped up. When I dropped him off, I went in and told the teacher about his accident and as I left he was showing his mates.

As I walked out of the main doors, Debbie was walking in with Dawn. I was so surprised to see her but I couldn't speak until she'd taken Dawn into her class. I was so excited; I walked slowly across the playground, watching everyone that came out of the door. I had just reached the gate and she came out. I was so pleased to see her; I was trembling with excitement. "Hello," I said first, "Are you all right?"

"Yes," she replied. "I've been away for a few days and I feel much better."

"I kept looking for you and hoping you'd ring me."

"I couldn't ring you because I wanted time to think about everything."

"Well, you look lovely."

"Thank you," she said, with that gorgeous smile back on her face. I wanted her again, desperately. As we approached Debbie's car, she said, "I have decided to-" then her phone bleeped. "Excuse me," she said as she answered it and pushed her hair behind her ear with one finger, like she'd done at the cabin, in the snow. I stood on the pavement, rested my arms on the roof of her car and waited. I watched the different expressions on her lovely face as she spoke. Then she turned the phone off and said, "I've got to go, I'm late. I'll see you tomorrow. I'll wait for you here." With that, she got in her car. As soon as the engine started, she drove off in a hurry. I walked to my car wondering what she had decided to do.

As I pulled onto the forecourt, my phone rang. It was Debbie. "I'm sorry," she said." I'm very late for a meeting and I need to talk with you. I want to tell you the reason for my decision. I haven't got the time today but could we meet somewhere for lunch, perhaps tomorrow, and I can explain?"

"Yes, certainly. If I don't see you in the morning," I said, "ring me, at the same time, on this number." She rang off.

All day I worried about the decision that she was talking about. Until about four o'clock, when Denise phoned.

"I'm sorry it's taken me so long to ring you back, I've been waiting for my roster to arrive in the post. I was hoping I had another back-to-back, but unfortunately I haven't for the next three weeks and I can't wait that long to see you."

I thought for a moment. "Can you meet me for a drink on Monday? I won't be here tomorrow."

"Yes, where?"

"Meet me at the Bridge Steak House in Earlshill, at midday."

"OK, don't be late, will you?" she said.

I put the phone down and sat back in my chair, wondering what I was doing. I'd told myself at the beginning of the game I would have one affair with each girl and here I was arranging a second. I sat there for ten minutes and the phone rang again. I answered it and, with a deep voice, I said, "Hello."

This familiar voice said, "Is the boss there?"

"Who is it?" I asked.

"Tell him its Lucy, he'll know who I am."

My heart started pounding again, as I put her on hold. I was dropping myself deeper and deeper into trouble but I couldn't stop myself. I pressed the button and said, "Hello, stranger, where have you been?"

"Hi," she said. "I've been away with Ivor, to Switzerland skiing. We had a great time, we came back Tuesday. Are you all right?"

"Yes," I said in a trance; I didn't know what to say.

Lucy carried on talking about Switzerland and then she said, "We met a couple over there, and I became very good friends with the girl, and she invited me to stay with her in France for a long weekend. I talked to Ivor about it and he suggested I go on my own because he is too busy at work. What do you think?"

I couldn't believe my ears. This was the girl that had said, no, I couldn't, it's impossible, and now she was asking me to meet her in France. "Whereabouts in France?"

"North," she said. "It's twenty minutes from Calais?"

"When are you thinking of going?"

"In about two weeks. I have to ring Colette and she'll meet me off the plane."

"Does this mean that you are flying from here?"

"Yes, why do you ask? We could fly together, and split up at the airport."

"What about Liz, at the customs desk?"

I heard Lucy breathe in quickly. "I never thought of that," she said.

"Leave it with me to work out something and I'll ring you back or pass your house next week. Is Ivor away soon?"

"Yes, he leaves Monday for three days."

"So it's safe to ring your house, then?"

"After the kids have gone to school, about ten, to be safe."

After I put the phone down, I counted the money that was left in the safe: there was £3626.99p, so I could afford a trip to France, but a long weekend? That was a bit more awkward.

I drove home that night not knowing what to do; Denise was madly in love with her husband's best friend; Lucy wanted me to go to France; and Debbie, I didn't know what was happening with her. I turned into Oak Lane and I could see behind me, in the mirror, flashing lights getting closer. I pulled over to let them pass. There were two police cars, an ambulance and two police motorbikes. I watched them pass and carried on. As I approached the T-junction at the end of the road, I could see an accident just up ahead. The traffic was quite bad and everyone was slowing down to have a look. At first I couldn't make out what had happened but, as I got closer, the police were directing the traffic around the two cars that were mangled together. I passed the accident and noticed one of the damaged cars was foreign—the number plates were different to ours—and it started me thinking. If that person in the car was French, they might want someone like me to take it back to France on my truck. I pulled away from the accident and started to make up a story in my mind. The car would have to be something different; if it was an ordinary car, it could be repaired here. To make the story believable it would have to be a left-hand drive, expensive car like a Mercedes or a Ferrari. The parts would be easier to get in France. The driver would have to be rich enough to pay a lot of money to take it back and it must be something I'd towed in to my garage.

I didn't say anything that night to Liz. I thought I would leave it for a few days and see if anything came of the trip first.

I didn't see, or hear, from Debbie, Lucy or Denise till Monday morning. Debbie was at the school and briefly said in the playground that she would meet me in the Red Lion at dinner-time on Tuesday. I drove straight into town, to get some parts for a car, and got back to the garage just after 11.30, only to be greeted by another massive bailiff, walking round and writing things down on a list.

"Can I help you?" I asked inquisitively.

He pulled out a card with his picture on and said, "I've been asked by the council to retrieve a sum of money that was due to be paid by November of last year, for rates on this property. The amount outstanding is £2608.09p; that includes bailiff charges."

My heart came up into my mouth. "Can we go up to my office and discuss this?"

"Yes," he said, almost with a smile on his face, as if he really enjoyed his job.

I opened the door and sat down at my desk. "What happens next?" I asked him.

"Well, you can either pay me in full now, or I will take this inventory back with me and give you thirty days to pay the said amount. If you fail to comply, we will come out with a van, sieze the items on this list and auction them off at a public auction, to raise as much as possible to reduce the amount. Then, after that, you will be asked for the balance at a later date."

I tried to reason with him but the best he could do was the thirty days. He left me with a copy of the list he'd made and a yellow sheet of paper with the charges printed out in full.

He left shortly afterwards and drove off in his new car, to visit some other poor hardworking person that was trying to make a living and, like me, probably had cash problems. It wouldn't have been so bad if he drove round in an old wreck of a car.

Then the phone rang; it was Denise. "Where are you? You promised to meet me today." I had completely forgotten.

"I'll be there in ten minutes, I'm sorry." I ran down the stairs and drove off to meet her. As I drove into the Bridge car park, I could see her standing by the door. She looked so sexy. I sat in the car for a few moments, just staring at her. The breeze was gently moving her brown curly hair over her eyes as she waited for me to get out of the car. I opened the door and waved. As I stood up, she smiled and waved back. She held the door open, waiting for me, and we went in together.

I glanced round the room to make sure no one was there I knew and Denise sat down in the corner. I ordered our drinks at the bar, went over and joined her. "Sorry I was late. I had a problem to sort out and I forgot everything else for a moment."

"How could you forget me?" she said, looking at me with those brown eyes. We talked for a while and then I said, "What are we going to do about the other night?"

"What do you mean?" she replied.

"Do you think it would be a good idea to go out again?"

"Why not?" she quickly said. "Don't you want to?"

"I do, but we nearly got caught when Andrew opened the door to the kitchen."

"I know that was a bit silly of me but I couldn't stop myself, something inside me said to hell with the risk. All day, of every day, I never stop thinking about you; no matter what I do, you are on my mind. I want to live with you, look after you and love you. While I was away last week, I had this vision, about moving abroad and living together, by the sea somewhere. I thought about Zante—we could rent a small house, just off the front in Argassi and walk on the sand together every day and night; we could make love whenever we wanted, in the sea or on the sand with a warm breeze on our backs. Just think of the all-over suntan we would have, the food, the drinks on the balcony just before we go to bed together and hold each other every night."

I didn't say anything for a while. I looked at the soft tanned skin on her face. She looked so excited. Her mouth curled up slightly at both ends and her lips were perfect and painted with a very pale pink, almost see-through, satin lip gloss. The small gap between them was just showing her brilliant white teeth and just above was the most perfect nose and eyes I could ever remember seeing on a girl. Her eyelashes were long and almost black to match her eyebrows. She seemed to blink in slow motion and it made those big brown eyes even bigger. Every strand of her curly hair was shining from the light above her on the wall. She took a sip from her glass of wine and slowly licked her lips with her deep red tongue and it slowly slipped back into her mouth.

I suddenly heard her say, "Are you all right?" and I realised I was in a deep trance. Denise had me hooked. The thought of living abroad with her was something any man would dream about.

I took a large gulp of my beer and said, "Before we sail off into the blue caves of Zante, aren't we forgetting a few things? Like Andrew, Liz, Mick, families, homes, businesses, jobs, money? In six months, or a year, we might not like each other, or we could be homesick."

"This isn't a schoolgirl crush I've got, it's a lot more than that—I love you; I have never wanted to be with anybody as much as I want to be with you," she said with a pained look on her beautiful dark face.

I didn't know what to say. I loved the thought of it all and, if I was going to run off with someone, it would have to be someone like Denise, who was attractive and tall, lovely personality, a good friend, someone you can talk to and have a laugh with. It was like that with Liz and me once many years ago. The money side of things didn't really matter if we loved each other, not that it wouldn't be a problem for us. It was all too much for me, what with everything else that was going on. I tried to explain that I fancied the idea but I wasn't going to say anything until I had given it some serious thought. For the while, I told her, it would be best if we carried on as we were.

Denise held my hand and said, "I really do love you." We carried on talking for about two hours and left just after three o'clock. I switched the radio off and thought about the conversation we'd just had, all the way back to work.

* * *

I never saw Debbie at Mick's school the next morning, so I waited impatiently until 12.30 and made my way over to the Red Lion to meet her for a drink and find out what she was going to do with John. She arrived at 1.30, just as I was thinking she wasn't going to make it. She kissed me on the cheek as she sat down on a stool next to me and apologised for being late. I ordered her a drink and said, "Shall we move over by the fire?"

As we walked over, Debbie said, "It's just like the one in the cabin, isn't it," and smiled. We reminisced for a while about that night and she started to tell me about her weekend away.

"I'm sorry I couldn't say anything the other day, but as it involves you, I didn't want to tell you bits. As you know, I went away that weekend, to my friend's house with Dawn and I had a long talk with myself about everything. I can't thank you enough for what you did for me on that Friday night. You were right in saying I couldn't go on like that, so I thought long and hard and decided to go back to John for a while, to see if he can sort himself out. He has promised me he will stop drinking and seek help from someone professional and I think he means it. But only time will tell. When I came back on the Monday night, we sat and talked for hours. I've set a bed up for him in the spare room and he'll sleep in there, not with me. To be honest, I don't want to be near him; it will take me a long time to get over the things he did to me. If he starts drinking again, I have told him I will leave him and I will take Dawn with me and he will have to take me to court to get her back. And with his present drinking problem, I don't think he would stand much chance, do you?"

I shook my head, and swigged at my drink as she carried on. "Something happened to me that day you took me out that has never happened to me before. I fell in love with a very nice gentle man."

I didn't say anything, because deep down I'd fallen for her and I wanted to hear what she had to say first.

"I thought about asking you to leave your wife, and Mick, to live with me but I don't think it would be fair to even suggest it. I am the one with the problems, not you, and I will have to sort it out on my own for now. However, I would like to see you now and again if it's possible and, in time, who knows? Things might change between you and your wife. If you asked me now, I would leave John today without a second thought but I know you can't. All I'm trying to say is I will wait and carry on, as I said, hoping that there is a small chance that one day we might be together. And I would be more willing to live on that hope than to have nothing." Debbie stopped and sipped her drink and I fell in love with her even more.

As she put her glass back down on the table, I gently put my hands on her rose-coloured cheeks, kissed her on the lips and said, "You've obviously thought about it a lot and I think you've made a very good decision. Will you tell me if he starts drinking or playing up? And definitely if he as much as looks at you with a frown? You don't deserve to be treated like that, you are a lovely person too, and very clever. I think what you said earlier was lovely and yes, I would love to see you and take you out again."

Debbie grabbed my hand under the table and said, "I promise I will tell you." We kissed.

We left the Red Lion about 2.15 because Debbie had to meet a client at three o'clock. We held each other and kissed. As we left, I made Debbie promise we could see each other every morning, even if we couldn't speak. She gave me one of those massive smiles before she left.

I drove back to work, with my head in the clouds, and then Roger phoned me from work and said that the petrol had run out again. I came back down to earth with a big bang.

# Chapter 11

Over the next few days, I bumped into Debbie at the school and she told me that John hadn't drunk anything at all and he was being nice to her, and Dawn. Then, on the Friday, Lucy phoned me at work and told me that Colette had phoned her Wednesday night, to see when she was going over to France. I told Lucy to arrange a weekend and let me know the Monday before she was due to go. Then I collected the cheques together I had been given and went to the bank.

As I was driving along, I thought about asking the bank for a loan. I parked the car, deposited the money, drew the wages, and asked the girl at the information desk if it would be at all possible to speak with the manager. She phoned him and asked me to take a seat, saying he would be down in a minute. I wandered around, looking at the posters on the wall. They said things like, 'If you need a loan for anything, just ask' and 'low cost loans available here'.

While I waited for the manager, I thought about what I wanted to say and what I didn't want him to know. The girl on reception said, "You can go up now, Mr Vaughan."

I made my way to his office and knocked on the door. I heard him say, "Enter," so in I went. I shook his hand and sat down opposite him at this big oak desk. Then he clasped his hairy hands together and leaned forwards on the desk. "What can I do for you?" he said, as he peered over his tiny round glasses.

"I could do with my overdraft raised, or a loan to help me through this quiet patch we've had. We are quite busy now but a few people are chasing me for money."

He lifted his hand and carefully placed it on his chin, with his elbow propped on the desk. Then he said, "Go on."

I explained to him that, in a few weeks, the money would start rolling in again. He opened a blue file that was on his desk and, as he looked through it, his head drooped and he scratched the top of his bald crown with his index finger. He flicked through the pages and lifted his head again. "How much is owed to you for work you have already done?"

This is where the real bullshit started. "Last time I looked, it was about £5,000. It may be more now, I haven't had time to bring the books up to date because I have been in the workshop. There's probably about £6,000 worth of fuel, underground in the tanks, and work in progress must be somewhere in the region of £4,000."

His eyebrows went up as he looked back at the file. I thought to myself, I've got this in the bag; it's going to take the pressure away for a while. He looked at me again and pushed his glasses back up his nose. "According to the figures I have here in front of me," he said, as he pulled a hanky from his pocket, "you already have £16,000 . . ." He sneezed twice and wiped his nose. My eyebrows went up then. I didn't realise I had that much, until he said, "Of our money." He put his hanky back in his pocket and carried on. "We paid a cheque on Wednesday for £7,234 for fuel and, unless you reduce the borrowing within the next week drastically, we won't be able to pay for the next delivery. So the answer is: no, I can't help you, I'm sorry."

I felt deflated; it was as if he'd stabbed me with his Parker pen. I smiled and shook his apelike hand again and left quickly, before he asked for the wages back.

When I got back to the garage, I gave the lads their wages and we locked up. I stopped at the Wooden Cross for a drink. A few of the lads were in there, telling their stories of the week as usual. I asked myself what they would say if I told them mine. I left about 7.30 and went home. I was going out with some of the lads for a drink at nine, to the Arden Oak.

While I ate my dinner, I casually mentioned to Liz that I'd pulled a car into the garage that was involved in an accident; the man that owned it was French and he'd asked me if I would take it to his house.

Liz looked up and said, "In France?"

"That's what I thought he said, but his English wasn't very good."

"If you are going over to France, I could come with you."

I'd hoped she wouldn't say that. "He's coming back to see me on Monday, with the couple he's staying with. Hopefully they can explain it better." I carried on eating my dinner and didn't mention it again.

Liz went to bed; I got changed and arrived at the Arden Oak about ten minutes late. Everyone was there, except Andrew. He had said, in the Wooden Cross earlier, that he would be here. I thought he might turn up later. We all had a laugh and, by eleven o'clock, I was ready for bed. I was worn out after the week I'd had, so I left and drove home. I must have been knackered; I was hallucinating. I thought I saw Andrew driving toward me, on the other side of the dual carriageway. I got home and went straight to bed. I was surprised to see Liz still awake as she was working in the morning.

I woke the next morning when I heard Mick in his room with the telly on. I got dressed and made him some breakfast, then dropped him at his swimming club. We were a bit late and I got to work at eleven, or just after. Lucy phoned me half an hour later, all excited.

"I'm going!" she cried. "I've been ringing all morning to tell you the good news. I'm going on Wednesday, this week. I'm flying in the afternoon. I know Liz won't be there, so will you be able to come?"

"I can't come on the plane with you but I'll come over on the train with my car, through the Eurotunnel. You'll have to give me the address and I'll meet you in a bar on Friday night."

"How will I know the bar?"

"When you get there, mention to your friend about going out Friday night and ask her where she is taking you. Tell her you want a couple of drinks first and a club after. Then ring me on the Friday, in my car, when I'm on my way, and I'll see you there."

"Brilliant," she said. "That way, Colette won't suspect a thing and you can come to the club with me."

"Hopefully, yes. Is she a bit broad-minded?"

"Well, if you could have heard her when we were skiing, apparently she loves anything in trousers."

"So, if we slipped off and you didn't go home till the morning, she wouldn't ring Ivor?"

"No, she wouldn't."

"Ring me Wednesday morning, after the kids have gone to school, with the address, and I'll see you in France." I put the phone down and started to look forward to the date.

# Chapter 12

IT WASN'T TILL the Monday night that I got round to telling Liz about my trip. She seemed very excited for me but was disappointed that she was working. Relieved, I explained that the French man was very rich and that he had a cousin with a garage in France that had worked on his car since the day he bought it; he would only trust them to repair it, I said, so I would leave Thursday dinner-time and catch the ferry Thursday night. I could sleep most of the way on the boat, drive through France on Friday, drop the car off, catch the ferry back late on Saturday and be home Sunday morning.

"Is it a good-paying job?" she asked.

"I told him it would cost him £900 and he gave me £200 towards the ferry and fuel costs. He's flying back tomorrow and ringing me Wednesday."

Liz looked at the calendar on the kitchen wall. "I'm working Wednesday, Thursday and Friday, so I'll swap with someone on Friday. Just make sure he pays you when you get there. We need the money; the mortgage is due again and we haven't got enough in our account, so you'll have to pay this one. The electric and gas are due as well."

This is what our marriage had come down to: it was not how much we loved each other, it was a case of who had the money to pay the bills on time.

* * *

Tuesday morning, I phoned to see what time the train would leave Folkestone and arrive in France and asked my mechanic to service my car so that it would be ready for the journey. Later that morning, I had a phone call from a bailiff, insisting I visit their office urgently to talk about a court summons, sometime that week. As I couldn't go on Thursday or Friday, I made the appointment for Wednesday at ten.

On the morning of my meeting I was very worried. I didn't even look out for Debbie at the school. I went straight to the garage and collected some papers, then went to the court. It took a while to find the office as I strode through the marble corridors. On reaching the reception desk, I was instructed to have a seat and wait for someone to come out to me. I sat in the waiting room on my own for ages; well, it seemed like ages. Finally, a man came out and told me to follow him. We went into a small room and I sat down in front of a small desk. He sat down opposite me, opened a huge file and flicked through the pages.

"Here we are," he said, pulling some papers out. As he looked at the first page, he said, "A company called Halsted has asked the court to retrieve the sum of £3.076, for parts supplied to your company." Then he turned the page and said, "We wrote to you on the first of December and we don't seem to have had a reply. Do I assume from that, you do not have the money?"

"I don't have the money at the moment, it's been very hard these last few months. Things are starting to look a little better but it's going to be some time before I can come up with large sums like that," I replied.

He turned the next page and said, "I understand, I have lots of people in the same boat. In fact, this file I have in front of me is only a few." I looked at it again: it was about three inches thick. I felt a bit more at ease after he told me that. "The best thing to do," he said, "is to make an offer of payment on a weekly, or monthly, basis. Something you can afford and then, if things get better, you can put up the payments. At least if you are trying to pay the debt off, the company will feel better and we will leave you alone."

It was as if someone had removed a large weight from around my neck. I agreed to pay £100 per month, signed a few forms, and then he asked me to go back in the waiting room while he made a phone call. I walked out, feeling a lot better. The room was full of people by this time. There was a man pacing the floor, three children running riot, a big woman on the far side of the room was crying her eyes out and the man next to her was trying to take no notice, as he read his newspaper. I watched him out of the corner of my eye. Every time he turned a page, he had a sneaky look at her. Sitting there was like a touchier for not paying your bills on time.

I was called back into the room. "Right," said the bailiff. "That's all sorted. Can you give me a cheque for the first payment? That will start the ball rolling."

I wrote one out, with my hand shaking, and he thanked me. I shook his hand and left as quickly as I could. I walked back through the waiting room and out into the corridor, followed the signs for the main entrance and left through the large revolving door. I felt like I had been released from prison. I ran back to my car.

As I put the key in the ignition, I noticed a pink piece of paper on my screen, in a see-through plastic bag. So I opened the door, pulled it from under the wiper blade and opened the bag. It was a parking ticket. I screwed it up and threw it on the seat next to me. I started the car and drove back, happy that was all over, but annoyed about the parking ticket.

It was dinner-time and I was hungry, so I pulled up at a pub and had a pint and a sandwich. While I was sitting there, I thought about the garage and the options I had. Do I go bankrupt, like most people do, or do I try and carry on a little longer and hope that things get better? I wasn't earning enough to pay the bills each week, never mind the old ones. In total, to get myself straight, I needed about £30,000 and I wasn't going to get that sort of money easily. I thought about re-mortgaging the house but, to be honest, I didn't want to tell Liz about the mess I was in. Another robbery was out of the question; I would end up with a heart attack if I tried that again. There was no point me putting the money in I was using for my dates because it wasn't enough and, besides, if it wasn't for them, I would probably go barmy with the worry.

I left the pub and went back to the garage, trying to forget about it and concentrate on getting to France. Then I suddenly remembered Lucy. I'd turned my phone off when I'd gone in to see the bailiff. She was going to ring me and tell me were to meet her. I looked at my watch: it was 3 20. She'd said she was going in the afternoon; there was nothing I could do because, if she had left, her mum would answer the phone. I didn't know what to do.

I still hadn't heard from Lucy by the time I left work that afternoon, so I drove past her house. Ivor was just pulling up on his drive, so I stopped and let the window down. He locked his Mercedes and came over to me. I said, "It's been a long time, how are you?" He smiled and said he was OK, as he put his briefcase down on the floor, and crouched beside it to peer in at me. "You look suntanned or something," I said, trying to get him to tell me about his holiday.

He smiled again. "We've been away skiing in Switzerland."

"Did you have a good time?" I asked.

"Yes, the weather was cold and sunny, as you would expect. Do you want to come in for a coffee?"

"No thanks," I said. "I've got to get home. How's Lucy and the kids? I bet they enjoyed it, didn't they?"

"Yes, in fact Lucy . . ." I thought, this is it, he's going to tell me now. " . . . Has gone to stay with a girl we got friendly with on the slopes."

"You mean, she went back again?"

"No," he said. "Colette lives in France, she's gone for a long weekend."

"That's nice. By the sea?"

"No, it's inland, it's a place called Les Hemmes, just the other side of the Channel. It's about thirty miles from Calais Airport. I was going to go but I've had too much time off work lately and I am so busy. I have to go to Holland on Monday and I have loads to do before I get there."

We talked some more and I left happier, knowing whereabouts I was headed.

When I got home, I played with Mick for a while and put him in bed. Then I had a shower, packed myself a suitcase and Liz and I had dinner. She went up to bed about nine. I waited for a while and found the atlas that we'd bought Mick one Christmas, so I could see where I was going in France. I found the airport and then I found the village where Lucy was staying; it wasn't far from the Eurotunnel entrance. I got into bed about ten and didn't fall asleep for ages, I was too excited.

The next day I woke early, thinking about France. I told Mick I'd see him in a couple of days when I dropped him at the school gates. Then I bumped into Debbie in the playground. "How's things?" I asked.

"Not bad," she said. "I still don't like him but he is trying to make an effort."

"Give it some time," I said. "At least things aren't as bad as they were."

"I've missed you", she said. "When can we go out together?"

"Soon," I replied. "I'm going over to France today to deliver a car. I should be back on Sunday, so I'll talk to you on Monday morning."

Her eyes got bigger as she said, "I could have come with you if you'd given me some warning."

"No, it's too long. John was suspicious when you stayed out one night, he would go mental if you stayed away for three nights. Mind you, it would be nice wouldn't it? Perhaps later, when things have died down a bit, I'll take you there."

"I will hold you to that," she shouted, smiling as I walked to my car.

When I got to work, everyone was working hard. I explained to them that I was going to Devon for a couple of days to a car auction and that I would be back at the weekend. I ordered some parts, opened a couple of letters and eventually left around noon. I had a slow ride down the motorway and stopped for something to eat about two o'clock, leaving a little after three, just as the head chef started shouting at a waitress behind the grill. I drove back on to the motorway and, within five minutes, there was steam coming from the engine. I quickly pulled over onto the hard shoulder and lifted the bonnet to have a look. One of the hoses had burst wide open. I phoned the police from the phone box on the motorway and they told me to wait with the car and said they would send a garage out as fast as they could. I explained that I had to be in Folkestone for seven o'clock to catch the Euro tunnel and was assured that someone would be there as fast as possible. I waited in the car for about forty minutes, until a tow truck pulled up behind me and this scruffy, long-haired teenager jumped out of his truck with an oily rag in his hand, walked over towards me dragging his feet and said, "What you done to your car, then?" He looked under the bonnet.

I said, "A hose has burst."

"Oh, has it now." He rubbed the oily rag up and down the wing of my car and said, "I don't think I've got one of those." I explained to him that I was going through the Euro tunnel at seven o'clock and he slowly walked over to his truck and drove it around to the front of my car, nearly causing an accident on the motorway as he pulled out. Two cars swerved to miss him. He reversed up to the front and dropped the two ramps down that stood up in the air on the back of the truck. "Can I have your keys, please," he asked, "so I can drive it up on the back?" I was beginning to worry now and I kept looking at my watch. "Don't panic, I will get you there on time," he said as he started the engine. "It sounds a bit worse than just a burst hose," he shouted as he shot up the ramps, onto the truck. Here we go, I said to myself, he's trying it on now; he's going to tell me the engine's knackered. Sure enough, as he climbed down, he said, "Your engine sounds like it's dropped a valve". I didn't say anything about me being in the same trade. I thought, I'd better get back to his garage first and see if has the hose.

We drove off the motorway and down a country lane to his shed in a field. He parked the truck, jumped down and disappeared around the back somewhere. I waited in the truck and he appeared with a hose in his hand. "You're lucky," he said. "I was sure I didn't have one for this model." He drove my car off the back of his truck and lifted the bonnet again. I stood and watched him as he fitted the hose. Then he filled the radiator with water and started the engine. Again I looked at my watch; it was nearly 5.30. I waited while he revved the car and checked to see if there were any other water leaks. After a few minutes, he said, "I wouldn't risk it but it's up to you."

I thought to myself, you're an arsehole. I was just about to say something and then I remembered my cheque book had the garage name on it. I kept quiet and waited to see the look on his face. "I'll risk it," I said as he slammed the bonnet shut. "How much do I owe you?"

He rubbed his hands together, with the same oily rag, and said, "Call it £95, all in."

I nearly fell over, the robbing bastard. "I'll have to pay you by company cheque," I said. I held it up in front of his face. He looked at it, read the garage name and said, "You should have told me you have a garage of your own." He went red and turned away. "Call it forty for cash."

I pulled out the money from my back pocket and paid him, smiling to myself as I climbed back into the car and drove off.

I pulled back on to the motorway and put my foot down to the floor, trying to make up some of the time I had lost. It was after six o'clock now and I was going to be late but I could still make it, if the road was clear. I pulled into the outside lane and sailed past everything. Then I started thinking about the night. Would Lucy be there first? And what would she be wearing? Would we smile secretly to each other? And who would speak first? I could talk to her with my Greek accent and no one would know I was English. Then there was the night, where would we make love? And for how long? How many times?

I just passed the sign for Bearsted, when there was a loud bang under the car. I quickly indicated and pulled off the motorway. This time I ground to a halt on the top of the slip-road and the there was smoke and steam everywhere. I couldn't believe it. Again I lifted the bonnet and looked in. I couldn't see anything for the smoke. I was beginning to think, it's all over, I'm never going to make it now.

I sat in the car and waited. After a few minutes, when everything had stopped hissing and smoking, I had a look in the engine compartment and noticed the fan belt had disappeared. It had obviously snapped and fallen off on the motorway earlier. I lifted the boot and found one in a compartment on the side, with the tools in. So I rolled my sleeves up and proceeded to fit the belt as quickly as possible. After 15 minutes, I crossed my fingers and started the engine. Everything seemed to be OK at first, so I shut the bonnet and drove down the road, looking for a garage to get some more water for the radiator. Every time the needle on the water temperature gauge got close to the red mark at the top, I turned the engine off and waited for a while, to let it cool down again. After about three miles, and four stops, I found a small petrol station and pulled in, let the engine cool down again and slowly filled the radiator. Just as the last couple of litres were going in,

I heard water running on the floor by my feet and across the forecourt. Something was leaking excessively. I looked under the car and noticed it was pouring out of the engine. The trip to France was all over. It was far too late to get anything done and I wasn't in the mood to try anymore. I asked the cashier of the petrol station if there was a place I could stay for the night. She told me to try the Red Lion down the road and then she gave me the number for a taxi firm in the nearby town. I went back out to my car and moved it off the forecourt, parking it around the back of the garage, then phoned the number she'd given me from the car and waited. After a few minutes, the cashier came out to see if I was all right and told me to leave the car there and, in the morning, one of the mechanics would have a look at it. I thanked her and she asked me if I would like a coffee while I was waiting for the taxi. I suddenly noticed she was very pretty: long, blonde, straight hair, nice slim figure and about 25 years old. I agreed and went into the shop with her. I waited by the counter while she made the coffee, then, when she came out from the back, we sat and talked for a while. She told me her name was Diane and her dad owned the garage; she worked for him as the secretary and cashier sometimes. I told her my name and that I had a small country garage as well. We obviously had a lot in common and I was amazed she knew so much about cars. She was a friendly girl.

The taxi sounded his horn as he stopped on the forecourt. I was sorry he came; I could have talked to her for ages. I thanked her for the coffee and walked round to fetch the overnight bag from my car. I made sure to lock all the doors and went back in to give Diane the keys. As I dropped them on the counter, I asked her if she was going out tonight and would she like to show me the town, as I was all alone in a strange place?

She smiled and clipped a tag on my keys, with my registration number on it. "Meet me in the Harvester at 9.30. You can have something to eat there and I'll have a drink with you."

"Perhaps you would eat with me, then," I said, "and tell me more about yourself."

"All right," she said. "I will, thank you." I turned and left, with a smile that was hurting my cheeks.

The taxi driver dropped me at the Red Lion. I asked him to pick me up at 9.15 and take me to the Harvester. I booked in for the night and went up to my room to get changed. It was a basic room, nicely decorated and fresh, with a single bed. I unpacked a few things and showered, then got dressed for dinner. I walked into the reception just as the taxi pulled up by the front door. I handed in my key and left.

I arrived at the Harvester a few minutes early, so I sat at the bar and ordered myself a large whiskey with lemonade, flicked through a menu and waited for Diane to arrive. I watched every car that pulled into the car park and every person that came into the restaurant, till about 9.45, then I ordered a table for two from the barman, still hoping that she would turn up. In no time at all, the waitress came over to the bar and told me my table was ready. I followed her to the far side of the restaurant and sat down, looking at the same menu. I glanced over at the bar and Diane was standing there on her own, looking around the room. I waved and she waved back. I was so relieved. She came over and sat down next to me.

"Sorry," she said. "We had a petrol delivery just as you left and I had to wait till they finished before I could lock the garage."

"It's OK," I said, smiling. "I've had to do it too and it always comes at the wrong time."

"Doesn't it just," she said, as she took her fur jacket off and slipped it over the back of her chair. She was wearing a black silk dress that touched every inch of her shapely body. As she sat down, she picked up the menu.

"Do you like red or white wine?" I asked.

She nodded. "Yes, I like both." The waitress came over and I ordered our meals and two bottles of wine, one red and one white. Diane looked at me and said, "Is your room all right?"

"Yes, it's clean and small but it'll be all right for one night." She looked at me again and smiled.

After we finished our meals, and most of the wine, I ordered two brandies and we sat talking for ages. In fact we were the last to leave. I paid the bill and we went out into the car park. "Can I give you a lift to the Red Lion?" Diane asked.

"Yes, please, if you're going that way."

I looked at my watch. It was almost midnight. As I got into her Escort Cabriolet, I suddenly wondered what Lucy might be doing in France. We drove off and all the way back I asked myself, shall I ask her in or not? Would she say yes or no? We pulled up at the pub and I asked if she thought we would be able to get a last drink.

"We can try," she said, locking the car and following me into the lounge. There were a few people still in there drinking, so I went to the bar. Diane said hello to a few people and then she came over and we sat on stools at the bar. I ordered two more brandies and sat chatting with her till about 12.30.

I asked Diane if she wanted a taxi, because of the amount she had drank, but she said, "No, it's all right, I'm already home."

"You live here?" I said, surprised.

"Well, my mum owns the pub and I stay here sometimes. My parents split up some time ago and, basically, Dad got the garage and Mum got the pub. I have my own house down the road but I stay here most nights; it's warmer.

"In that case," I said, as I held my brandy glass up, "one more."

"No, I've got to go to bed. Thanks for a lovely evening though, I've really enjoyed it." She kissed my cheek and stood up.

Diane said good night to the bar staff and left the lounge. I had one more brandy, paid the bill and went up to my room, collecting the key on the way. I got undressed, climbed into bed and lay there for a while, looking up at the ceiling, with my hands behind my head, wondering if she would come to my room in the middle of the night.

The next morning, I awoke with the phone ringing next to my ear. "Good morning," a voice said. "It's Diane here, are you awake?" I looked at my watch, it was 7.30.

"Yes, just about," I said, wondering where I was for a moment.

"Your breakfast will be ready in half an hour."

"Thank you," I said wiping my eyes, trying to focus.

I put the phone down and quickly got dressed to go downstairs. Diane was at the reception desk, on the phone. She put her hand over the mouthpiece and said, "It's through there," pointing to a door. "I'll join you in a moment." I went in and a young girl in a black waitress uniform showed me where to sit. I ordered coffee and toast and Diane came and sat with me. "Thanks again for last night."

"It was my pleasure." I added, "If you don't fix my car today, we can do it again tonight."

She laughed. "Well, it's hard to get parts delivered out here," she said. "I'll leave at 8.30, one of the mechanics can have a look when they come in, and I'll ring you later."

Once I'd finished breakfast, I went back up to my room.

It was about 9.30 when the phone rang. "Hello, it's Diane here. Your core plug has rusted and dropped out. I've ordered one and, unfortunately, it will be here before dinner, so when it's ready, I'll come down and collect you."

I thanked Diane and put the phone down. While I was waiting, I decided to phone my garage, to see if everything was OK. I didn't tell them where I was, only that I was having a bit of trouble with my car and that I would ring them on my way back.

Suddenly it hit me—Lucy was going to ring me from France. I needed to tell her I wasn't coming and my phone was in the car. I tided up my room and walked to the garage. It was a fair walk but I wanted some fresh air. I arrived at the garage just as they were checking the car. Diane looked surprised to see me and said, "I would have fetched you."

"It's all right, I needed a walk. I suddenly realised I hadn't got my phone. I'm waiting for an urgent call from France." I went out to my car and picked my phone up off the floor. It was under my seat. I was horrified to see the battery was flat and I didn't have the charger.

One of the mechanics went out in the car for a test drive while I waited in the shop with Diane. I thought about staying another night. I couldn't go home earlier than Saturday night because I'd told Liz I wouldn't be home till Sunday and there was no way I was going to chance a trip to France with all the trouble I'd had with the car. Lucy wouldn't know where I was, in fact, no one would know where I was, except Diane. As I sat there, thinking long and hard, my car pulled up outside on the forecourt. One part of me wanted it to be knackered, so I wouldn't have a choice, and the other part wanted it fixed, so I would.

The mechanic walked in and held the keys out in front of me. "It will be all right now," he said. "We thought the head gasket had gone but I've given it a good run and it seems fine."

I thanked him, took the keys and turned to Diane. She looked almost sad as I asked her for the bill. "Does this mean goodbye?" she said.

I still didn't know what to say. I paused for a second or two and said, "What if I stay?"

"If you stay, I could return the meal; you paid for last night."

Diane made up my mind for me. "OK, where?"

"At my house," she said. "I'll cook tonight, at 8.30. Bring some wine." She scribbled her address on a petrol receipt.

I drove off down the road and the car seemed fine. I drove past the Red Lion and carried on. I had some time to kill, so I drove around and had a look at the town; it was a nice quaint little place. I stopped in a bar and had a drink or two and eventually made my way back, about six o'clock, to my room.

I had a lie down but I couldn't sleep; I was too excited. I showered and changed and lay back on the bed, checking my watch every other second. Then I drove over to Diane's house. I parked on the big red paved drive, in front of the gigantic white garage doors, and rang the doorbell. Diane opened the door, wearing a short black waitress uniform and a white ribbon in her hair. She looked a picture. I went in with two bottles of champagne and a bunch of roses. We kissed in the hall, a very passionate kiss. I had that feeling of excitement and lust. I was free from everything and everybody. No one knew where I was. I was locked in a massive house, with a beautiful 25 year old girl, two bottles of champagne and the whole night ahead of us.

We went through into the dining room and the oval table was laid out with gold cutlery and crystal glasses. There were two candelabras lit, one at each end. The candles were flickering in the dark and the seats were at both ends of the table, so we could face each other. I was stunned. Diane sat me down and disappeared into another room with the champagne and flowers. I opened my napkin, placed it on my lap and waited, looking around at all the beautiful paintings on the wall and the antiques standing on top of the mantle. There was a chandelier above the centre of the table. I had never in my life been in such a magnificent room before.

Diane appeared pushing a trolley. Steam was billowing out from the chrome-covered dishes. She pushed it up to the middle of the table and disappeared again. The smell was amazing. Then she reappeared with two plates. She placed one in front of me, one at the other end of the table and sat down.

I looked at her, with the candlelight reflecting in her eyes, and said, "You are marvellous. How on earth did you manage to cook all this in a few hours?"

She put her hands up, shrugged her shoulders and said, "It was nothing." She looked down at her empty glass and said, "The champagne." As she stood up, I asked if I could put some music on. "Help yourself," she cried as she disappeared again. I looked through her CD collection and found 'The Best of Kenny G' and put it on quietly, as Diane walked back into the room with a bottle in each hand. She placed one at each end of the table, then she said, "This is my favourite." I stood up, closed the cupboard gingerly and asked her to dance with me. She came over and we danced very close, holding each other like we would never let go. We kissed softly as the music played and slowly moved round and round on one spot. I put my hands on the back of her dress and felt a zip that went all the way down and hoped I could unfastened it later. The record stopped and Diane sat down as the next song started. I poured some champagne into her glass as she held it up by the stem, then she tipped it to her lips. My appetite was lost by now and the animal in me just wanted to make love with her on the table. I glanced at my watch. It was only 9 30; we still had hours left, even if I had to go back to the Red Lion on my own. I sat opposite and poured myself a drink, staring at Diane at the other end of the table. She walked over to the trolley and pushed it towards me. As I lifted the lid, the steam rose into the air. The smell was tremendous. Diane lifted the bowl and scooped six oysters onto my plate and then she walked backwards with the trolley, looking deep into my eyes. I picked up the clamp, to hold the oyster, and, with the golden fork, I flicked one out onto my plate. By this time, Diane had put some on her plate and was eating them with her fingers. Holding them up in the air and dropping them into her mouth. I took a sip of champagne and ate another. They were delicious.

When I finished the last one, she said, "Would you like some more?"

I wiped the sides of my mouth with the napkin and said, "No, I will save myself for the main course."

She grinned at me and drank all the champagne that was left in her glass, then poured some more. I felt so relaxed and didn't want this night to end. I sat back in the carver and picked up my glass again. Diane took the plates out and came back in with two clean ones. We danced again, even closer than we did before and this time we undressed each other slowly. I pulled the zip down and Diane's dress dropped to the floor. She was naked apart from the ribbon in her hair. I took my jacket off, while she unfastened my shirt slowly and kissed my chest, as each button was undone. When Diane got to my trousers, she flicked open the clip. My hands were on her shoulders and she slowly slid the zip down to the bottom. They dropped to my ankles and she slowly pushed down my pants, then placed my solid erection in her mouth, sucking it hard. She put her hands on my buttocks and pushed me deeper into her mouth. It was sheer filth but I didn't complain. I couldn't take any more without me spoiling her dinner. I pulled myself out and Diane stood up. She waved her finger at me, from side to side, with a smile and a seductive look on her face, then she told me to sit down and wait. Naked, I sat down in my chair and Diane pushed the trolley forward again. I placed the napkin on my lap. This time it didn't feel right, with a huge lump in the middle. Diane lifted the lid and served lobster next. We drank some more champagne and we both knew this was the moment we had been waiting for. Diane stood up and slowly walked round the table towards me. As she stood next to the table by my side, she pushed all the dinner plates into the middle, sat on the end and lay back, opening her legs wide. I kissed and licked the inside of her thighs, working my way up slowly to the top, softly touching and stroking her legs. My ears started ringing. I tried to take no notice and carried on. The ringing got louder and louder. I opened my eyes to see where it was coming from. It was a little table next to my bed in the Red Lion. I quickly closed my eyes again but the dream had vanished completely.

I answered the phone, distraught, and Diane asked me if I was going round. I looked at my watch and it said 9.50. "I'm coming, I'm sorry, I must have fallen asleep. It was that long walk I had to your garage this morning." I threw the phone down and ran down the stairs, dropped my key at the reception desk and left in my car, speeding off down the road. I stopped at the shop to get two bottles of champagne; I thought at least that part would come true. When I found the house, it didn't look anything like the one in the dream. It was a lot smaller and there was no big drive to park my car. I had to leave it on the road. I rang the doorbell, and Diane answered it. She was wearing tight jeans and a short top that showed off her tanned stomach. She looked nice; I could see her shapely figure. I went in and apologised for being late. The table was laid and we sat down to eat straight away. Diane had made spaghetti bolognese. It was nice but it wasn't my favourite dish. The cold champagne helped to wash the taste away. We talked for a while and Diane cleared the table and took everything out to the kitchen.

When Diane came back in, she had a cigarette in her hand. "I didn't know you smoked," I said.

"I don't normally, this is a special one." It looked like she had just found it on the floor. "It's grass," she said, as she inhaled a good part of it and closed her eyes. "It helps me to relax." Then she offered it to me.

"No thanks, I stopped smoking some years ago and it wouldn't take a lot to start me off again after the last few months I've had."

"Has it been hard, then?" she asked. I explained to her about the garage going through a bad patch and Diane told me about her father going through it as well. We drank some more champagne and, at about midnight, Diane asked me if I wanted to stay the night. I thought for a while, looking at her. I didn't know anything about her sex life and the last thing I needed was AIDS or a bad dose of the clap to take home. Besides, after that dream the night had kind of lost its edge.

I said "No". She looked surprised. "I think I'll get back to the Red Lion, I've got a lot to do tomorrow. I've had a lovely time and it wouldn't be fair to either of us if I stayed, would it?" She looked at me, all dejected. "If I stay tonight we both know what will happen. Then I will go back home to my wife and son and we will probably never see each other again."

Diane interrupted me and said, "Don't say that, we don't live a million miles away."

"I think it would be best if we just say goodnight, and leave it at that, don't you?"

Diane nodded and stood up. "Yes, you're probably right," she said. I thanked her again for the meal and walked out to the hall. We stood behind the closed front door. I said goodnight, kissed her on the lips and opened the door. "I'll be down in the morning before I leave, to pay you," I shouted as I opened the car door and got in. Diane waved and I drove back to the Red Lion.

The next morning, I lay in bed staring round the room. I was pleased I didn't stay the night but I lay there for five minutes, thinking what it might have been like to have had sex with Diane. I climbed out of bed and got myself ready to leave.

As I was throwing everything in my bag, there was a knock at the door. I opened it and Diane was standing there. "Your breakfast is ready," she said with a smile. I asked her in but she refused, so I left the door open while I packed the last few things away and followed her down the stairs. We sat and ate breakfast together in the dining room. I paid the hotel bill and we left. I followed her to the garage in my car and filled up with petrol. Then I went in to her office behind the counter and paid for the repair at the same time.

"This is it then," she said.

I felt sad at the thought of not seeing her again. I nodded. "I'm afraid so. I've got your phone number. Can I ring you from time to time for a chat?"

"Yes and if you are ever down here again, please call in and see me It's been nice."

I held my arms out and she came around the desk and kissed me for the last time.

I made my way back towards the motorway. It was just after 10 o'clock and I was on my way back to my garage. I had been on the motorway for about two and a half hours when I noticed the water temperature gauge was creeping up again slowly. I didn't have long to go so I slowed down and tried to nurse the car along in the slow lane. It started to slow down, on its own, and the smoke started to pour out the back and this time I managed to pull off the motorway and find a telephone on the side of the road. I rang my garage and asked Roger to bring the truck out and fetch me. It wasn't too far away. I gave him directions and sat in the car until he arrived.

We loaded the car on the back of the truck and he took me back to the garage. As we were travelling back, Roger asked if I'd had a good time. I told him that I went to Devon and the car broke down on the way back. He looked at me and said nothing, as if he didn't believe me. I asked him if everything was OK at work and he said yes, that we were very busy at the moment and had got some good jobs in. When we got to the garage, we unloaded the car and put it inside, ready for the mechanic to work on it Monday, and I borrowed the spare car to use at the weekend.

I was on my way home when it suddenly dawned on me; I wasn't expected home till tomorrow morning, so I pulled into the Hare and the Hound pub for a drink. I sat at the bar on a stool and Janice asked me if I wanted my usual and poured me a double whiskey and lemonade, in a tall glass, with ice.

Janice and Peter had been friends of mine for years. They'd been landlords of three different pubs since I first met them 15 years ago and Janice, or Jane as she likes to be called, was on my list for a special night out.

I sat there drinking for about an hour, telling Jane the story of what had happened to me on the motorway and that I didn't want to go home that night. Her face lit up. She told me Peter had gone away for the weekend playing golf, wouldn't be back till Tuesday and there was a room empty I could have for the night. I asked her to book me a meal at eight and she showed me to my room. I had a shower, went back down to the bar at 7.30 and sat on the same stool, until Jane called me through to the dining area. I ordered a steak and, at about nine o'clock, when I had finished, I went back into the bar and sat talking with Jane while she served other customers through the night.

At 11.30, when every one had gone from the bar and there was only one couple left in the dining area, she poured herself a large brandy from the optic on the wall and sat next to me at the bar. The waitresses finished, tidied up and, at twelve o'clock, there was only me and Jane left. She locked the doors from the inside and turned all the lights out, except the small lamps on the wall by the open fire. Jane poured two large brandies this time and we moved over and sat down next to the fire. We chatted for ages. She told me that Peter was having an affair with a waitress and he didn't know that she'd seen them in the kitchen on the side one night, when she'd come home early from her friend's that it didn't really bother her and how they lived separately. She told me how she'd nearly had an affair with a customer and how he kept asking her out, night after night, and she almost met him at another pub in town but lost her bottle at the last moment and didn't go in.

Jane was a little older than me, only by two or three years. She was a typical landlady, masses of long blonde hair and a big bust that was always on display to the public. Her figure was tremendous. She worked out every other day at the local gym. When she stood up to get some more brandies, I couldn't stop myself from glancing at her backside. She was wearing tight blue trousers and a half-unbuttoned blue silk shirt. I sat by the fire and waited till she came back with the drinks. She placed one in front of me and squeezed past, so I could have another look, then she placed her glass on the table and sat on my lap, put her arms around my neck and said, "Will you give me one on the pool table?"

I was taken back a little; it came as a shock to be honest. I jokingly said, "Do you mean a game?"

"I can't play pool," she said and kissed me. I carefully put my hand up the back of her shirt and felt her solid body. It was warm and smooth. I worked my way up to her bra strap and she smiled as we were kissing. Then she said, "It's at the front." I looked down at her cleavage and was getting very excited at the thought of holding her naked in my arms, with that large bust pushed hard up against my chest. Jane stood up and sat back on my lap, with one leg either side of me. Then she forced my head into her chest. I kissed each one in turn, as I unfastened her blouse from the top down, then came the moment I had been waiting for. I unclasped the bra and they fell out. I licked her big, red, erect nipples first, then held one in each hand and, with my thumb, gently massaged them as Jane ripped open my shirt and forced it down my back. I kissed my way up her neck to her wet lips and licked the inside of them softly. Jane ran her fingers through my hair and down my back, then moved her hips backwards and forwards slowly.

My penis was banging on my trousers, shouting, "Let me out!" I ran my fingers down her back and felt the shape of her firm cheeks on my lap. Then, with one hand under each thigh, I stood up, lifting her into the air. She wrapped her legs around my waist and her arms around my neck and then I carried her over to the pool table, still kissing her, and carefully placed her on the edge. She lay back, with her hair evenly spread over the pool table and her legs dangling over the side.

Jane pushed the cues off the table while I pulled the zip down on her jeans and unfastened the button. I eased them down her legs to reveal her blue, silk, skimpy panties. I unfastened my trousers quickly and they dropped to the floor. Jane opened her legs and I leaned over her and kissed and licked her nipples again, at the same time as I rubbed my erection on her still-covered vagina. Then I slowly worked my way down to her navel and pulled down her panties. I threw them on the floor as her legs opened again and I stuck my tongue in between her juicy lips and licked her until she went wild, groaning and shouting, "More! More!" I felt her hands in my hair and she pulled my head up. I licked her stomach and then her nipples. Then, as I kissed her lips, I felt myself enter Jane and travel deep inside her. Her legs wrapped themselves around my waist and she held me in place with her strong leg muscles, still groaning and panting with ecstasy. My heart was racing ten times faster; we were both hot from the open fire and soaked in perspiration. We licked and kissed each other until I came, still locked in with her strong legs.

We lay in that position for a while, holding each other. We said nothing. I could hear the fire crackling in the hearth as the panting slowed down and we kissed softly.

Eventually, I stood up. Jane lay still for a while and then sat up, still on the edge of the pool table. She put her arms over my shoulder and around my neck. "Are you OK?" I asked.

She kissed my ear. "Much better now," she whispered.

As I held her tight in my arms, I said, "I wanted to ask you out for an evening of romance sometime. Would it be possible?"

"Yes, I don't see why not," she said. "That would be lovely."

"Could you stay out for a night?" I asked.

"Definitely," she replied. "Where're you going to take me?"

"I don't know yet. Somewhere nice."

We gathered our clothes together, got dressed and sat by the fire again. We finished our drinks and talked a little longer, then I glanced up at the clock on the wall over the bar. It was 2.30. Jane told me that she must go to bed because she had to be up early to organise the breakfast in the morning. We kissed once more and I went up to my room while Jane locked up and turned everything off.

I had a shower, climbed into bed, fell asleep almost immediately and woke up when the door knocked in the morning.

I opened it and Jane burst into my room and kissed me, "Thanks for last night," she said. "I was beginning to think my sex life was over. It's been a long time since I did it with Peter."

I followed her down the stairs and went into the dining area for my breakfast. The waitress brought me coffee and, while I was waiting, Jane came over and sat with me. "Where are you going to take me, then?" she said. "I can't wait."

"I'll have to think of somewhere special. I'll ring you next week."

"It would be better if you came in for a drink," she said discreetly. "Peter will be back late Tuesday. I'm working Tuesday night behind the bar, on my own. Try and sort something out and tell me then." The waitress arrived with my bacon and eggs and Jane left the table to speak to someone else that had come down for their breakfast.

When I finished eating, Jane came back and sat down again. I asked her for the bill but she wouldn't let me pay. "No," she said. "It's on the house. After the way you handled your cue on the pool table last night, I wouldn't hear of it." I shook my head in disbelief and smiled. "Spend it on me when we go out," she said. I thanked her and went up to get my things from the room. I eventually left about 9.30 and made my way home, trying to get my story straight about France before I spoke to Liz.

I parked my car on the drive and Andrew's car was in the corner by the garage. A cold shiver went straight though me. I opened the front door and threw my bag on the floor. I started to shake with anger at the thought of them spending the night together. The kitchen door opened and Liz came out laughing, which riled me even more.

"Hello," she said. "Andrew's just come round to take us swimming. Have you had a good trip? You look shattered." It was the anger in my face. Then Mick came out with his towel rolled up under his arm.

"Hello, Dad." He dropped his towel on the stairs, jumped up and clung to me, hanging on around my neck. "I've missed you, Dad," he said in my ear.

I didn't know what to say. It all looked very suspicious, or was it just me? I decided not to say anything for now and kissed Liz on the cheek. "It's been a long journey," I said and walked into the kitchen.

Andrew was sitting at the table, eating beans on toast. "How did it go? Liz told me all about your trip to France. Was it worth it?" he said, as he put the last fork-full of beans in his mouth.

I switched the kettle on and said, "I think so. He paid me in cash but my car broke down on the motorway this morning. I managed to get it back to the garage and leave it there."

Liz picked up a mug off the draining board and said, "What was it like in France?" I sat down at the table and Mick sat on my lap with his arm around my neck.

"It was cold and wet. I didn't take much notice really. I dropped the car off and he introduced me to his family. Not one of them could speak English. I got there about midday Friday and had dinner with them, then left about tea-time, found a room for the night, fell fast asleep till Saturday morning and started back after breakfast. The ferry crossings went to plan and I came back £700 richer.

Then Mick said, "Did you bring me a present?"

This was my first mistake. "I did, but I've left it in my car at work. I'll bring it home with me tomorrow night."

Liz brought me my coffee over, put it on the table and said, "Did he pay you in Euros or English money?"

"English money, of course. He went to the bank while I was there. He was so pleased to see his car, I thought he was going to pay me double."

I took a sip of coffee and then Liz said, "Roger rang me from the garage on Friday and said you were having some trouble with your car."

I started to worry. I had the feeling they were firing questions at me because they didn't believe me. "It was only an overheating problem. I pulled into a garage and they looked at it for me."

"I didn't know you could speak French as well," Andrew said.

This was my second mistake. "Luckily for me the mechanic was English," I said quickly. "I had lost a bit of water, that's all. He changed a hose and I was on my way again in minutes. Anyway, what's been happening here?" I thought I had better change the subject.

Liz said, "Andrew took me out for a drink on Friday night, because we were bored. Denise has gone to New York and you were in France, so we went to the Wooden. The usual crowd was there—we had a nice night." Liz picked up Andrew's plate and put it in the sink.

Then Andrew said, "Come on then, let's go for a dip." Mick jumped off my lap and Liz got her coat. I told him I was going to get my head down for a couple of hours. "I'll see you later," said Andrew and they left me alone.

I sat in the kitchen and finished my coffee, wondering if anything was going on between them. After about ten minutes, I decided to follow them to the swimming baths, to see if I could catch them doing anything.

While I was driving, I thought of all the things Andrew had said about not being able to have an affair, when he was talking about the naked woman in the house, while he was cutting down the tree that day in her garden and about all the times I came home and he was at my house. Then there was that time, a couple of weeks ago, when he was going to meet everyone in the pub, but never turned up and I thought I saw him on the other side of the dual carriageway. It was him, he knew I was out, so he went to see Liz instead. New Year's Eve, he was dancing with Liz all night. It all started to fall into place.

I parked the car in the car park away from the baths and made my way over to the side window. I watched and waited furiously behind a big tree outside and then Mick came out from the changing rooms on his own and dived in the pool. The longer I waited, the angrier I got. It was a good job Mick could swim exceptionally well. He was on his own and they weren't watching him at all. After about five minutes, Andrew and Liz came out together, laughing. They held hands and jumped in the water together. Mick was at the other end of the pool by this time and couldn't see what was happening. I was shaking with anger and couldn't watch any more, so I walked back to my car and left them to it. As I drove back, I thought more and more about it, annoyed with myself for not realising before.

I sat in the car on the drive and a thought suddenly occurred to me—I was getting wound up at those two fooling around and I was doing the same. But it was as if they didn't care; they wanted to get caught. Mick was undoubtedly going to see them at some stage and tell me. I went indoors, unpacked my suitcase and waited till they came home.

It was nearly three hours before they got back from the swimming baths. When I heard the car pull up, I watched through the front bedroom window behind the lace curtains. Andrew dropped them off on the drive and drove off. I still wasn't sure what to say to Liz. I heard the front door open and close. Then Mick shouted, "Dad, we're home!"

I went down the stairs and Liz asked me if I'd had a good sleep. "Yes, thank you," I answered, quite sharply. It was nearly three o'clock and I didn't want to speak to Liz in case I said the wrong thing. I told Mick to get his football, so we could go over to the park and I could think for a while on my own.

Liz asked if everything was OK and said, “You sound annoyed.”

“I must be more tired than I thought,” I said as we walked out of the front door.

“See you later, Mum,” Mick cried, as the door slammed behind us.

As we were playing football, I asked Mick if he'd had a good time at the baths and he said, “Yes, but it wasn't as good as the last time Andrew took me.”

“When was that, then?” I asked, as the ball went flying past me into the bushes.

“It was a few weeks ago when you went away.”

“Did Mum come with you?”

“No, it was just me and Andrew. We went to the swimming baths in Hallford, with the big slides, it was great fun. I was a bit scared at first, so I went on the small one twice and then the big one about five times!”

We kicked the ball about for an hour and then we decided to go home. We stopped at the shops and I bought Mick some sweets and we arrived home in time for tea.

As usual, Liz went up to bed at nine o'clock and I fell asleep watching the telly and woke when she went to work at 4.30. The telly was still on and I sat thinking more about Liz and Andrew. By 7.30, I had convinced myself that there was nothing going on but I would watch them both and let it drop for now, until I had definite proof.

Mick came down dressed for school and had his breakfast while I got ready for work. I dropped him off in the playground and his parting words were, "Don't forget my present from France, will you, Dad?" I walked back to the car thinking about what I could get him from the shops, as I bumped into Debbie. I winked at her. She smiled and nodded her head as if to say, "wait for me". I stood by the gate and she came out after she had seen her little girl into school. She asked me how I got on in France and I quickly told her the same as I'd told Andrew and Liz. As we walked towards her car, I couldn't stop myself looking at her. She was gorgeous and every time I saw her I felt so different. She asked me again if we could go out soon. I briefly explained that it would be very soon. I was thinking about where Lucy was and if she had got back from France yet.

I drove to work and, just as I turned the corner to the garage, the phone rang. It was the girl herself. "Hello."

"What happened to you, then?" she said, with a sharp voice.

"I'm sorry, I tried but the car broke down and I didn't get out of England." I told her I would explain when I saw her and then she told me she would be on her way home in the afternoon. It suddenly occurred to me that she was still in France.

"Could you bring me a present home for Mick? I'll explain this to you as well but get him something with the price tag on it, from France. Something like a car, or a football—it must be from there, and have French writing on it."

"All right," she said. "I'll bring you something back. Meet me tomorrow at the same pub as before for a drink and you can explain it all to me."

We said goodbye and I parked the car on the forecourt and went in to see what had happened while I was away. Roger gave me the mail and the mechanic told me the water pump on my car was leaking and that one had been ordered. I told him to check it all over because I was going back down to collect the car that I bought while I was away, in the next few days. Then I went up to my office and opened all the mail. The worst letter I had was from the bank, telling me I was overdrawn and that they wouldn't pay anything else until I put a large amount of money into the account.

When my car was fixed, I went out and collected money from some of my customers and paid it into the bank. It wasn't nearly enough but it was all I could get.

Late in the afternoon, I had a phone call from Denise. "You promised to take me out again," she said, "and I'm flying off to India in seven days."

"It's not possible at the moment," I told her. "When will you be back?"

"I'm going for a week," she replied. "I won't see you for a whole fortnight."

"It's a bit awkward at the moment. I've just come back from France and it's going to be hard for me to get out. I need to spend some time at work and home. As soon as you come back, I promise I'll take you out again."

We talked for a while and Denise mentioned she was going to New York for five days, after her trip to India. Now, that would be a romantic weekend, I thought. I wanted to ask her if she thought Andrew and Liz were having an affair but I couldn't bring myself to say it. After a while, I put the phone down and eventually went home.

It was about eight when I drove past Lucy's house. Ivor's car wasn't on the drive and I remembered him saying he was going to Holland today, so I phoned her house. "Can you talk?" I asked quickly.

"No," she said. "I think you must have the wrong number."

"Did you get me something for Mick?" I asked.

"Yes." Obviously there was someone there with her in the house.

"Can you throw it out the bedroom window?" I asked.

Then she said, "Yes, it's OK," and put the phone down.

I waited in the car and eventually the bedroom light came on and the curtains opened. Then the window opened and Lucy's hand came out and dropped something onto the ground. I sat for a few moments, then got out of the car, looked up and down the road to make sure no one was watching me, and slowly walked past the drive and onto the grass. I picked it up, then walked back to the car and got in quickly. I opened the bag and looked in. It was a Renault car in a box, with French writing on; exactly what I wanted. I drove home and parked on the drive and, before I locked my car, Mick opened the front door, with a big grin on his face.

"Have you got it?" he said.

"Yes." I gave him the bag and he opened it as he walked into the front room.

He pulled the box out. "Thanks, Dad," he said, then he opened it and showed his mum.

"That's nice," she said. "Aren't you a lucky boy? Daddy didn't bring me anything."

I froze for a second. "I didn't really have much time for shopping. I wanted to get home. You can have the seven hundred pounds."

Liz laughed and said, "I'm only joking".

I picked up the car and pointed out that the number plates were different to ours and the writing on the box was French—so that Liz would know it could only have come from France. Mick pushed it around on the carpet for a while and took it up to bed with him.

He took his car in to school to show his mates the next day. I didn't see Debbie.

At midday, I arrived at the pub to meet Lucy but she didn't show. I drove back to the garage, worried in case something had happened to her on the way to meet me. I rang the house from my mobile and Lucy's mum answered. "Is Ivor there?"

"No, I'm sorry, who is it?" she asked.

"It's Nick."

"He's gone to Holland."

"It doesn't matter, I was just ringing on the off chance he fancied a drink tonight."

"He won't be back till Thursday night."

"No problem, I'll ring him then. Are you all right?" I asked. "I haven't seen you for ages."

"Yes, I'm fine. Lucy has had to go down to Devon. Her friend's husband has passed away and she has gone down to look after her for a couple of days. She left this morning early on the coach."

"Never mind, I'll ring them at the weekend. Is that the friend in . . ." I was struggling to think of a place in Devon. "Bude?"

"No, it's a place in Woolacombe, called Mortoe, I think."

"Oh, I know, with a bed and breakfast."

"It's a caravan park, it's on the right as you go into the village."

"That's right, I remember them telling me now."

"Yes, it was a shame, he was only 41," she went on to say. "He was having an affair with a local girl when his heart gave up."

Lucy's mum was one of those people that never stopped talking and loved gossip. She told me about her illness and how bad she was on her last holiday in Cyprus and where she'd been, in full detail. I talked to her on the phone for ages; I couldn't get her off. I had the information I wanted though and eventually I said goodbye to her after about twenty minutes and hastily put the phone down.

# Chapter 13

I THOUGHT FOR a long while when I got back into my office: it was all getting out of hand. Denise was careless and desperate for me to take her out again. She could get us both into trouble. And Debbie: if I was true to myself, I was falling in love with her. I knew she loved me and, out of all of them, I would have loved to take her out again. I had been thinking about her a lot. John didn't deserve her; she was amazing. Then Jane at the pub: she was desperate for sex; she would probably hound me for more, now we had done it once. I hadn't seen Julie for months, which was a pity; I had fallen for her as well.

I opened the safe and counted the money again: there was still over £3000 left. I thought about Lucy for a while and decided that if I couldn't have Lucy in France, I would have her in Devon, or at least I would try—I had to find her first.

Again, I lied to Liz. I phoned and told her I was going down to Southampton to collect a car in the morning, early. I did say I would try to come home on the night and that I would ring if I didn't think I was going to make it.

I still had the same aggravation at work. I'd sold another car off the forecourt that day and paid the proceeds into the bank. I left for home about six but popped into the Hare and Hound for a drink on the way. As I walked through the door, I suddenly remembered that Jane was waiting for me to tell her when we were going out. I had forgotten all about it. I couldn't stop, so I carried on up to the bar. She was standing there with a big smile on her face. I ordered my usual and sat on a stool.

"Well, when?" she asked, looking over her shoulder.

"I haven't worked anything out yet, I've had a busy couple of days and I haven't had the time to plan it properly. I've got to go out tomorrow but as soon as I get back, I will, I promise."

Jane served another customer and I looked over at two lads playing on the pool table. I thought of Saturday night, then I talked to Jane a bit longer and left for home about seven.

I woke at four o'clock in the morning and got myself ready quietly. As I kissed Liz on the cheek, while she was sleeping, I heard her say, "See you later."

I crept into Mick's room, kissed him too, and with a snore, he turned over. Then I left with my overnight bag, just in case, and took off. I drove down the motorway smoothly, checking the temperature gauge all the way. Nothing went wrong. I arrived in Mortehoe at 8.30 and parked on the side of the road, overlooking the long sandy beach, and gazed out to sea. With the window open, the smell of sea air was strong and refreshing.

I loved the seaside; it had always intrigued me as a child, when I had visited with my parents for summer holidays. I locked the car, ran down the steps and slowly walked along the beach. There was a chill in the air and the breeze was quite breathtaking. It had obviously rained in the night and the beach was covered in small dents where the drops had bounced off the sand. There were only two other sets of footprints in the sand and they had evidently walked together, with a dog that ran off in different directions, no doubt to fetch a stick. I could see where the dog had brought it back and run off again.

I walked for about half an hour before deciding to turn back. There were other people walking towards me now and up on the road a number of cars were pulling up to look at the sea. I climbed back up the stairs and walked down to the cafe, just across the road, and sat by the window, still fascinated by the view.

I ordered myself a breakfast with coffee and sat staring out to sea while I waited. In the distance, I could see a few boats bobbing up and down and the sun was trying to come out from behind the clouds. It looked like it could be a nice day. The waiter walked up behind me and placed the tray on the edge of the table, then pushed it on a bit further. It looked delicious. I was so hungry I couldn't wait and I started before he could put the bill under the ashtray. It was burning my mouth but I couldn't stop. I devoured it in minutes and washed it down with the coffee.

I looked down on to the road in front of the cafe, watching all the cars go by, and noticed a white van with writing on the side pull up at the zebra crossing. It said 'Sea View Caravan Park'. I looked at the passenger and was shocked to see Lucy sitting there. I couldn't believe my luck. Here we were at last, together. I was so happy, I jumped up, paid the bill and ran to my car. Just as I started the engine, I could see in the distance the same van coming back towards me. I quickly pulled out and drove down the road to turn my car round and, as it passed me, I followed it along the winding roads to the caravan park and up the drive to the booking office. I watched the woman get out of the driver's side of the van, slam the door and look down the drive towards me. As I pulled up behind her, she shouted, "We're not taking any bookings for a while, I'm sorry."

Lucy hadn't got out yet. I waited patiently as the woman walked away. Then I realised she wasn't in there. I shouted to the woman, "Sorry, I just saw your van on the sea front, I thought I recognised your passenger from Birmingham."

With a very sad expression on her face, she forced a smile and said, "She is from there, I've just taken her to the station to go back home." I was lost for words, except thank you. I got back into the car, reversed into a space, then drove off, back down the drive to the road, wondering what to do. I looked at my watch. It said 9.45. Then I thought, perhaps it doesn't leave till on the hour.

I drove back into the town as quickly as possible along the winding roads, crossed the crossing where I'd first seen them and stopped just after, by the kerb. I let the window down and asked a man the way to the train station. "Just round this corner," he said, and pointed. I drove off and pulled into the car park and found a space almost immediately, jumped out of the car and glanced at my watch again: it was just after ten. I ran across the car park and into the small station. The porter was walking towards me with a flag in his hand. There was a train pulling out of the station.

I asked if it was the train to Birmingham and he answered me with a Cornish accent. "It stops there, yes." I was so annoyed, I wanted to hit him, although I knew it wasn't his fault. Then he said, "Do you know, that's the first time that train's left on time for weeks." At this point, I definitely wanted to kill him.

"Where does it stop next?" I asked.

"That will be Chapelton and after that Umberliegh."

"Thank you," I shouted as I ran back to the car and drove off like a man possessed. I screeched round the bends and drove like an idiot for a while and then realised, after I'd nearly knocked four people and a dog over, that I wouldn't make it. The roads were far too narrow. I turned the car round and went back, a lot slower. As I stopped at the same zebra crossing to let someone cross, a thought entered my head, like a bolt of lightning. Lucy had come down on the coach and would probably go back on a coach. "It's the coach station, not the train station," I said to myself. Again I turned the car round, nearly knocking over a bollard, and drove back in the same direction. Just before the train station was the coach station. My heart started pumping again. I parked the car and ran in to the booking office. There were a few people waiting and some kids running riot around the seats. The smell of diesel was horrendous. Behind the desk was an elderly man, sitting there with a sandwich to his mouth, chewing slowly like a camel.

"Has the bus for Birmingham left yet?"

He looked at me with a blank expression on his face and it seemed to take him ages to answer. Then he said. "No," with a mouth full of food. "It's just about to," he said, spitting bread all over me.

I turned and ran out to where all the coaches were parked. I could see three men talking in front of the coach that was ticking over. The door was still open and there were people on it waiting to go. I asked one of the drivers if I could look on the coach for someone. By this time, the man from the booking office had followed me out, shouting, or spitting, "You can't go on there without paying!" I quickly jumped up into the coach and slowly walked along the narrow aisle, looking from left to right as I went. At the back, I could see someone holding a newspaper up. I smiled and when I got to them, I pulled down the paper to find an Indian couple sitting there.

"I'm sorry," I said. "I'm looking for someone." He nodded his head as I turned and walked back to the front, upset and disappointed. As I got to the top of the steps by the door, Lucy walked up them, with a look of astonishment on her face.

"What are you doing here?" she said. I was so pleased to see her, I grabbed her and kissed her in front of everyone on the coach, to a loud cheer. We climbed off the coach, embarrassed, and Lucy said, "What's happened?"

"Nothing," I said. "Where is your suitcase?" The coach driver was just putting it in the cupboard in the side of the coach. "I'll take that," I shouted. As the driver looked up, I pulled it out of his hand. I grabbed Lucy's arm and said, "I'll take you home with me in the car."

We turned to leave and the man from the ticket office was by the door. "Hope you're not going to ask for your money back," he cried, waving his sandwich at me. I couldn't be bothered to argue with him.

We hurried out to the car park and got in the car, after I threw her case onto the back seat. Then Lucy said, "Are you going to tell me what's going on?"

I started the engine and said, "Let's find a nice little pub and I'll explain everything to you over a drink."

We drove inland for a while and found a place called the Sailor's Arms. Lucy sat down while I got the drinks. It was a nice quiet old pub, dark and small, but warm and very cosy. We sat for hours talking. I explained about my ordeal trying to get to France and Lucy told me how she had waited in the bar in France for me to arrive, how she had worried about me and how when I spoke to her on the phone about Mick's present, when she was at home, she had just got in and received the phone call about her friend in Devon. Luckily, her mum was still there with her and told her to go down on the coach. Then I told her about me thinking she'd gone back on the train and my rushing around to find her. We had a laugh and a couple more drinks and then I asked Lucy if she had phoned and told her mum that she was coming home on the coach.

"Yes," she said. "I phoned last night but my mum said, 'Stay for another day if you want, there's no need to rush back', and I left it like that. Why?"

"Well, I came down this morning, hoping to catch you and see if we could stay for that one night together."

She smiled and said, "You crafty thing—where?"

"Well, I don't know yet, we'll have to find somewhere, won't we?" We finished our drinks and left.

We drove down the coast, into Wadebridge, and found a quaint little harbour, called Padstow. I parked the car, and we sat looking out to sea. "Do you want to stay here?" I asked Lucy.

"Yes, I don't mind," she said looking out of the window. "It's lovely."

I looked at the clock on the dashboard in the car; it was just after six o'clock. "Wait here—I'll book us into a hotel for the night then." I got out of the car and, as I walked, I phoned Liz from my mobile. I told her I had collected the car but that it was too late for me to come back, so I would stay and travel up in the morning. She didn't sound too disappointed. After I said goodbye, I turned the phone off.

The first place I tried said 'No Vacancies' on the window, so I tried the hotel next door. "Sorry," the lady said. "We are fully booked this week, try the Ship down the road." I thanked her, and left.

The Ship was fully booked as well. So I went across to the Harbour Hotel. "Hello," I said. "Do you have any rooms vacant for one night? The lady behind the desk shook her head from side to side, breathed in noisily through her puckered lips, and then with a Cornish accent said, "'Tis the offshore party tonight, you see."

"What is the offshore party?" I asked.

"Well, my dear, if you look out to sea, you'll see a fine big white boat called Stow Away. 'Tis once a year it comes to the 'arbour and folk round err go out to the captain's party on board. There's not a room vacant this time of year."

I had the feeling that she did not want to say she had a room, but there was a 'maybe' in her voice somewhere, so I asked, "Is there a small chance me and my pregnant wife who is in the car could attend this party?"

She puckered her lips again, drawing vast amounts of air through the small hole, and said, "Not without an invitation like this, you won't." Then she pulled two tickets out from behind her desk and held them up.

"Do these two tickets have a room with them?"

"Arr, that depends, don' it."

"How much would it depend on?" I asked.

She looked at me with a smile on her very lined face and said, "'Bout £30 each, would be the price."

"Will this price enable my wife and I to have a room?"

"Well, you see," she went on to say, "my 'usband and I got two extra tickets for my sister and 'er 'usband to attend, but unfortunately they can't make it, see."

"So, would it be possible for us to have their room?"

She looked me up and down and said, "You look like good folk. At £50 a ticket, it's possible."

I was so pleased, I said, "Right then, we'll have them. Can we get something to eat before we go?"

"No need do that, there's food aboard."

"Thank you very much," I said. "I'll fetch my wife in."

"What your names be?"

"Rodgers," I said, looking at a picture on the wall painted by S Rodgers, "Simon Rodgers."

"And your wife?"

"Lucy." I walked towards the door, feeling shattered after all that, and went out to the car.

As I opened the door, I heard Lucy say, "Did you find somewhere?" I got in the car and started the engine, laughing. "What's the matter?" she said.

"You would never believe me if I told you." I reversed the car and drove nearer to the hotel and parked it in a space opposite.

"What happened then?" Lucy asked.

"You see that fine ship, as the lady in the hotel put it?"

"Yes," Lucy said curiously.

"Well, we are going to a party on it tonight."

"You're right," she said, "I don't believe you."

I laughed again. "The only way I was going to get a room here tonight was to agree to go to the captain's party."

"Honest, what do you mean?"

"Let's get into our room and I will explain." We got out and I locked the car and walked around to grab Lucy's bag and her hand, then we walked across the road to the hotel. "You're married to me and your name is Lucy Rodgers,

OK?" Just as I pushed the door open I said, "And by the way, you're pregnant."

I felt her pull me back. "What?"

I looked at her and said, "Just a little bit pregnant."

We walked up to the desk and the lady came over to us. "Hello, my dear, do ee want to follow me up the stairs and I will show ee to the room?"

I couldn't let go of Lucy's hand, in case she ran off. I gripped it tight. I could still feel her trying to get free as we walked along the landing to the room. The lady opened the door and said, "What was your names? Sorry, I've got a terrible memory."

"I'm Steven and this is Lucy," I said as we walked into the room.

The lady looked puzzled and said, "I told you I've got a bad memory, I thought you said Simon earlier."

I must have changed colour to a deep red. Just before she shut the door, I said, "My driving licence says Simon, but all my friends call me Steven, it's a long story."

"Oh, I see," she said with a puzzled look on her face, then pulled the door closed.

"What's going on?" Lucy said as soon as the door shut.

"All the rooms are fully booked because this time every year, apparently, that boat I showed you comes into the harbour and the captain throws a party for some reason, for the locals. Her sister and husband were going to the party and they got them some tickets, but they can't make it, so I had to buy the tickets off them in order to get their room."

"Why am I pregnant, then?"

"I thought it would sound better if there was a pregnant woman in the car and the old lady would help me find a room for the night. It worked for Joseph and Mary."

"You're amazing," Lucy said, shaking her head. "What are we going to wear for this boat party?"

"I'm just going downstairs to find out."

Lucy sat on the bed and I went downstairs and rang the bell on the desk. The lady came out from the back room. "Hello, my dear, is everything all right?"

"Yes, fine thanks. I was wondering what to wear tonight, as we haven't brought a lot with us."

"I hadn't thought of that," she said. "I'll ask my 'usband, just a minute." I waited, and looked around the reception at the posters and pictures on the wall, until she came back out. "My 'usband said he 'as a dinner suit you could borrow, 'e's about your size, and I'll ask someone in the 'otel if they can lend Lucy something, and bring it up."

I thanked her and went back up to the room. As I opened the door, Lucy jumped up off the bed. "How did you get on?" she asked.

"It's all sorted, they're going to lend us something to wear."

We talked for a while and then I put my arms around Lucy's waist. I was just about to kiss her when the hotel owner knocked on the door. We both jumped. I opened it. The lady walked in, laid a suit on the bed and a dress for Lucy. "I thinks these will fit ye both, why don't ee try them on and then come down and meet my 'usband in the bar, when you're ready, and have a drink?" I thanked her again and she left, closing the door as she went.

Lucy picked up the dress and said, "This is nice," and held it up in front of herself in the mirror, then looked at the label.

I picked up the suit and said "'Tis nice, is net?" We both laughed. I pulled Lucy on to the bed. She landed on top of me screaming, "Keep your filthy 'ands off me, you blackguard!" in a Cornish voice. Still laughing, we kissed and cuddled on the bed for a short time, then Lucy said, "Let's go down and have a drink first, to get me in the mood."

We stood up and quickly tried the clothes on, then went down to the reception. I rang the bell and the lady came out again. "'Tis you," she said. "Follow me."

"What's your name?" I asked quickly.

"My name is Beth and my 'usband is Jim." We followed her into the next room and up to the bar. Then Beth called Jim over. He was a tall, rugged-looking man, with a big thick silver beard and masses of hair to match. He shook Lucy's hand first and said, "My missus tells me you'll be coming aboard with us tonight."

Lucy smiled and said, "It sounds lovely,"

Then Beth smacked his hand and said, "You can let the poor girl go now."

He smiled and said to me, as he grabbed my hand and shook it with a strong grip, "'Tis a pleasure to meet folk from up north down 'ere."

"It's very good of you to let us come to such an exclusive party," I said, still shaking his hand.

"You'll 'ave ter tell me your secret," he said. "'Ow did ee manage to get those tickets off the missus?"

"She's a capitalist and a very fine judge of character," I said, laughing again.

"'Oh, I can see us getting on splendidly tonight, I've been looking forward to the party for months." Jim eventually stopped shaking my hand, luckily, before it fell off.

Lucy and I sat on the barstools as Jim went behind the bar. He said, "What would be ee poison then, me hearties?" I had a whiskey and lemonade, as usual, and Lucy asked for a white wine and soda. I looked at her and said quietly, so that no one would hear me, with a grin, "Is that a good idea, darling? Don't forget the baby." Lucy looked like she was going to kill me and then she kicked me in the shin. "Ow!" I shouted as Jim put the drinks down on the bar.

"Do ee be OK?" he said. I nodded, as Beth walked back into the room and sat by us.

"Jim," she said. "I forgot to tell ee, Lucy is pregnant."

"Congratulations, my lovely." Then he drank a full glass of rum and slammed the glass down. "To the little one," he said, leaning on the bar with both hands. I told him we'd only found out a couple of weeks ago.

"It was a bit of a shock, to be honest."

Lucy reached for her drink and said under her breath, "It was a bigger shock to me."

Beth suddenly stood up. "I'd better go and get myself looking pretty. I'll knock on yer door when it's time to be goin', should be 'bout eight." As she went, I looked at my watch; it said 7.30. We finished our drinks and went back up to our room. We didn't have time for any distractions. We showered separately and got ready in our loaned clothes. Lucy looked lovely in her long red evening dress and I looked quite smart in my dinner suit, Lucy said.

We sat on the bed and waited. Beth knocked just after eight and shouted, "We'll meet you downstairs in reception."

As we stood up together, I kissed Lucy, holding her tight. She pulled back and said sarcastically, "Watch the baby." I smiled and then she said, "Wait till I get you home, my lovely."

I lifted my eyebrows. "I can't wait."

Lucy slipped a thin jacket on and we left the room and went down to meet them. Beth looked lovely for an elderly lady. She was probably about sixty and Jim, with his thick silver-grey beard, looked like an old fisherman, with a row of medals attached to his chest. Jim shouted goodbye and we all left together.

It was almost dark now and we only had to walk across the road and wait until the little boat picked us up by the steps. I put my arm around Lucy while we were standing there. It was a still night but there was a chill in the air. Lucy pointed to some untidy lads fishing on the harbour wall next to us with bits of string dangling in the water. As we looked around the harbour there were different coloured lights above the shops and houses. People walked slowly looking in shop windows with their arms around each other; some were eating fish and chips out of newspaper. There were crowds sitting outside small bars, laughing and singing as they drank. A few fishermen were working in their boats, with people looking down on them from the top of the harbour wall. The sea was very calm and there was a perfect reflection duplicated around the edge. Lucy put her hand around my waist. I had a relaxed feeling, as if nothing could touch me. We were looking forward to a nice night on board a big boat that we could see in the distance and we could hear the pup-pup of the smaller boat getting nearer and nearer.

As we waited, some other people had arrived that I hadn't noticed. I was amazed by the view and quite excited.

The boat stopped at the foot of the steps with smoke puffing out from the small engine at the back. Jim got into the boat first and held his hand out for Beth. "Come on, my lovely," he said. I was steadying her by holding her arm and she almost leaped in. Then Jim held his hand out for Lucy, as the sailor sat Beth down. Lucy wasn't sure and grabbed my hand. I could feel her shaking as she stepped into the boat, very carefully holding onto Jim, and waited for me. Then I followed. We climbed over the seats, holding each other tight, and sat at the back with Beth while Jim helped some more people in carefully. Then when we were all seated the boat turned around and set off towards the ship.

As we got closer the music got louder and, looking back, the harbour got smaller. "Isn't she a fine vessel?" said Jim.

Lucy held my hand all the way, as tightly as possible, and wouldn't let go for anything. "Are you all right?" I asked.

"A bit cold," she said with her teeth chattering.

I took my jacket off and wrapped it around her shoulders. "Is that better?"

"Yes, thank you."

As we pulled up at the bottom of the ship's steps, the music was quite loud and every now and again it got louder in short bursts. Jim stood up and grabbed the rails and helped everyone onto the steps at the side of the boat. Beth went first and then Lucy. As I got to Jim he said, "I will say to the cap'n that Beth's kin couldn't make it, so we invited our friends from up north, OK?"

"Yes, and thanks for letting us come with you both."

He slapped me on the back and said, "Enjoy yourself, laddie." I went up first and Jim followed. As we got to the top, I realised why the music had gotten louder and quieter. It was every time someone opened the sliding doors and walked into the party. We all waited for Jim to go first and then we followed. Lucy passed my jacket back and I slipped it on before I walked in.

The ship was massive. As we walked through the door I noticed a live band singing at the other end of the room. There must have been at least a hundred people in there already; a lot were dancing. Across the room I could see Jim bent over, talking to an Arabic looking man with two foreign girls on his lap, then he leaned to one side and waved. Lucy waved back. I couldn't stop myself from looking around the room as we all shuffled past the bar in a line: it was magnificent. A waiter gave us both a glass of pink champagne; we stood and sipped it, amazed at the size of our surroundings.

Jim called us over and we shook hands with the Arab. "This is Mr Ahmed," he said. Lucy smiled and commented on the boat. He grinned and said with a foreign accent, "Thank you, get yourselves some more champagne and please, have a good time." He clicked his fingers and over came the waiter with a tray full of drinks.

Jim picked up a glass and said to me, "Do ee want to come outside?" Then Beth asked if they could get warm first and join us shortly. I picked up a full glass and we walked to the door. It automatically slid open for us to go out onto the deck.

We stood by the rails outside and I asked Jim about the ship and Mr Ahmed. "Well, as far as I can make out, ee was the kin of a very wealthy sheik, and when ee was at university in England ee always came here for weekends. Now one weekend, ee meet a girl from the 'arbour, fell in love and one day they married. Ee took her off to Saudi with him to live, on the understanding that ee would bring 'er back at least once a year. Now ees father died some years back, in fact, folk round 'ere said ee was shot by Mr Ahmed in there, but no one knows for sure. Anyway, after a couple of years, he started coming back to England by sea. Hence the name of the ship, Stow-away. Ee took someone away from Padstow." I smiled as he carried on. "Ee throws one large party for folk, while ee's 'ere." Just then the door opened and Beth and Lucy came out, I asked Lucy if she fancied a walk around the deck and she nodded. "I'll see ee in a short while by the pool," Jim said and we walked off.

"Are you warmer now?" I asked Lucy.

"Yes, thanks, it must have been the breeze across the sea in that small boat," she replied. I stopped by the rail and grabbed Lucy's hand. As she turned I put my arms around her waist and kissed her. I felt her hands on my back holding me tight as we looked out to sea. It was black; all we could see was the full moon and the reflection on the calm water. We carried on to the back of the boat arm in arm. The more we walked, the quieter the music got and we could hear splashing and laughing as we turned the corner. We could see a kidney-shaped swimming pool steaming and lit up, with a few people in there, swimming around, enjoying themselves. Standing on the side were four waiters with trays of drinks and towels over their arms so that people could dry themselves as they came out of the pool. We stood on the side watching for a while, and Jim appeared with Beth.

"Haven' ee got any trunks, matey?" he said to me.

I flinched at the thought of it and said, "No, thank God."

"Do ee want some?" Jim clicked his fingers and called a waiter over. "Can ee find my friend some trunks for the pool?"

I shook my head. "Don't worry about me, I'm quite happy standing here, I hate water."

"Well, I think 'tis time I went in," he said, rubbing his hands together.

"Ee must be mad," commented Beth. "'Tis in the warm my old bones need to be," and she turned and left.

Jim disappeared into the changing rooms and I said to Lucy, "Let's get out of here before he comes back."

We walked around to the other side and I noticed some spiral stairs that went down to the next deck. Still holding hands with Lucy, I said, "Let's have a look down here." We walked down as another couple ran up giggling. When we got to the bottom it was very quiet and a bit darker. We carried on walking for a while and stopped by the rail on this side of the ship. We could see the harbour; it was still lit up and, above the harbour in the hills, were houses with their lights on. It was so romantic. We kissed again. I put my hands on Lucy's backside and tried to slide her dress up, but she stopped me.

"Someone might come," she said.

"I will, if you let me," I jokingly said.

"No, not here. Wait till we get back to the hotel tonight." We kissed a while longer and walked some more. The further we walked, the darker and quieter it got. It was obviously the living quarters. All the doors were dark-coloured louvre doors and just up ahead we could see the light from a room shining though the slats in lines onto the deck. Lucy whispered, "Let's go back now, it's a bit scary."

As we turned, I could hear someone talking. It seemed to come from that room, then the talking got louder. I put my finger to Lucy's lips so I could hear what they were talking about and all of a sudden it stopped and went quiet. All we could hear was the water lapping against the ship and a very faint drum of the music up on the next deck. I kissed Lucy again and all of a sudden we heard two loud cracks. We both opened our eyes at the same time, staring at each other, still with our lips touching. We froze in that position for a second. The whites of Lucy's eyes lit up. We didn't know what to do. The light went off in that room. We were both terrified. I pulled Lucy backwards and tried the knob on the door behind me. It turned and clicked open. I pulled Lucy into the room and slowly closed the door. We were shaking with fear as we stood there in the dark waiting for something to happen. I put my hand over Lucy's mouth when I heard a door creak and click and then footsteps. They got louder and louder. Lucy was shaking like a leaf. I put my other hand on the back of her head and pulled it into my chest. She grabbed my lapels and then the walking stopped outside our room. I could feel Lucy's mouth open wide as if she was going to scream. I pressed her head as hard as I could into my chest and we heard another click. I turned my head to look through the slats. I could just see someone lighting a cigarette, then the walking started again and slowly got softer. We stood there for a little longer and I took my hand away from Lucy's mouth and held her tight in my arms. She wouldn't lift her head from my chest until I eased her away a little. I put my finger back on her lips. Her eyes were still big and staring at me. I turned around toward the door, feeling for the handle. Lucy was pressed hard against my back. I pulled the handle slowly and it clicked open. I could feel Lucy jump at the noise. Carefully, I pulled the door open enough to look down to where the light had been. It was total darkness. Lucy grabbed my arm. I pulled the door a little more to look the other way—it was dark and quiet that way, too—then I forced the door open all the way. Lucy was still holding my arm tight. We moved forward slowly and stopped looking up and down the deck, with our backs to the cabins.

"We must get back to the pool," I whispered. Lucy nodded once, terrified, with her eyes still staring at me and nothing else, then slowly we eased our way back towards the stairs, one step at a time. I took a step and then Lucy took a step. It seemed to take ages. Not saying a word, we shuffled along the deck till we got to the bottom of the steps. We waited for a second until I was sure the stairs were clear. I slowly turned to Lucy and whispered again. "Give me your hand." She placed it in mine. I could still feel her shaking. I looked up the stairs and turned back to Lucy. "When we get back by the pool, we will be all right." I jerked her hand and ran up the stairs with Lucy close behind.

As we stepped onto the deck, we could see people running around and jumping in to the pool. We walked quickly towards them and, as we passed a waiter, I grabbed two glasses of champagne off the tray and we stood by the rail at the edge of the deck. I drank mine in one, as Lucy sipped hers, looking around. I put my arms around Lucy's waist again and she laid her head on my shoulder, looking out to sea.

"What are we going to do?" she asked, then looked at me. "We will have to tell someone."

I looked around the deck and said, "The best thing to do is get off the boat first and then we will decide what to do." She put her head back on my shoulder and we stood there thinking.

All of a sudden there was a loud slap on my back. It made me jump and, as Lucy lifted her head, she threw up all over the deck. It was Jim. "Are thee both all right?" he said, then he grabbed the glasses out of our hands and said, "Oh, my dear, no sea legs, aye?" then laughed as he called the waiter over and pointed to show him what had happened. He put down his tray, ran off and came back with a big water hose and blasted the mess over the side.

I walked Lucy to a bench and sat her down. Jim followed us and sat next to Lucy. As she moved closer to me, she said, "I'm sorry, I-"

"Don't worry," Jim interrupted. "You aren't the first tonight, my dear, and I'm sure you won't be the last." With that he stood up and walked off.

"Are you OK, now?" I asked, taking off my jacket.

Lucy lifted her head and said, "I thought it was-"

"I know, don't worry." I tried to be calm, as I placed my jacket around her shoulders and held it there. "Do you want me to get you another drink?"

Lucy nodded. "Please."

"Do you want to go inside for a bit?"

"No, I'll be all right, now," she said, wiping her nose with her hanky.

I walked over to the waiter and he asked me, "Is the lady all right?"

I took two glasses and said, "Yes, thank you." He stared at me; I had the feeling I'd seen his face before. I walked back to Lucy, puzzled, and sat down with a frown on my face.

"What's the matter?" Lucy asked.

"Nothing, I thought I'd seen that waiter's face before." I gave her the drink, then we stood up and walked slowly back towards the dance room.

As we approached the doors, they opened and Beth walked out "Hello, I 'eard ee aven't been too good, my dear."

Lucy half smiled and said, "I feel much better now, thanks."

We stopped by the rail and I looked into the room as the door shut. Then Beth said, "It's too warm in there. 'Ave ee seen Jim on ee travels?"

I explained that he was with us about fifteen minutes ago and she walked off towards the back of the ship. Lucy turned to look out to sea and we held each other. I asked Lucy if she wanted to go to the front of the boat. "No, thank you," she said. "I've seen enough. I'm staying here until we go."

I smiled and kissed her as Jim and Beth walked towards us. "You found him, then?" I said.

"Ee's always somewhere else." Jim laughed and they went inside. We followed and I asked Lucy for a dance. The music was a lot slower now and we walked onto the dance floor. We held each other and danced for a while, not speaking a word. As we turned around and around, I was looking at everyone in the room, thinking to myself, it could have been anybody; any one of these people could have been in that room. I'm sure Lucy was thinking the same.

The record stopped and we waited for the next to start when I heard Jim behind me. "'Tis my turn," he said pulling

Lucy off me. She smiled and held her arms out as a waltz started. I turned to walk off and Beth was behind me.

"May I have this waltz?" I asked her.

"I thought ee would never ask."

We moved around the room like Fred and Ginger. I caught a glimpse of Lucy, frowning and looking disgusted with me for letting Jim step in—and on her toes a number of times.

Knackered, I sat down with Beth. A waiter came over and placed some more drinks on the table in front of us. I asked him to leave two more, as Lucy came over limping with Jim holding her arm.

"I mus' be pissed," Jim said as Lucy sat down and held her right foot.

"It's probably me, I haven't waltzed for ages," Lucy said politely.

Beth looked up at Jim and said, "You've always had two left feet."

He sat down and asked Lucy if she was all right and she smiled at him. We sat drinking and talking for a while as the room started to empty. "Where is everyone going?" I asked Beth.

"Oh, 'tis that the time already?" she said and stood up. "Come outside, 'tis the firework display."

I pulled Beth's chair back, as Jim did for Lucy, and we went outside. The fireworks had already started. The black sky was covered with coloured sparkles from the exploding rockets. Lucy stood, leaning on the rail, and I stood behind her with my arms under hers and our cheeks touching each other's, looking up at the fireworks as they fell down into the sea.

After five minutes, Beth said she was going back in and Lucy shivered and said, "I'll come with you."

As she turned, I whispered, "Don't say anything to Beth." Lucy shook her head and followed her.

The crowd of people around me was thinning out and I noticed Jim had disappeared again. I made my way back into the dance room and sat down next to Lucy. Beth was dancing and looked like she was enjoying herself. The door opened and Jim walked back in and sat down. He looked over at Beth and then he looked at his watch. "I think it's time we were making a move."

Lucy stood up and said, "Yes, it must be late," grabbing her coat off the chair.

Jim looked up at Lucy and said, "'Tis no need for thee to be comin with me and the missus; thee can stay a while if thee want and come back on 'nother boat."

"No," she insisted. "We'll come back with you. I need my rest carrying this around." She patted her stomach. I dropped my head in case Jim saw me smile and Lucy walked off to the toilet.

"Does she be OK, now?" Jim asked.

"Yes, she gets tired easily," I said, still smiling.

Then Beth came back. "Lucy be all right? She went past me like a hungry shark."

"Yes," I added. "She's tired." Jim stood and held Beth's jacket up and she gracefully slipped it over her shoulders and then Jim walked over to Mr Ahmed as Lucy came back.

We collected our things and in turn thanked Mr Ahmed for having us at his wonderful party and then we waited by the doors until a waiter came over and told us the boat was ready. Jim thanked him and we left. As we walked back down the steps, I looked back at the harbour. I could see it wasn't as lively as it had been earlier. There were just a few streetlights on and some coloured lights above the shops and bars. We slowly climbed back into the boat and started our journey back. It was even colder than before. I held Lucy as tight as I could in my arms; I had given her my jacket again on the steps getting into the boat. I sat there, with only the thought of a cosy bed and Lucy all to myself, keeping me warm. Jim was trying to sing 'row the boat ashore' and Beth was trying to hide behind Lucy in embarrassment.

It wasn't long before we reached the harbour. I had to admit I was looking forward to putting my feet back on land again. Jim stood up first, a bit shakily, and the boat started to sway a bit. He climbed up the steps almost on his hands and knees and stopped by the streetlight just above us. I helped Beth up first, then Jim came back down the steps and held his hand out for her. Over she went and up the steps. I moved over and Lucy squeezed past me, hanging on, and Jim held out his hand again. Lucy was just about to grab it, when all of a sudden she stopped and gasped.

"What's the matter?" I asked as she turned, still holding me.

"He's got blood on his cuff," she whispered.

A cold shiver went down my spine but there was nothing I could do. I grabbed his hand and jumped onto the steps, pulling Lucy behind me, and we ran up the steps together.

"What's the matter?" asked Jim.

"Lucy felt sick again," I said quickly.

"Let's get her in the warm," Beth added as she grabbed Jim's arm and hurriedly walked across the road to the hotel.

Lucy pulled my hand back as we followed and said, "I'm not staying there with him."

"Let's not jump to any conclusions yet, we don't have anywhere else to go remember and besides, he could have slipped shaving." I must admit it started me thinking. Where was he when Beth couldn't find him? Did he really like swimming? Or was that just to get rid of Beth? He looked dry enough when we were talking to him afterwards. And what was he whispering to Mr Ahmed?

By the time we got to the hotel, he was guilty. We walked in and Beth told Jim to get us all a warm drink. As soon as he said those magic words, "'Tis time for brandy, how's about a nightcap, my lovelies?" he was excused. I'd let him off. I didn't care if he had got anything to do with it, if, in fact, anything did happen.

We all walked through to the bar and sat down; there was no one else in there. Jim got the drinks. Beth stood up and said she would be back soon. Then Jim said, "What would ee like to be drinkin'?" I ordered a double brandy, and Lucy had a single.

Lucy turned to me and said, "What are we going to do?"

I held her hand and said, "Nothing at the moment."

Jim came over and put the drinks down on the table. He pulled the chair out as if he was going to sit down and said, "Just a minute, I must make a phone call."

Lucy looked at me, and as he walked away she said, "I told you there was something funny about him. Who is he ringing at this time of night? He's going to-"

"No, no . . . don't be silly, you won't sleep tonight. On the other hand, I don't want you to." Lucy half smiled. "Look," I said. "We were tired and perhaps our imaginations got the better of us. We are off the boat now. We only heard a couple of clicks, we didn't see a dead body. Perhaps whoever it was in there was listening to the radio, turned it off, closed their suitcase, turned off the light and left."

Lucy looked at me and said, "All I can say, then, is it was a bloody big suitcase."

I took a sip of brandy as the door flew open and in came Beth with a plate of sandwiches. She placed them on the table and sat down. "Where's the old fool?" she said.

"He's gone to make a phone call," Lucy answered.

"Oh, ee's gone to ring 'is sister in America. 'E rings about this time every week, 'tis the only time 'e knows 'e can catch er in, 'tis tea-time over there."

Lucy looked at me again and smiled. It was the first time I had seen some colour in her face since it had happened. Then, after a few seconds of silence, she said, "He doesn't shave."

"These look nice," I said as I picked up a sandwich and bit into it. Lucy took a sip of her brandy as Jim walked into the room.

"'Tis all shipshape over there. Everyone seems to be splendid," he said smiling. As he approached, he threw a gun onto the table. Lucy coughed and nearly choked on her brandy. "Do ee like that?" he said. "I found it in the 'arbour, 'twas on the sand one day when the tide was out."

I looked closer while Lucy was still coughing into her hanky. It was a rusty pistol-type gun that was very old and looked as though it hadn't been fired for hundreds of years. Then Beth said, "Not that old thing again, put it away and 'ave a sandwich." Lucy calmed down after she realised what it was, and we all sat talking for a while, until Beth said, "'Tis my bed I be needin'. 'Tis me to be up in a few hours for the breakfast, so I'll see thee both in the morning."

Then Lucy said, "I think I will come up with you," and kicked me in the other shin under the table as she stood up. "Don't be long, will you."

"No, I'll be up in a minute," I said, rubbing my leg with tears in my eyes.

As they left Jim said, "One more?"

I held my empty glass up. "Just one," and he went behind the bar with it. I was feeling a bit worse for the amount of drink I'd had and my eyes were getting very heavy. When he came back, we sat and talked about the pistol, Cornwall, Birmingham, Devon, his family in America, then all of a sudden I heard a noise—the sound of glasses banging together—and a lady spoke to me.

"It won't do ee any good sitting there all night." I opened my eyes as Beth pulled the curtains back. With a headache, and squinting my eyes, I realised it was morning. There was a half-empty bottle of brandy on the table in front of me and as Beth picked it up she said, "Do ee want to have a quick wash before your breakfast? Lucy is eating hers." Then it hit me. I closed my eyes and dropped my head in my hands, shouting to myself, you've missed your night with Lucy again!

I went into the breakfast room and Lucy was sitting on her own at the table, eating. "I'm sorry," I said, and sat opposite her. "I must have fallen asleep talking to Jim."

"It doesn't matter, it was not meant to happen, was it?" she said with a look on her face that would have burnt anybody's toast.

Beth came in with my breakfast and put it down on the table in front of me. "What time did Jim come up?"

"'Twas about four in the night, I be thinking. He stumbled across the room and got into bed fully clothed, he did. 'Twas the second his 'ead hit the pillow he moaned like an old shipwreck and I couldn't be wakin' him. So I 'ad to put up with it till I gets up, don' I."

"I'm sorry, we had a good chat."

"Well, if ee's makin' a noise, I know he's not dead, dun I." she said with a grin, then she turned and left. She looked remarkable considering she'd had no sleep.

We didn't speak for a while, then Lucy said, "To be honest, I fell asleep straight away, as well. The door was locked on the inside and there was a chair wedged against the handle."

"Was that to keep me out?"

She leaned forward and whispered with a serious look on her face, "No—Jim. I'm still not sure he didn't have something to do with that murder."

I tried to laugh it off and said, "Just because he had blood on his shirtsleeve."

"Shhh!" Still whispering, she said, "Before we went downstairs to the lower deck, he said he was going for a swim. Did you notice he wasn't wet when we were talking to him after I was ill? And didn't you wonder where he kept disappearing to? It was all a bit strange, don't you think?"

"Let's just forget it, we can't tell anyone. If we told the police, we would end up in the papers and what would Ivor and Liz say to that? Let's just finish our breakfast and head for home."

Beth took our plates away and Lucy and I sat talking for a while. We finished our coffee and I went up to our room first to get changed. I left Lucy talking to Beth, hoping she wouldn't be long; we still had some time left. I showered and got ready. After thirty minutes I went back down. Lucy and Beth were still engrossed in conversation. I sat back down and listened for while. From what I could make out, they were taking about having babies and things like that. I tried to interrupt—there was an empty bed upstairs—then Jim walked into the room holding his head with both hands and groaning, "'Tis help I need." I pulled the chair out for him to sit down as the waitress came over with a black coffee. I couldn't stop smiling; he looked awful.

Beth turned to him and said, "'Tis your own fault," then she turned away and carried on talking to Lucy.

Jim poked his tongue out at her with a disgusted look on his face as he scratched his chin through his beard and said, "'Ow do ee feel?"

"All right," I said.

"I 'eard ee slept in the chair all night. I tried to wake ee but there was no response."

"I'm used to sleeping like that at home," I explained.

Then he turned and called the waitress back. "'Tis my bacon and eggs I be needin," he shouted.

"It's coming in a minute," she replied and walked off into the kitchen.

"'Twas a good night on board," Jim said, looking at me for a response.

I noticed Lucy's ears prick up as he spoke. Then she looked at me as if to say, "It wasn't for me". "I enjoyed myself, I've never been to a party on a boat before."

Lucy looked at me again as she stood up and said, "Shall we make a move? It's getting on."

I nodded and drained the last bit of coffee from my cup. Beth stood up and said, "I must be get'n' on, too." Jim still sat with his head in his hands.

"I'll settle up with you when I come down. We'll collect our things and meet you at the reception desk."

"OK, my dear," she said and walked away as Jim's breakfast arrived.

"We will leave you to enjoy your breakfast and see you in a while," Lucy said as she walked off, then Jim nodded and started to eat.

I followed Lucy up stairs, hoping we could spend a little time together. I pushed open the door to find Lucy packing her things away in a small suitcase. Quickly I did the same and pulled Lucy onto the bed and said, "How about it, then? We still have some time left."

She looked up at me and smiled. "'Tis too late, my lovely, last night was the only chance you had for a few days, if you know what I mean." I was still annoyed with myself for falling asleep last night.

We messed about on the bed for a few moments and then we collected our things and made our way down to the reception desk. Lucy pinged the bell and out came Beth looking a little worse than she had earlier. "All set, then?" she said as she opened a drawer and reached for the bill. "All together it comes to £128 with the drinks that you had."

I paid her in cash and Jim walked in from the dining room, still holding his head. "Just off, are we?" He lowered his arm just long enough to shake our hands and then he put it back on his head. "'Twas lovely to meet thee both," he said. "Come back some time and see us again." He turned to Beth and said to her, "Give them a card so they can tell us when the baby arrives."

I took the card from Beth, kissed her on the cheek and said, "Thank you for all your help and a lovely night, we enjoyed it." Then we turned and left, waving as we opened the door and walked out onto a busy road and towards the car.

We made our way out of the town and up the hill towards the main road, looking back at the view of the sea. I turned the radio on softly and Lucy said, "Can you stop somewhere? I'd like to ring my mum."

"I've got to get some petrol, so you can ring her from there."

"OK," she said, and let her head fall back against the headrest.

We had been travelling for about five minutes when I pulled into a station and Lucy got out, just as the news was about to start. I opened the glove box to get my cheque book and the man on the radio said, "Good morning, everyone, this is the ten o'clock news." Then he paused: "A man was found washed up on the shores of Devon this morning by a passer-by. He had been shot twice in the head. Police are treating it as murder and-" I turned it off quickly, as a horrible feeling went through me from head to toe. I could just see Lucy in the window of the filling station on the phone and hoped that the radio wasn't on in there. I got out of the car, put the petrol in as fast as I could and ran in to pay. As I wrote the cheque out, I could hear Lucy talking on the phone, then she put the receiver down, went out of the shop and got back in the car. I followed and, as I approached, I could feel Lucy's eyes following me.

"You will never guess what," she said as I got back in the car.

"I know, I've just heard it." I started the car and pulled away.

"Well, what am I going to do?"

"Nothing," I said. "Just forget it."

Lucy was quiet for a second, then she said, "What are you talking about? I will see him when I get home."

"Who?"

"Ivor, he's back early."

"Oh, I thought you meant . . ." I stopped and thought, shall I tell Lucy or not?

"What did you hear?" Lucy said with a worried look on her face.

"I'll tell you in a minute. What's wrong with Ivor?"

"Mum's just told me he came home yesterday and phoned Jackie in Mortoe to talk to me. She must have told him I left yesterday for home on the coach."

Again I went cold, then hot, and I felt worse than when I'd heard about the man that was found dead. I pulled over into a lay-by. "Do you know her phone number?"

"Yes, it's in my diary." Lucy searched through her handbag and pulled it out. "What shall I say? I can't tell her I spent the night here."

"Tell her you missed the coach and you stayed in a hotel for the night and that you didn't want to bother her because of her bereavement, etc."

Lucy looked puzzled. She sat there thinking with her finger in her mouth, tapping her teeth with her nail. "Can you find me another phone box, then?" She was still deep in thought as I pulled away.

"Do you want to use my phone?" I held it up in front of Lucy.

"No, I'll ring her from a payphone.

It wasn't long before we found a phone box in the town. I pulled over and waited nervously while she called her friend.

It was a while before she came back and got in the car smiling. "Is everything all right?" I asked.

"Jackie didn't speak to him at all yesterday, she was out till late at her friend's caravan. She hasn't spoke to Ivor since the night before her husband died, so I don't know what mum was on about."

Feeling a little bit better, we pulled off again. "Why don't you ring Ivor at work and tell him you're on your way home soon and you'll see him tonight?"

"That's a good idea. Will you stop again? I'd feel better if I knew."

"Let's have a drink and you can ring from there."

We found a place with a small door into the lounge called the Duck Inn. I ordered the drinks and Lucy made the phone call.

With a big grin on her face, Lucy sat down, took a sip from her drink and said, "He tried to ring last night but couldn't get through. He assumed that we were out together."

"So everything is OK, then?"

"Yes," she said, with a sigh of relief.

We finished our drinks and headed for home. We pulled on to the motorway and Lucy seemed to get a bit randy; she started to stroke the inside of my leg with the tip of her fingers softly and worked her way up my leg. I wasn't sure if I should tell her to stop, so I pulled over into the middle lane and slowed down a bit. Then she fumbled about with my zip. I slowed down even more, between two large trucks. The one behind me started blowing his horn, while Lucy was trying to find mine in my pants. I drove on, pretending to take no notice, and the truck behind me pulled out and started to overtake me still blowing like mad. I must have cut him up. Then I realised it was too dangerous, so I told her to stop before we had an accident. She looked up at me and said, "'Tis a feel I'd be wantin'."

I pushed her hand away and tried to fasten my zip back up and said, "You will have to wait, then, won't you, till next time."

We laughed and joked about me falling asleep and Lucy locking the door. Then Lucy said, "What were you going to tell me earlier?"

I'd forgotten about the news report and I'd hoped Lucy had too, but now we were miles away and it didn't seem to matter so much. I said, "On the news, when I had the radio on and you were on the phone to your mum, they said that a body was discovered on the beach in Devon." Lucy breathed in sharply, put her hand over her mouth and stared at me with those big eyes of hers. "It doesn't mean it was from the boat, they just said that someone found a body. It could be someone who'd had a heart attack, or just drowned." I didn't think it would be wise to tell her about the two bullet holes.

# Chapter 14

WE CARRIED ON down the motorway into Birmingham and I dropped Lucy off at the bus station with a kiss at about 2.30 before driving back to the garage.

I sat in the car on the forecourt for a while, scared to go in, in case something else had happened while I was away. Then Roger came out of the body shop with his hands in his pockets and walked towards me—not looking too happy, I might add. I opened the door and stood up. "Everything all right?" I asked.

"No, not really."

"What's happened?"

"A bailiff came round this morning, demanding money for the electric that you owe. I tried to ring you on your mobile but there was no answer."

I had that sinking feeling again. "So, what did you do?"

"What could I do? I had to go to my bank to draw it out and pay him in cash. He wouldn't accept it any other way. He wanted to disconnect the supply."

"I'm sorry, how much was it?"

"Four hundred and eighty pounds. Apparently you sent a cheque and it was returned unpaid."

"I'll get it out of the petrol money and give it to you."

"How deep in the shit are we?" Roger asked with a worried expression on his face. "Do we have to start looking for new jobs, or is it just tight at the moment?"

"It has been tight for ages. There isn't enough money coming in to pay the bills. We have a good month and we have three bad months and it's hard to make up the difference."

Roger lifted one hand out of his pocket, scratched his head and said, "Why didn't you say something before?"

"What do you want me to say? I don't think it's as bad as it sounds, we just need to shift some of the cars off the front and have a couple of really good months and we'll be back on top again." I thought it best not to tell him everything in case he started to look for another job. "Do the others know about all this going on?"

"No." He shook his head and put his hand back in his pocket. "I took him up to your office and he waited up there while I went to the bank."

"Don't worry, it will be OK soon," I added, trying to reassure him. "I've been talking to a friend of mine for the last couple of weeks and I've bid on some more cars at the right price. Have we got much work in at the moment?" I asked as I pulled my briefcase from the back seat.

"Yes, we have been busy and there are some cheques in the drawer."

"See, it's getting better already." With a straight face, Roger nodded and walked back into the garage. I followed him into the workshop and collected the mail and the cheques from the drawer, shouted hello to everyone and went upstairs to open the letters. I counted the money and got everything ready for the bank in the morning.

I arrived home about 7.30. I told Liz and Mick how I'd got on at the auction and I took my dinner into the front room on a tray. I had just sat down to eat it and the phone rang. I answered it and a voice said, "Hello, it's Nigel here, I need to speak to you urgently."

"What's the matter?" I asked.

"I can't talk over the phone. Are you going to the Wooden Cross tomorrow night after work?"

"I could be."

"Good, I will see you then, you've got some explaining to do." I replaced the receiver and carried on with my dinner as if nothing had happened but I was worried about what he'd said.

I woke Friday morning, still worried and, as normal, dropped Mick of at school and then went to the bank. I tried to ring Nigel two or three times during the day but couldn't get through on his phone in the truck. I paid the wages and gave the money back to Roger—he seemed to be a bit happier—and left about five o'clock for the pub.

As I walked in, I could see Nigel out of the corner of my eye, sitting reading his paper. So, trying not to look too concerned, I ordered myself a drink at the bar and he came over. "You've been caught," were his first words.

I turned and said, "What you on about?"

"I think we had better sit down."

I picked up my glass and followed him to a table. "What do you mean, I've been caught?" He put his glass down, leaned over towards me, then he started, looking round to make sure no one was close. "A truck driver on the M5 motorway travelling north, has seen someone in a car with a girl by his side, half-naked, giving the driver a good time, as he put it." I kept a straight face as he carried on and realised why the truck driver was sounding his horn on the motorway coming back from Devon. "Now, what happens in our trucks, when one driver looks down into a car and see something like this, he calls on his CB radio to all the other drivers in the area to look out for a certain car with a particular registration number coming up behind them, because there's something going on in the car. On this occasion, unfortunately, I was travelling south about five miles further on and didn't see anything, but I heard the registration number." Then he paused to take a gulp of beer. He must have known I wanted to say something because he put his other hand up to say 'hold on, I haven't finished'. Then he put his glass back down on the table and carried on, wiping the froth from his top lip. "Now, correct me if I'm wrong, but the registration number I heard was yours. Now, as I've seen you up north in a motorway cafe with a dark-haired attractive hitchhiker, if I remember correctly and as, apparently, this was a dark-haired girl, half-naked and by your side, and as your wife is blonde, I was wondering what was going on."

Now it was my turn and the answer had to be a good one; the last thing I needed was this banded about later when everyone came in telling their stories of the week. "Oh, is that all? I thought I was in trouble." The expression his face was a puzzled one; his eyebrows drooped in the middle above his nose. "I must go to the toilet first. While I'm up, do you want another drink?" I asked him calmly.

He nodded, "Yes, please, and a bag of salted nuts." I walked over to the bar casually; inside I was worried sick. I ordered the drinks and, while Mary the barmaid was pouring them, I popped to the loo.

While I was standing there on my own, everything went through my mind from being caught red-handed miles and miles away, to how I was going to explain this one.

I collected the drinks and nuts and sat back down. "How's the family?"

"All right, thanks, and don't try to change the subject." I took a large gulp of my drink and smiled nervously.

"I went down south to a car auction the day before to see what was for sale. Didn't buy anything, to be honest, it was all a load of crap, and while I was there I met another car trader from up here, called Tony. Now, he bought three cars: a Jaguar, Escort and Montego. Instead of him paying to have the cars delivered, he takes his mechanic and secretary with him and they bring them back. Anyway, we all left together, and I was behind the secretary who was driving the Montego; the others had driven off and gone. As she pulled on to the motorway at Exeter, great clouds of smoke appeared from the back of her car and she pulled over onto the hard shoulder, so I stopped behind her. It was obvious that the engine had overheated, so she gave me

Tony's mobile phone number and I phoned him quickly to tell him what had happened. He was about three junctions ahead and said he would come back; she was to stay with the car till he arrived and I couldn't leave her there stranded. We waited for twenty minutes and she started to get more and more angry and she borrowed my phone and rang him back. She started shouting abuse at him, saying things like, 'It's not fair', and 'You bastards always leave me behind with the shit' and then something about being home for tea-time. Anyway, to cut a long story short, we managed to drive it a bit further, left the car at the next junction and I brought her back with me. As to having a good time, she is a tart, she's plastered in make-up and her dress was no thicker than your leather belt. She never stopped moaning all the way back. I don't think sex entered her ugly head and it never entered mine." Nigel licked the salt off his fingertips and screwed the bag up, dropping it into the ashtray. "Tony phoned me today to thank me for taking her home and apparently the Montego was scrapped. Just down the road from where we left it was a garage and they fetched it in for him and the estimate was more than the car was worth." I took another mouthful of my drink and waited for a response.

"So nothing happened?"

"No," I said with a smile. "And the girl in the motorway café was a hitchhiker, cold and wet. I just asked her if she wanted a coffee to warm her up and afterwards I dropped her off at the next junction." The look on his face was enough to say he believed me. So I added, "She wanted to repay me for giving her a lift and she asked me back to her house." His face dropped again and I quickly told him I was joking. We laughed it off. By this time some of the others had arrived and we moved back over to the bar to talk with them.

Just before I was leaving, Nigel said, "I'm glad we spoke, I was worried. We've been good friends for years and I wouldn't like anything to happen to you and Liz."

"Don't worry, everything is fine, but if I don't get home soon it won't be." I shouted goodbye and left, breathing a long sigh of relief.

On Saturday night, Liz and I went out for a Chinese meal with Denise, Andrew, Sandra and Henry. Denise was off to India on the Sunday afternoon. I sat opposite Denise. She winked at me every time our eyes met and kept running her bare foot up and down my leg softly, under my trousers.

We had a nice meal and, as we were leaving, I said goodbye to Denise and she whispered, "As soon as I get back, I want you." I held her tight in my arms, wished her a pleasant trip and we went home.

# Chapter 15

On Monday, Debbie walked towards me in the playground with her head down. I didn't speak to her as normal and carried on slowly to the gates. I waited for a few minutes and she didn't come out, so I walked over to my car and sat waiting. After about five minutes, I could see her walking towards the gates still with her head down, so I jumped out of the car and walked up behind her. "Debbie," I shouted but she carried on walking. I shouted again. "Debbie, it's me, hold on!" By this time I had caught her up and I grabbed her arm. "What's wrong? I was calling you." She turned round. Her head was still down and I could hear her sobbing. I lifted her head. I couldn't believe my eyes: she was black and blue and, just above her right eye, was a cut about an inch long, still bleeding. "Has John done this to you?" Debbie burst out crying and nodded. If he were standing next to me, I probably would have killed him with my bare hands. I wanted to hold her tight but there were other parents about. I started to shake with anger; I had to think quickly. "Can you drive down the road?" Debbie nodded again. "Follow me." I helped her into her car and then ran back to mine and pulled away with Debbie behind me. I turned into the park entrance, stopped, and she pulled up next to me. My body was still shaking. My teeth were locked together as I flexed the muscles in my jaw. I ran over to her car. Debbie stood up and again burst into tears. I held her close as she wept on my shoulder. "Can you tell me what happened?"

She lifted her head, wiping her nose with a tissue and sniffing, trying to catch her breath. Then she said in a broken voice, "It . . . was . . . last night . . ."

I pushed her hair behind her ear with my finger, as she pulled another tissue from her sleeve, gasping for air in short bursts. "Calm down and try to tell me what happened."

"It was . . . last night, about 8.30, when he came . . . home from work. As soon as the front door slammed shut, I knew . . . he had been drinking. I've been through it a thousand times before. I was preparing . . . the dinner, then the kitchen door crashed open. I was scared and too frightened to turn around. Luckily, I'd put Dawn to bed. 'Where the fuck's my dinner?' is all he said." The tears were building up in my eyes by this time and I was still shaking all over. "I put his dinner down on the table in front of him and he grabbed my wrist, then he pulled me down onto his lap, trying to kiss me on the neck. I managed to struggle free and get out of the way. Then he started shouting 'I want you, bitch!' trying to unfasten his trousers, then I ran up the stairs." Debbie's voice started to break again so I pulled her into my shoulder as she burst into tears.

"Don't worry, he can't get you now." I stroked her hair until she stopped crying, wiped her nose on a tiny bit of crinkled tissue and carried on.

"When I opened the door to go upstairs he picked his dinner plate up and threw it at me and went wild—'You fuckin' bitch, come here now!' I ran as fast as I could up the stairs into Dawn's room, more scared than I've ever been in my life. Dawn was crying and screaming as I tried to wedge a chair against the door. Then he started banging on the door until it cracked at the top. The crack got bigger and bigger until his fist appeared through a hole, covered in blood. I grabbed Dawn and we hid in the wardrobe but I couldn't stop her screaming. Then we heard the door smash in. First, I thought he went into the en-suite, so I pushed the door open and we tried to run out, but he was standing in the room. He grabbed Dawn off me and threw her on the bed, then he took a swipe at me and punched me on my chin. I fell to the floor and hit my head on the cupboard next to the bed. Then he kicked me in the leg and ran down the stairs." Debbie's eyes started to fill up again.

"The bastard!" I was so angry. "Where is he now?"

"I don't know. He left the house and I haven't seen him since. I locked all the doors and got into bed with Dawn. She stopped crying and fell asleep eventually."

"Is she all right this morning?"

"She's tired but I had to put her in school so I could find somewhere to stay for a couple of days."

"Have you told anyone?"

"No, I'm too embarrassed. I made Dawn promise not to say a word to anybody at school either."

I kissed her forehead and said, "Don't be silly, it's not your fault." Then she dropped her head again. "I will find you a place to stay tonight. Go back home and collect some things for you and Dawn from the house; not a word to anyone, OK?" Debbie nodded while she wiped her nose. "Don't put your clothes in a suitcase, find a carrier bag or something like that, in case the neighbours are watching, collect Dawn at dinner-time and meet me at the Plough in Stratford at two o'clock in the car park. Don't say anything to the teachers, just take her out."

"What shall I do if he's at home?"

I pulled the phone out of my pocket and phoned his workshop. "Hello, is John there?" I asked.

"Yes, I'll just get him for you," a girl answered.

"No, it's OK, I'll pop in and surprise him. Don't worry, but thanks." Debbie looked at me with a black, half-closed eye. "He's at work, so I will go first to your house and park at the end of the drive while you go in and I'll wait till you have finished in case he comes home."

Debbie kissed me on the cheek and got back into her car. I drove off first with her close behind. She parked her car and ran into the house quickly, while I waited.

After about five minutes, she threw three bags in the boot, jumped back into her car and pulled away. I followed her to the end of the road and then made my way to work.

As I drove back I calmed down a bit and was trying to think what I could do to the bastard that might help

Debbie. Beating him senseless was all I could come up with at first but common sense told me he would only do it again later.

I pulled on to the forecourt and went straight up to my office, still deep in thought. Then I remembered my cousin in London and his parting words every time I leave him—"If you want anything or anyone done just let me know". I opened my phone book and stared at his name on the page, undecided what to do, then I phoned him.

"Hello, Don, its Nick here.

"Hello," he said. "How are you?"

"All right, thanks, yourself?"

"Yes, how's the family?"

"Everyone is OK."

Then he said, "To what do I owe this pleasure?"

"I need some advice but I don't think it's a good idea to talk about it on the phone. Can I come down this afternoon?"

"Yes, by all means." He paused. "Oh, hang on a minute, I've got to meet someone in Milton Keynes at four o'clock, do you want to meet me there? It's on your way."

"Great," I said, then he gave me the address and explained to me roughly where it was.

I messed about in the garage for a while with very little interest; Debbie was all I could think about and how she must have felt when all this was going on. I started to get angry again.

It was about 1.15 when I left and made my way over to Stratford to meet Debbie. I arrived a little ahead of her and waited. At 2.30 I started to worry, in case something had happened.

Her BMW pulled into the car park and I watched her go past behind me in my door mirror. She stopped about six cars further down the line. I waited for a few seconds to make sure no one was following her, opened the door and stood up. Then she got out of her car and ran over to me. We kissed, holding each other in between the cars, and she sobbed again on my shoulder. "I hate that bastard and all he's put us through." I held her tighter and asked her if Dawn was in the car. She nodded and wiped her nose with a pink hanky.

"Get your things out of the car and I'll get you both booked in."

Debbie walked back to the car and I went into the hotel. I registered us in the book as Mr and Mrs Smith—it was the first name that came into my head—and waited by the entrance. As they came through the door, I told Debbie to cover her bruised eye with her hand. I walked them over to the lift and we got in. We didn't speak for a while and I noticed Dawn, the little girl, looking up at me as she held her mum's hand. "Hello," I said, trying to be friendly. "I'm your uncle Nick." I held my hand out to shake her's and she hid behind Debbie. The door opened and we found the room almost opposite the lift. I unlocked it and stood by the door. Debbie pushed Dawn in first, so I tapped her on the back and as she turned I whispered, "I won't come in, I will see you later. It's not good for Dawn to see us together." She stepped back pulling the door to and I kissed her again, and left.

It was a little after three o'clock when I left the car park and I arrived at Milton Keynes just before four. I found the house almost straight away. Don's Ferrari was parked on the drive, so I stopped on the road and waited, watching the front door until it opened. Don shook the hand of an elderly man and, as he walked to his car, he waved to me while unlocking his door. Getting in with his black briefcase, he reversed off the drive and pulled level with me, opened his window and shouted, "Follow me." So I did. We drove out in to the countryside for a few miles and stopped at a pub called the golden Lion. I parked next to him in the car park and he came and sat in my car. "What's wrong?" were his first words.

"I need some advice. I didn't like to say on the phone, you never know if anyone is listening in. When I left you last time, again you said if you need anything or anyone done to contact you. What did you mean?"

"Exactly that. Why, what have you got yourself into?"

"Well, I have a friend who has been badly beaten by her husband." Don screwed his face up and said, "What's he like?"

"He was a friend of mine, a good friend some years ago. I hadn't seen him for a long time and we met up last New Year's Eve. Debbie, that's his wife, told me then that he drank too much. The more he drinks, the nastier he gets. The other night he broke the bedroom door down and punched and kicked her badly and she had to grab their little girl and run away from him and hide until he went out. I've got them in a hotel at the moment."

Don shook his head from side to side and said, "I have a friend up your way who hates blokes like him. He owes me a few favours; I'll speak to him tomorrow and let you know. Are you involved with this girl?"

"I won't lie, I've been out with her once and, yes, she is a very attractive girl that shouldn't be treated like a punch bag every time he drinks too much. She hates him. They live in separate parts of the house. It's been going on for a long time, apparently. She hasn't told anyone this time; she's too afraid to."

"Where does he work?"

"He's a mechanic, in a garage not far from me, and he obviously doesn't know we've been out together."

"Have you told anyone about her?"

"No, only you."

"Are you positive?"

"Yes, I have not told a soul."

"Good, make sure she is OK. Firstly, do you need any money?"

"No. I've got some, thanks."

"Wait until you hear from me. I will see you tomorrow. Write down on a piece of paper his address, at work and at home, and if he has a hobby, where he goes and drinks, things that will help us to decide what to do with him. I'll ring you as soon as I have spoken with my friend, and we'll meet you somewhere. When we talk on the phone, choose your words carefully."

With that, Don got back into his car and drove off. I drove back to see if Debbie was all right.

I parked the car and made my way up to her room and knocked on the door. There was no answer, so I knocked again a little louder this time. Still no answer, so I went down to the reception and said to the man behind the desk, "I came in earlier with my wife and daughter. I've just tried the door and there's no answer. Can you tell me if they went out?" He turned and looked behind on the wall and said, "There's no key so they should still be in their room. Would you like me to ring the room for you, sir?"

"Yes, please, if you could," I said, afraid in case something had happened.

He picked up the phone and dialled the room number. "Hello, your husband is here and wants to come up." It suddenly struck me she might be thinking it was John.

"Tell her I forgot to tell her about the log cabin up north."

He repeated me word for word and then he put the phone down and said, "If you go up now, she will be waiting for you by the lift, sir."

I thanked him and made my way up. As the lift door opened, Debbie was standing there. "I had to say that in case you thought it was John."

"I did to start with," she said grinning.

"How are you?" I asked as I put my arms around her.

"I'm all right. Dawn is fast asleep; she is probably worn out from last night."

"Have you eaten anything today?"

"No, I'm not really hungry," she said quietly. "Dawn will be when she wakes, I'm sure."

"Well, take her down to the restaurant, then both of you get some sleep and I'll be back in the morning. Don't worry about John, he won't find you. I'm the only one that knows you're here. Don't ring anyone tonight and I will ring you before I come up in the morning."

Debbie looked up at me and said, "OK." She looked a bit more relaxed. Her eye was a deep purple and the cut on her head was drying up. We kissed quickly and I told her I had to go. Debbie asked me to stop a bit longer but I didn't think it would be a good idea. I didn't want Dawn to see us together.

On my way out, I stopped at the reception desk and gave the manager £200 and asked him to let them have what they wanted in the restaurant when they came down later. Then I left and made my way home.

I drove past Debbie's house. John's Land Rover was on the drive in front of his boat and so I carried on.

As I pulled onto my drive, I half expected to see Andrew's car there and was shocked when it wasn't.

I made myself a drink as Liz served the dinner and, after it was eaten, we sat and talked for a while. Mick showed me his certificate he had got at school for swimming. I told him how proud of him I was and promised to get him another frame so he could hang it on the bedroom wall with his other three.

At nine o'clock they went to bed as usual. I sat up and while I was watching the television I put together a list for Don, as he had asked.

While I was driving to work the next morning, Don phoned. "Can you meet me in Warwick about midday at the Queen's Arms and bring me the paperwork I asked you for?"

"Yes," I answered, a little startled. "Is everything OK?"

"Fine," he said, and went on to give me vague directions.

When I got to the garage, I phoned Debbie at the hotel. She told me she felt a lot better and I briefly explained I was going to talk to someone and that I would call in later on my way back.

I left for Warwick about eleven o'clock and eventually found the Queen's Arms just before twelve. As I pulled into the car park, I could see Don's car and next to it was a big red Bentley with the roof down. I parked up, found the lounge and went in. Don was at the bar and next to him was a black man, who looked bigger and meaner than Mike Tyson—he was huge. As I approached them, Don turned and introduced him. "This is my friend, Savage." I looked at him and as I shook his massive hand, I thought to myself, I wouldn't like to be on the wrong side of him. Then Don said, "Shall we sit over here? It's a bit more private." I followed them and we all sat down in the corner.

Don spoke first, almost whispering. "I've explained the situation as best as I could. There are two options open: it can be arranged for this person to get a good hiding but, to be honest, it only works for a while and then it will probably happen again later."

"What's the other option?" I asked.

Then, even quieter, Don leaned forward and said, "An accident."

"What kind of an accident?" I asked innocently, then Savage leaned forward and with a very serious look on his face, his teeth clasped together and a very deep voice he whispered, "A fatal accident. Bastards like that don't deserve to be alive."

I froze. All I could do was stare at him. He meant every word; I could tell by his expression. I smiled. "I couldn't do that." Don asked me if I had jotted a few things down. I stood up and pulled out the folded sheet of paper from my back pocket and dropped it on the table in front of him. I suddenly realised what I was getting myself into. Savage was a professional killer and he wasn't here to be messed about. Don unfolded the paper and they looked at it together.

"Where's he keep his speedboat?" Savage asked.

"On the drive in front of his house."

They looked at each other and then Don said, "1978, Isle of Man."

Savage almost smiled, I think. His cheeks moved up slightly and then he said, "Yes, that would do it."

Wondering what they were talking about, I stood up. "Can I get either of you a drink?"

They lifted their heads together and Savage said, "Not for me."

Don shook his head. "You get yourself one—you look as if you need it."

I walked over to the empty bar. "A large whiskey, please." While I was waiting, I thought about what they'd said. My hand was trembling as I paid the girl for the drink. I knocked it back in one then, placing the glass back on the bar, I asked for another.

Again I paid and, with my drink, sat back down. "What's the chance of him using his boat soon?" Don asked.

"He often takes it down to the Cotswolds. Why do you ask?"

"We were just trying to work something out." I took a sip of whiskey while they whispered to each other. Then Don said, "In the next couple of days, his boat will disappear off his drive and, two or three days after, it will be left somewhere close to his house, so he will find it again. Now, I need you to convince his wife to go back to him for a couple of days. We will frighten him enough to leave her alone. She must act normal to her neighbours and friends." I took another gulp from my glass. "Then," he said, "you must drop hints to him about going out with him the next time he takes the boat out and try to get a few friends together, make it a day out. The rest you can leave to us, OK?" I nodded, still in a daze about what I was doing, and finished my drink.

They whispered some more and then Savage stood up and said, "I must go, I've got some money to collect before five o'clock." I stood up and held my hand out to shake his enormous hand. Then he left, pulling his jacket together and fastening the middle button.

Don folded the sheet of paper I'd given him and slid it in his top pocket. "Don't worry, it will be sorted," he said with a smile on his face. He could probably tell I was terrified.

"Am I right in thinking he does this sort of thing regularly?" I asked foolishly.

Don lifted his eyebrows once and stood up. "I must go, too. Will you be all right? You look a little pale."

"Yes," I said standing up "It's a bit hard to swallow, all this." We walked out together.

As we approached the cars, Don turned to me. "It will be all right, just get them back together and don't say anything to err . . ."

"Debbie."

"Yes, Debbie—about the boat. I'll be in touch tomorrow."

I sat in my car as Don's Ferrari disappeared off down the road, so I made my way back to Stratford trying to work out how I was going to get them back together.

I walked into the hotel reception; the same man was at the desk. "Could you tell Debbie in room 103 I'm coming up?"

"They're in the restaurant, sir," he said pointing to the door, so I made my way in.

I sat with them for a short while and asked Debbie if she was OK. She told me she was a lot better and a bit more relaxed. We chatted a little longer then I left, telling her I would see her in the morning.

The following day, I drove back to the hotel, worried about telling her to go back to John. I made my way up to her room after telling the receptionist to let Debbie know I was on my way up. As the lift door opened she was standing in the corridor. "How are you?"

"I'm all right," she said as we walked towards the room. Debbie put her hand on the handle to open the door.

"Debbie, I need to speak to you without Dawn listening."

She looked at me, then she pushed the door open. "Stay in bed a little while longer, Mummy's just outside the door if you want me." She pulled the door closed again. "What's the matter?" she said, looking at me with a big grin and that lovely smile I hadn't seen for ages.

"I've spoken to a friend of mine about John." The smile disappeared. "He is going to get a good hiding."

"Good," she said clenching her fist and with a hateful look on her face.

"I need you to go back to him for a short while."

"No way," she said shaking her head. "I don't care if I never see that bastard again as long as I live."

I put my hands gently on her cheeks and looked into her eyes. "Now, listen to me first, I know it is going to be hard for you both and I wouldn't let any more harm come to either of you. No one knows what's gone on in the last few days and if anything was to happen to him, people would be suspicious if you weren't at home."

Debbie turned, looking out of the window, leaning on the frame. "How long, is a few days?" I heard her say into the glass.

"Seven, ten tops." Her head dropped and then she turned back.

"I couldn't. What about Dawn?"

"Most of the time she will be at school and he'll be at work. It's only the nights and, as I said before, he will be frightened off."

"What happens in seven to ten days, then?"

"I can't tell you at the moment, but it will be better for you and Dawn." Debbie walked towards me with tears trickling down her cheeks; I put my arm around her waist and lifted her chin with my finger. "I wouldn't ask you to do anything like this if it wasn't necessary." I kissed her tears and then she sobbed on my shoulder. "Listen, I'll see if I can arrange something else," I said quietly in her ear.

Then Debbie lifted her head and said, "Ten days, not a day longer."

I held her tight and said, "It will be all over soon."

I quickly stepped back as the door opened. "Mum, are you coming in yet?"

"Yes," Debbie said wiping her eyes. "I'll be with you in a couple of minutes, darling." As the door clicked shut, Debbie said, "Will you come in with me and tell Dawn?" Nodding, I followed her into the room.

Dawn was sitting on her hands on the edge of the bed, watching cartoons on the telly; Debbie sat next to her, and softly placed her arm around her shoulders. "Mummy's going to take you home today, would you like that?"

Dawn waved her head vigorously from side to side. "No, I want to stay here with you."

Debbie carried on. "We can't stay here for ever, we've got to go home sometime."

"But Daddy's there, I don't like Daddy," she cried. Debbie pulled Dawn's head onto her cheek. I felt so sorry for them as they sat on the bed together.

I knelt down in front of Dawn and said, "I've talked to your daddy and he is so sorry for hurting you and your mum. He said he will go to the hospital to see the doctors because he hasn't been very well lately and he wants the doctors to make him better, and he asked me to ask you to come home because he misses you both so much."

The tears rolled down Dawn's face as she looked up at Debbie and said, "Daddy won't shout at me again?"

Debbie shook her head, wiping the tears from Dawn's cheeks. "No, darling, he won't shout at us anymore."

With that promise, Dawn said, "Shall we go home, then?"

That huge lump was in my throat again and I couldn't say another word. I walked into the bathroom and got myself a glass of water. Then I heard Debbie say, "Shall we put all our things back in the bags?"

Before I went back into the room, I looked through the opening in the door. I could see in the mirror on the wall that Debbie was cuddling Dawn and I heard her say, "It will be all right."

As I walked through, I said to Debbie, "I will go down and tell the reception you're leaving and meet you both downstairs." Debbie nodded and carried on packing their clothes into bags.

After I had settled the bill, I waited. Eventually the lift door opened and they stood there like two refugees. We shouted goodbye as we walked across the reception area and left.

While Debbie was loading her car, I told her I would follow her back so far and then go on ahead to make sure John wasn't at home. We didn't kiss, in case Dawn saw us.

I'd just pulled out onto the road when my phone rang. It was Don. "How's things?" he asked.

I had to think carefully. "All right, on her way home as we speak."

"Good, apparently your mate will be seen after dinner today, so I'll ring later."

I had to speak quickly, but be careful how I said it. "Is there a slim chance he could be laid up for a couple of days after seeing the doctor? They didn't want to go back." It went quiet for a second.

"I'll ring you back later," and then he hung up.

I followed Debbie part of the way, carried on to make sure John wasn't home, and waited. Her BMW pulled up behind me and as I pulled away she flashed her lights. Then I made my way to work.

About four o'clock, while I was upstairs in my office wading through some paperwork, the phone rang.

"There was no need for your mate to go and see the doctor. Unfortunately for him, a car fell on him earlier at work and they took him straight to the hospital for X-rays on his chest. He might have to stay in for a while. Anyway, I've got to go, speak with you later."

As I put the phone down, I couldn't stop myself smiling and, of course, I was relieved that Debbie didn't have to stay with John, so I phoned her. "Hello, it's only me. John's going to be in hospital for a few days. He's had an accident at work. His boss will probably ring to tell you what happened so go and visit him and I'll see you in the morning."

It went quiet for a second and then the only words she could say were, "Thank you . . ." and, "I love you so much."

I carried on for a while with the paperwork, trying hard not to think of Debbie and those words "I love you". It was almost impossible. I collected all the cheques together, filled in the bankbooks and looked at my watch. It was too late to bank them, so I added up a few figures to see how the garage was doing. I was surprised: it wasn't as bad as I thought and there was plenty in the bank.

I left for home about seven o'clock, with my bankbooks so I could go in the morning on the way to work.

I dropped Mick off at school the next day and bumped into Debbie in the playground and whispered as we passed each other, "Meet me in the entrance to the park." I thought it best if no one saw us together at all and I carried on in my car.

After a few minutes, Debbie pulled up behind me and got out, running towards me with her arms full stretch. "How are things?" I asked as we embraced each other.

"Much better. I couldn't believe it when you told me he was in hospital, I was so relieved."

"Did you see him?"

"Yes, I went to see the bastard last night. He was trying to be nice but I just felt sick. I stayed with him for a few minutes and I had to leave. The doctors X-rayed him but nothing was broken unfortunately. They did say they would keep him in for a few days, thank God."

"Now you can tell Dawn her dad's in hospital seeing the doctors. I'm going to see his boss today and I'm sure he will tell me what happened so I will go and see him this afternoon, you go tonight and I will see you here tomorrow morning after school. I don't want anyone to think there is something going on between us." Debbie nodded once sharply, looking into my eyes, and then I heard my phone ring in the car. I leaned through the window to answer.

"Don here, is everything all right?"

"Yes, fine, thank you."

"They tell me at the hospital John's in for the week. His wife will be pleased, I would think."

I smiled and looked at Debbie. I was amazed how he did everything. "I'm going to see him this afternoon," I said, choosing my words carefully. "I think when he gets out of hospital, I might try and convince him to take the boat down to the lake."

"Good idea, I would come with you, but the boat is going away tonight and won't be back till Wednesday, so I'll have to see. I'll speak to you soon, bye."

After replacing the phone, I walked over to Debbie. "That was my friend. John will be in hospital for a week at least. Can you still visit him at night and try—I know it's hard—to be nice?"

"I despise him," she said with a look of hate on her face.

"It will be all over soon. Try, please." We kissed once and left.

I drove to the bank on my way back to the garage and deposited the cheques, then carried on to work. Everything seemed to be OK, so I drove to the garage where John worked and, sure enough, his boss told me what had happened briefly, then I made my way over to the hospital. As I walked towards his bed, I could see him lying on the top of it, watching the television at the end of the ward, bound in bandages around his chest. The anger started to well up inside of me as I got closer and closer. I didn't relish the thought of speaking to him but I had to pretend I knew nothing.

"What happened to you? I just popped in to see you at work and they told me about your accident." He looked up and painfully smiled at me as he pulled himself up in the bed with the chrome bar that hung above his head.

"I don't know, I jacked a car up, put the stands underneath the chassis as I always do and climbed under to work on the exhaust. I was only under there a couple of minutes when the car came straight down on me, pinning me to the floor and crushing my chest. I couldn't breathe for ages; the pain was dreadful. As luck would have it, the jack was still underneath otherwise I'd be dead. There was a big black guy standing close. He pumped it back up again and dragged me out by my feet."

I stood listening to him go on about the stands being next to the car and how sure he was that he had put them under. "Never mind, as long as you are OK now, that's the main thing," I said sarcastically. "When do you think you'll be out?"

"They haven't told me yet. In fact, I don't know why they're keeping me in. I wanted to take the boat out this weekend down to the lake; it's going to be nice apparently."

Great, I thought. "Well, you can go the weekend after."

"I can't, it's my birthday then."

"Even better." I said. "I will get a few people together and we can have a party. I will take a barbie and some drinks, it will be a good day. You can take the boat."

"Good idea," he said. "I'll be 40. I will look forward to that, mate."

I left shortly after that, clenching my fists and walking as fast as I could to get out. The word 'mate' kept ringing in my ears; it made me feel sick.

I'd done everything that Don had asked me to do. Now it was down to him and Savage.

# Chapter 16

THE NEXT DAY I dropped Mick off at school and waited in the park for Debbie. She arrived a little after me, so we strolled along for a while holding hands. It was a nice bright, sunny day and she said, "John told me last night that we are all going down to the lake for his birthday. What's going on? I wouldn't spend a day with him after all the shit he put us through."

"It's all part of the plan."

"What plan? What's happening?" We stopped.

"I can't tell you yet," I said. "You will still have to trust me."

"Anyway, his boat was stolen last night off the drive, so that's the end of that idea," she said. It was hard for me not to tell Debbie everything, but for her own sake I had to keep quiet, at least for the time being.

"Have you reported it to the police?" I asked.

"No, I'm not interested."

"You must report it and tell the insurance company. They will send you a claim form and you can give it to John, he can fill in the details. It must be worth a lot of money. Is it insured?" I asked casually.

"Yes, it's insured for all sorts. He can't take it on the lake unless he has full cover, in case of accidents."

"Well, I would if I was you."

"All right, if you think it's best, I will do it when I get back," she said. We walked and talked for a while, then Debbie went home and I went to the garage.

I was washing my hands to go home when the phone rang. It was Don. "Meet me on Monday at the Bull's Head in Lapworth, around two o'clock. I've got to see a client at four and there's a fair bit to talk about." He said everything was OK and he would see me then.

Not much happened over the weekend. I had a drink on Sunday lunch-time with Andrew. He told me Denise was away and due back Wednesday that week, so I mentioned to him about taking John's boat out next Sunday. "Great," he said, then he told me he would ring round and get a few of the others interested.

On Monday morning, I met Debbie in the park and explained to her that I was going to see my friend today about John and that I would meet her on the following morning to explain. She told me she had been to see John in hospital again over the weekend and how upset he was over his boat.

I left the garage at lunch-time and arrived just before two in the pub car park. There was no sign of Don's car, so I went in and had a drink at the bar while I waited. Don walked in just after two o'clock. "I don't have long, can we sit over there, out of the way?"

"Yes, do you want a drink?"

"No, thanks, I need a level head." We walked over to a little table in the corner and sat down opposite each other. Don stubbed his cigar out in the ashtray and leaned forward.

"The boat will be placed on someone's drive, not far from where he lives, the early hours of Thursday. The people that live there will be away and the house will be empty. John will be released ten o'clock Thursday morning. Can you or Debbie collect him and take him home past the house, so he'll recognise the boat?"

"Debbie has got a tow-bar on her BMW."

"Good, tell her to collect him from hospital but you must make her go past the house, without telling her about the boat; that way he will see it and knock on the door. When there's no answer, he'll hook it onto the car and take it home." I sat watching his lips, listening to every word he spoke without moving in case I missed something. "Tell Debbie to ring the police and tell them they found it in a car park and they won't bother with it anymore. Is that all clear?"

"Yes," I said, still concentrating.

"Now, on Sunday, let him go down to the lake on his own—you mentioned before he has a Land Rover." I nodded. "Debbie has to pretend she has something to do before she meets him there later. Are there a few going?"

"Yes, it's his birthday."

"How unfortunate," Don said with a grin. "Do you know anyone with a remote-controlled car?"

"Yes, we bought Mick one last Christmas."

"Brilliant, can you make sure all the batteries are new and take it with you on Sunday?" My throat was dry by now and I was finding it hard to swallow, so I had a sip from my beer and put the glass back on the table. "In the boot of my car, there is another remote-controlled car and a handset with flat batteries. On Saturday night, can you charge the batteries that drive both cars and take everything with you? Don't, under any circumstances, change the batteries in my handset for yours."

"Why?"

"I'll come to that in a moment." Don glanced at his watch quickly. "Now, listen carefully, this is the important part: in the handset that I give you, there is a yellow chip. When the time is right, this means when he is in the boat on his own and on the water far away, someone in an orange anorak and green shorts will come along. He will act a bit simple, he will speak only to you and ask if he can have a go with the remote-controlled cars. You will obviously say yes. By this time, the battery that drives your lad's car will be flat—make sure it is—if he don't play with it, you do it, it has got to be flat. So that you both know who you are, there's a code: he will suggest swapping the batteries from one handset to the other so he can play with the car I give you in the car park when we go outside. You will say, 'Why don't you swap the yellow chip?' and he will answer, 'I never thought of that'. This is the man that worked on the boat. He has fixed a remote-control unit to the engine and, when he pushes the lever on the handset forward, it will cut a groove out of the spark-plug lead, which will send an electric spark to the engine. Then, when he pulls the lever back, it will cut the petrol pipe and the boat will catch fire and explode. You will all be shocked and that will be the end of Doreen's problems."

"Debbie's problems."

"Sorry," Don added. "So you won't have to do it, OK?" I was so relieved. "While you're all looking out at the boat, the man in the anorak will disappear," Don said, as he looked at his watch again and stood up. "Is everything clear in your mind?"

"Yes, I'm so pleased I haven't got to pull the trigger," I said, almost smiling.

"Come out to the car with me, then, I must get off." I drank the last of my beer and followed him into the car park. As he opened his boot, I could see the handset next to the car; it was a Ferrari like his. I smiled at him and he said, "I'm sorry, I couldn't resist it." As he closed the boot he said, "it would be a good idea to take out the chip and keep it somewhere safe, perhaps in your car." I nodded. "Now are you sure you will remember everything?" he said.

"Yes, Debbie will collect him from hospital, drive past the house, collect his boat. Then Sunday he will go on his own. We will all go in separate cars, Debbie will follow later and I will wait till a man in a green anorak appears."

"No! It's orange anorak, green shorts."

"Sorry, orange anorak appears and swaps the chip, then boom."

"Good, if you have any problems, let me know and I will meet you here Friday." Don looked at his watch again and said, "I must dash, I'll speak with you soon," and opened his door. "Oh, I almost forgot . . ." He gave me a small piece of paper; I looked at it and tucked it in my top pocket. "This is the address, the boat will be on this drive and tell Dorothy not to be late."

"Debbie."

"Sorry, I was never very good with names," he said smiling. "One other thing, the tablets he gets from the doctor are strong sleeping tablets. Make sure Debbie—see I got it right in the end—make sure she gives him the exact amount, they will keep him asleep till Sunday." He waved and drove off.

I placed the car in the boot and removed the chip from the handset. As I held it in my hand, a shiver went through me; I dropped it in the door pocket and made my way home.

Tuesday morning, after dropping Mick off at school, I waited in the park for Debbie to come. I didn't see her in the playground and her car wasn't on her drive as I drove past her house. I waited till 9.30 and left for work worried.

During the day I phoned her mobile phone a few times but there was no answer and I worried even more. I drove past her house on the way home and the car still wasn't there at eight o'clock. I sat in the house wondering were she was, still concerned in case John had discharged himself from the hospital and gone home. At nine o'clock, I told Liz I was popping to the shops to get a bottle of whiskey and drove past the house—still nothing.

I sat watching the television till late, thinking about where she could be. I thought about ringing the house but if John was out of hospital he would answer the phone. All night I dozed and woke up worrying about her.

Wednesday morning, feeling very tired, I woke Mick and got him ready, hurrying him all the time. Eventually we got to school and, as we pulled up, I could see her car by the gate. I was relieved but still worried. I walked Mick to the entrance as Debbie came out smiling and talking to another mother. I could see she hadn't come to any harm, so I made my way back to the car, hoping Debbie would follow me to the park.

I waited at the entrance as usual and she followed me in. I was so pleased to see her, I leaped out of the car before she could open the door and asked, "Where have you been? I was so worried all day yesterday and last night, I haven't slept."

"I'm sorry, I had to go to Manchester to collect some papers for a very big case we are involved with. I'm sorry, I didn't think, I'm not used to having anybody worry about me," she said and kissed me on the cheek.

We walked across the park for ages. "We've not really talked about your job, have we?"

"No," she said. "It's quite interesting sometimes. We are working on a case at the moment: organised crime. That's all hush-hush, that's one of the reasons I had to fetch the papers yesterday and they're very confidential."

Slowly we walked back towards the cars, holding hands, laughing and joking. I'd completely forgotten about John until Debbie asked about him. "He's coming out on Thursday morning. I need you to fetch him."

"Do I have to?"

"Yes, it would look much better if you did it, as the dutiful wife."

"And what then?"

"I want you to get him at ten o'clock and take him home. The doctor will give him some tablets to take. They're sleeping tablets. Give him the exact amount as prescribed on the bottle and he will sleep all the time."

"Can't I give him the lot in one go?"

"No! Just give him the right amount and leave the rest to me."

"All right, but I'm going to leave him as soon as I get the chance."

"I know, this is what I've been talking to my friends about." Debbie looked confused. As she walked towards her car I shouted, "When you've picked John up, drive down Manor Lane. I will be parked off the road. When you go past me I will know that everything is OK." Debbie waved as she got into her car and drove off.

The day passed quite quickly. Work wasn't as bad as it had been lately so I made my way home at eight o'clock.

Andrew's car was on the drive. I filled up with anger immediately; I slammed the car door shut, walked to the house as quickly as I could, fumbling with my keys, and dropped them on the floor. As I bent down to pick them up, the door opened. Denise was standing there. "Hello," she said. "Andrew and I just popped in, how are you?"

Feeling a bit calmer and relieved, I went inside. "I'm fine, have you had a good trip?" I asked.

Denise spoke quietly. "I've missed you, that's why I had to come around, I couldn't wait to see you." She kissed me on the side of my mouth and tried to lick my lips as the lounge door opened.

"I thought I heard the front door close," Liz said, looking a bit suspicious.

"It's only me," I added and carried on into the kitchen, with Denise following behind.

We all sat at the table talking and drinking for a while and they left about ten o'clock. Denise was shattered from her trip and, to be honest, I was too, after the night I'd had worrying about Debbie.

Thursday morning, I woke as the alarm went off. I carefully edged my way out of bed, not wanting to disturb Liz, and made breakfast for Mick. I took him to school and then drove to Manor Lane. I passed the house and, sure enough, the boat was on the drive as planned. I carried on to the cul-de-sac further on, drove down it, parked behind a car so I wouldn't be seen and waited. Debbie drove past just after ten o'clock with John, so I drove up to the end of the road and watched Debbie's BMW pull up outside the house where the boat was. I waited for a while and watched John get out of the passenger side of her car and run up the drive. Everything seemed to be going to plan, so I made my way to work.

It was early afternoon when Debbie phoned. "How's things?" I asked.

"I did everything you told me to do, collected the bastard from hospital and took him home the way you told me to. Did you know his boat was in that road on someone's drive?"

I hesitated for a second. "No."

"I couldn't believe it, he made me take it home. Anyway, he's in bed now. I gave him a tablet. It was so hard not to give him the whole bottle," she said. "He is looking forward to Sunday now! I'm not coming."

"Meet me in the morning at the park. I will talk to you then." Debbie agreed and I put the phone down.

Looking at the phone, I sat in the quiet at my desk, slumped in the chair and clicking the top of my parker pen, asking myself if I should call it all off and why I was involved in the first place. My stomach churned at the thought of the boat exploding into millions of bits with him on it. Then I went cold all over: what if it all went wrong and someone else got hurt? It wasn't long before I thought about Debbie and what she'd been through with him beating her up. I was in too deep; she was on my mind all day long, from the second I woke to the time I fell asleep. It had been a long time since I'd felt like this over a girl. Some days I found myself smiling, as I thought of Debbie's smile, how I rushed to get to the school to see her face, knowing that would keep me going till the next day, and the sound of her voice made me so happy—all my problems disappeared when I was with her. Then I thought about Liz and how nasty I had become towards her every time she spoke to me. I felt angry with her for having an affair behind my back but I wasn't sure that she was. I was going mad with jealousy, hate, love, sex, lying, cheating, scheming and now, on top of all that, murder. I wanted to talk to someone about it all, but I soon realised I was on my own. I tried to think of something else, but it wouldn't leave my mind. I wondered if I would leave Liz after all this and live with Debbie or Denise. The game I started had gone wrong; it was supposed to be a bit of fun.

The phone rang, so I answered it quickly, hoping it would take my mind off it all. It was Mr Simpson from the VAT office. "Your cheque is late, Mr Vaughan."

"I'm sorry, it will be in the post tonight."

As I put the phone down, the door opened and Roger brought me in a cup of coffee. I was so glad to see him. "How are things downstairs?"

"Fine, we've just finished the TVR respray, you can ring Dennis and tell him to fetch it if you want to." I made the phone call, talked to him for a while and soon forgot about everything, until I got home about seven—Mick was playing outside the house with his remote-controlled car. I felt very strange as it bumped up and down the kerb; it made me shiver as he pulled the lever backwards.

Liz put my dinner on the table while I poured myself a large drink. We ate together for the first time in ages. "I'm taking you out for the day on Sunday."

"I'm working," she said sarcastically, as if it was my fault. "Well, don't worry, I'll take Mick, then."

"Where?"

"It's John's 40th birthday; he's taking the boat down to the Cotswolds on the lake. I just thought we could pack a picnic and have a day together; it's something we haven't done for ages."

"It's not my fault, you are the one that works all hours. I'm surprised you aren't working Sunday."

"Couldn't you swap with someone?"

"With who?"

"Forget it, then!" I shouted and threw the rest of my dinner in the bin, my plate in the bowl and stormed out of the house and into the garden.

We had become very short-tempered with each other lately. I sat there for a few minutes trying to cool down, then Liz came out to me. "I've just spoken to Jenny from work. She said she will swap Saturday for Sunday, so I can come."

I sat there for a second. "All you had to do was ask someone," I said as Liz stormed off.

I heard her shout, "I'm going to bed."

Mick came out into the garden, excited. "Where we going?" I told him about the day out and he went up to bed happy.

I woke in the chair with a stiff neck. Liz had gone to work, so we got ready and left for school. I saw Debbie in the playground; we didn't speak, so I carried on to the park. I waited a short while until she turned the corner and parked behind me. We walked for a while. Debbie was very quiet. "What's wrong? He hasn't started-"

Shaking her head, she interrupted me. "No. I'm not coming on Sunday, I just can't. Birthday or no Birthday, I can't bear him, I don't want to be anywhere near him."

"I want you to come. I want you to be near me. He'll be out on the boat all afternoon showing off. Come later, come about three o'clock. Tell him you have to do something first and you will follow him. You need to be there."

"Why, what's going to happen?"

"You'll know soon enough. There's nothing I can tell you."

We walked a bit further, quietly, then out of the blue she said, "OK, I will come later in the day."

"Oh, good, you won't be disappointed, and leave Dawn with someone, don't bring her with you."

"He will go mad if she's not there."

"If he says anything, just tell him she wasn't well."

"I hope you know what you're doing," Debbie said, looking at me straight-faced. I had the impression she had worked out what was going to happen.

"I won't see you till Sunday. Be there for three o'clock." We kissed by the cars and held each other as if we would never see each other ever again.

I made my way to work after stopping at the bank to get the wages. Don phoned about midday to tell me everything was set and that he would speak to me next week sometime.

I left work at about five o'clock and made my way to the Wooden Cross for a drink with my friends. They spoke about Sunday and how they were all looking forward to it so we arranged to meet at ten in the car park at the Bear Inn on the main road.

After a few drinks I made my way home and played with Mick until he went to bed. Then, as normal, I fell asleep in the chair till morning.

On Saturday, when I awoke to the sound of the cartoons on the television, I decided to go for a quick run. I hadn't been for a few months and when I got back to the house I could tell. It took me nearly twice as long. I had a quick shower, Mick and I got dressed and I took him to work with me, stopping off at McDonald's on the way for a breakfast. We ate it in the car park and carried on to the garage. While I was busy in the workshop, Mick washed my car, leaving a few dirty patches all over it. Then, after I'd washed it again, we went home about one o'clock.

I didn't do a lot that afternoon, except watch the telly with Liz and Mick. I started drinking heavily when they were in bed, hoping it would help me sleep, and at midnight I staggered to bed. I lay awake for hours and couldn't stop thinking about the boat on the lake.

# Chapter 17

LIZ NUDGED ME and said, “I’ve made you a coffee, it’s nearly 8.30, you’d better get up.” It took me ages to come round and realise where I was. “I’m going to leave some clothes washing while we’re out and I’ve just found a piece of paper in your top pocket with an address on it. Can I throw it away or do you want it?”

Still rubbing my eyes, yawning and tasting my tongue, I eventually answered, “Leave it on the side in the kitchen, I’ll have a look when I come down.” I heard Mick in his bedroom getting dressed and, while I was drinking my coffee, he came into the bedroom.

“Come on, Dad, we’ll be late, I want to be the first on the boat. Is it fast?” I felt sick again. He reminded me of the day I had ahead of me, as I nodded.

It wasn’t long after that I walked into the kitchen; Liz was making sandwiches and flasks of coffee for the picnic. “I don’t want any breakfast, thanks, but I will have another coffee.” Mick was eating Cornflakes on the other side of the table as I sat down.

“Are you all right? You look a bit pale,” Liz said, as she placed my coffee down in front of me.

"I think I drank too much last night."

We started to load the car. "Is everything here?" I asked as I placed things in the boot.

Liz shouted, "Yes, course it is!" Then she got in the car and slammed the door.

"Where's the remote-controlled cars, then?"

"Don't bother with those, they'll have enough to do . . . if we ever get there," she said sarcastically.

"I'll get them. I spent all night last night charging them up for the kids to play with," I shouted back and went in the house.

After I carefully placed them in the boot, we eventually set off, just after 9.30. I checked that the yellow chip was still in the door pocket as we drove down the road.

We were the first to arrive at the Bear Inn car park. All the others came shortly after and we started the journey to the lake in a convoy. It was a nice sunny day for the time of year; we had a good journey, except Liz and I didn't speak all the way there. We pulled up at the lake a little after midday; Mick was hanging out of the window looking at all the boats moored by the side of the grass. As we went in the entrance, there was someone reversing a Range Rover backwards down the jetty. The trailer was submerged under the water and the boat was floating off with someone else steering it.

We carried on along the long stretch of grass that ran out between the lake and the moored boats, past all the parked cars and caravans around the edge, and parked at the end on a nice big piece of grass, next to another jetty, from where the water-skiers started.

Lucy, Sandra, Denise, even Julie, had come. It was nice to see Julie; it had been a long time. All I needed now was Debbie for the whole set. The girls spread out all the blankets, food and booze, while Andrew sorted out the small barbecue. Then I went off to find John and his boat. I walked along the rickety old wooden jetty to the end. John was out on the lake speeding around the small island that was in the middle. I noticed he had some other people with him, so I stood on the end waving, trying to attract his attention. Mick and some of the other kids had walked up behind me, and then they all started shouting at the top of their voices. Eventually he waved and carried on, so I went back to the others and sat down on a blanket with a can of beer.

After ten minutes or so, I could see John's boat crawling along slowly as it came in on the other side of the grass. I could see him fastening it to the side, smiling and talking, and then he came over with the other people that were with him in the boat. Here we go, I thought, I must make it look as if I like him. I stood up and introduced him to the people he didn't know and he introduced the others. We all sat down and they picked up a couple of drinks. I noticed John didn't.

We talked for a while and I heard Simon talk to John about the boat. I heard him say something about the size of the engine then John replied, "I'll show you in a while." I started to panic in case he found the device that had been fitted to it.

It wasn't long before I heard him say to Simon, "Do you want to have a look, then?" As they stood up, I started to worry. I decided to go with them and pretend I was interested too. I stood up and looked around; everyone seamed to be enjoying themselves. Even Liz was smiling, but then she was talking to Andrew while he cooked beef burgers on the barbecue for the kids.

As we walked, John looked down at his watch. "Where's Debbie?" I asked.

"She will be here later. She had to go into work for an hour or two."

The nearer we got to the boat, the more I panicked, trying to think of a way of stopping him opening the engine compartment. "When do you take the boat back out?"

"Now, actually," he said, looking at his watch again. "Can I show you the engine later?"

Simon stopped. "Yes, no worries," he said, as I breathed a sigh of relief.

"We only get thirty minutes on the lake before I have to come off and let the other boats go on. It's like a rota system, so we all get a fair go," John explained to Simon. "If anyone wants a go at skiing, tell them to meet me on the end of the jetty. I'm just going to warm the boat up." We walked back to the others as John started the boat and slowly pulled out onto the lake.

"Are you going to have a go?" I asked.

"No, I don't think so, it's too cold and dirty. I'm not that good. If I keep falling into that water I will probably be ill."

"John said, if anyone fancies a go at skiing he will meet you on the jetty in five minutes," I shouted.

I sat and watched him as the boat lifted at the front and took off at high speed across the water. I stood up. Now was a perfect time for the anorak man to appear—John was on his own.

It suddenly occurred to me that Mick wasn't playing with his remote-controlled car and that the batteries must be flat. Quickly I went to the car, opened the boot and placed both cars on the ground and next to them the handsets. The yellow chip I placed in my pocket and sat back down.

After a couple of laps, John came into the jetty. All the kids waited patiently at the end for a go in the boat. Andrew was trying to force a wetsuit over his legs, with Ivor helping him, as John placed some of kids in the boat and took off again.

Nervously, and holding the yellow chip in between my fingers in my pocket, I sat watching the boat go across the water. Then it came back in and John swapped the kids, then took off once more. I watched terrified in case something went wrong. They all waved, laughing as they went past us. Andrew walked down to the jetty, with a water-ski under his arm, and waited. I wanted to shout, "Don't go!" but I couldn't because everyone would know there was something wrong.

Those thirty minutes were the longest I'd ever spent in my life. I was so relieved as the boat came back in and John tied it up again.

I calmed down as we sat talking and Mick asked me if he could play with the cars. I felt my pocket. I could feel the chip was there so I said, "Yes, let the others have a go." I looked over at Liz. She was still engrossed in a conversation, this time with Simon.

"Dad, this one doesn't work!"

"Leave it there and I'll have a look in a moment." I started to look round for anorak man, because John was sure to warm the boat up again soon. I went over to the other remote-controlled car and pretended to look at it, slipping the yellow chip into the handset and put the Ferrari in the boot.

By now I was starting to fall apart. My hands were shaking. I looked at my watch every five seconds. Where's this bloke? I continually said to myself. I walked over to the jetty, hoping he would see me, and then I walked back to the car and waited—nothing. I had to calm down so I walked on a bit further, back towards the entrance, pretending to look at the boats moored at the side. Just to the left of the entrance I noticed a clubhouse, so I went in. "A double whiskey, please." As the girl poured it, I looked around the room and sat on a stool by the bar. Every time someone walked in, I stared at them. I was going out of my head; losing the plot. After the second double whiskey, I paid and walked back towards the others, feeling a bit more relaxed.

"Where have you been?" Liz shouted, as I got closer.

"Looking for a toilet."

John pointed and said, "There's one in the clubhouse."

"I found it eventually," I answered.

Then I heard Liz say under her breath, "The toilet, or the bar?"

I sat down and started to talk to Henry about work. I needed something to take my mind off it all. Then he told me about the house he and Sandra were buying, in great detail. Still glancing around, I tried to listen to him. Out of the corner of my eye, I could see Andrew holding the Ferrari in his hand; I jumped up as he placed it back in the boot, thinking of an excuse quickly. "I'm sorry," I said screwing my face up. "I've got cramp in my leg." Henry laughed.

I glanced over at John as he looked at his watch first, then the entrance, to see if Debbie had come yet. I noticed Mick's car was still going strong. Some of the other kids were having a go with it over the bumps and into the grass.

"It's time to ski again!" John said aloud, as he stood up. My stomach turned over slowly.

Liz had been drinking quite heavily by now and I heard her say, "Can I come in the boat?"

"It's not a good idea, you will probably fall overboard," I said.

Luckily John didn't hear her and carried on walking towards the boat. Liz glared at me. "I need some fresh air," she said angrily. As I watched him untie the rope and pull away slowly, I looked around. Still no anorak man. Then I noticed the car had been abandoned. Mick and all the other kids were looking for fish at the water's edge.

Time was passing by now and I was getting very frustrated again: there was no sign of Debbie or the anorak man. I watched John go around the island again and then he came into the jetty to pick up one of his friends that wanted a spin.

It was about 3.30 when Debbie's car pulled up on the grass at the other end of our cars. I watched as she got out, collecting a few things from the boot. She came over and sat down. John's boat pulled up at the end of the jetty and, as he came over, I heard him say, "It's about time." Debbie smiled at him nervously and carried on talking to Liz, who was well on her way by now.

Where is this man? I asked myself, still looking all the time. I decided to go for a walk again towards the clubhouse. I heard Ivor and Henry say they would come with me, and Liz shouted, "Don't be long!" Her voice grated as we walked off.

As we entered the club, Henry said, "Anyone for a drink while we're here?"

"A large whiskey, please," I said walking towards the toilet, looking around the room again, while Ivor sat at the bar. I walked back into the room, still worried in case the anorak man didn't turn up. We sat there for a while before we went back to the others and I had another couple of drinks.

"You're knocking them back a bit, aren't you?" Ivor said, a little concerned.

"I'll be all right!"

As we walked back slowly, I could see that John's boat was tied up again. We got back to the others. By this time, I had to sit down. I felt a bit light-headed; it was a mixture of not eating, fresh air, nerves and, of course, the amount of alcohol I'd had.

"Anyone coming for a ski?" John shouted. My heart came up into my mouth again. I stood up looking around. It must be this time, I said to myself.

I heard Andrew say, "Not yet, I'll have a go next time." Then I heard John say, "This is the last time, I will have to take the boat out of the water after this." I walked around frantically looking for the orange anorak man. The kids were all playing by the jetty, looking into the water and trying to splash each other. Liz was slurring a bit and so were some of the others. Time was running out—I was panicking.

John put some petrol in the tank of his boat from a big green jerry can, then started it and slowly went out onto the lake to warm it up. Debbie kept catching my eye, with an inquisitive frown on her face. It was at this point I thought about doing it myself. It was the perfect time. He was on his own, no one else was on the lake and the boat was full of petrol. I watched him go around the island in the middle. I thought I had enough drink inside me, but I just couldn't pick up the receiver. I looked over at Debbie. She still stared at me with the same inquisitive look. I was shaking from head to foot. Henry was trying to put Andrew's wetsuit on, balancing on one leg. Everyone was laughing as he lost his balance and fell backwards. Andrew had disappeared. I looked out to the boat to see if he was on it. I couldn't be sure; I could only see John. Again, I looked for the orange anorak and then decided to walk up to the clubhouse. I walked quickly. Everyone by now had drunk too much and wouldn't notice if I disappeared. I hurried to the club. Where is he? I kept repeating it to myself. It must be done now. If that boat comes out of the water Debbie will have to go home with him and I will have failed. I made my mind up to do it; something inside me snapped. I turned back, looking out to the boat. I was almost sprinting. Nothing else mattered and all I could see in my mind was the lever on the handset. As I approached my car, my head was pumping. I was shaking with fear and anger—I wasn't sure what it was. I reached into the boot and moved the cover that I'd laid over the car. I froze when it wasn't there. I pushed the toolbox to one side, threw the blanket out of the boot—it was gone. I looked around the inside of the car—still nothing. As I turned, I could see Andrew on his knees with his back to me and the Ferrari was next to him on the ground. I started to rush towards him as he stood up and slowly pulled the aerial up, out of the handset.

I looked out to the boat, but it had disappeared behind the island. I waited. It seemed to take ages to come out the other side. I looked back at Andrew as he gingerly kicked the back of the Ferrari.

Everyone turned as the boat exploded into millions of bits. Andrew unknowingly had done it.

I looked out to the lake. There were bits of boat everywhere landing in the water. Everyone stood up to see what had happened. There was a deathly silence all around; even the kids stood and looked out at the rubble dropping from the sky. All except Mick. I couldn't see Mick. I looked to see if he was with Liz. She wasn't with the others.

"Who was on the boat?" I screamed.

Ivor shouted, "I saw your Mick, Liz, and John on it just now."

No one spoke, no one could speak, including me, and the tears welled up in my eyes as I started to run towards the jetty. I ran and ran and dived into the lake, swimming as fast as I could towards the island. All I could think, was what have I done to my own family? I swam, still crying as I got slower and slower. I thought about Mick and when he was born, all those years ago, and how we idolised him. It was the only other time I could remember crying as Liz held him in her arms for the first time; all the work we had done to make him into a little man with a personality of his own. The first word he said was "Dad", and the first steps he took were towards me. It was all gone. I had killed him and Liz, all because of a stupid game I had to play.

I was foolish to even think I could do something like this. I was beginning to feel like a lead weight by now and very tired. My arms had stopped, my legs were hardly moving and I was taking in vast amounts of water through my nose and mouth. I tried to stand on the bottom, but the water was too deep; I couldn't feel it. I couldn't feel anything with my feet. I tried one last effort to get my head out of the water. I pushed my heavy legs and arms once more.

It worked—my head just popped out of the water long enough for me to hear Mick shouting, "Hang on, Dad, I'm coming!"

I opened my sore eyes. I could just make out Liz standing on the island, looking into the water. Then I swallowed more and more water. I was drained. I felt myself sinking slowly down deeper. My lungs felt like they would explode at any second, as I slowly gave up. Then something grabbed my hair.

THE END

Thanks to friends and family that helped with
Information, stories and ideas,

COMING SOON THE SEQUEL
MANY RETURNS

More problems for Nicholas to sort out, before he has a date with a stunningly attractive young waitress, who with out knowing it, is an exceptional and very mysterious girl.

It turns out that the name she's using is not the one she was born with.